W9-BDL-833

"You may kiss the bride."

Matty had no time to think. Dave placed a hand to each side of her face and drew her toward him and kissed her. She grabbed his arms and gasped. Their mouths opened to each other.

The heat and rhythm were instant and powerful. It was all she'd remembered. It was much more.

The kiss ended only because they had to breathe.

Why had he kissed her that way? Why had she kissed him back? Habit? Instinct? Desire?

The only thing that mattered was her fear that Dave would think she'd asked him to marry her because she still wanted him. She'd have to make sure he understood she still saw the marriage as strictly a business deal.

"I now pronounce you husband and wife," the judge said. "And from the looks of it, just in time!"

Dear Reader,

Many people read romance novels for the unforgettable heroes that capture our hearts and stay with us long after the last page is read. But to give all the credit for the success of this genre to these handsome hunks is to underestimate the value of the heart of a romance: the heroine.

"Heroes are fantasy material, but for me, the heroines are much more grounded in real life," says Susan Mallery, bestselling author of this month's *Shelter in a Soldier's Arms*. "For me, the heroine is at the center of the story. I want to write and read about women who are intelligent, funny and determined."

Gina Wilkins's *The Stranger in Room 205* features a beautiful newspaper proprietor who discovers an amnesiac in her backyard and finds herself in an adventure of a lifetime! And don't miss *The M.D. Meets His Match* in Hades, Alaska, where Marie Ferrarella's snowbound heroine unexpectedly finds romance that is sure to heat up the bitter cold....

Peggy Webb delivers an *Invitation to a Wedding;* when the heroine is rescued from marrying the wrong man, could a long-lost friend end up being Mr. Right? Sparks fly in Lisette Belisle's novel when the heroine, raising *Her Sister's Secret Son,* meets a mysterious man who claims to be the boy's father! And in Patricia McLinn's *Almost a Bride,* a rancher desperate to save her ranch enters into a marriage of convenience, but with temptation as her bed partner, life becomes a minefield of desire.

Special Edition is proud to publish novels featuring strong, admirable heroines struggling to balance life, love and family and making dreams come true. Enjoy! And look inside for details about our Silhouette Makes You a Star contest.

Best,

Karen Taylor Richman, Senior Editor

Please address questions and book requests to:
Silhouette Reader Service
U.S.: 3010 Walden Ave., P.O. Box 1325, Buffalo, NY 14269
Canadian: P.O. Box 609, Fort Erie, Ont. L2A 5X3

Almost a Bride

PATRICIA McLINN

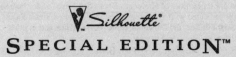

SPECIAL EDITION™

Published by Silhouette Books

America's Publisher of Contemporary Romance

To Toby,
a very special reader.
Thank you for your loyal support.

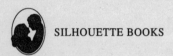 SILHOUETTE BOOKS

ISBN 0-373-24404-5

ALMOST A BRIDE

Books by Patricia McLinn

Silhouette Special Edition

Hoops #587
A New World #641
*Prelude to a Wedding #712
*Wedding Party #718
*Grady's Wedding #813
Not a Family Man #864
Rodeo Nights #904
A Stranger in the Family #959
A Stranger To Love #1098
The Rancher Meets His Match #1164
†Lost-and-Found Groom #1344
†At the Heart's Command #1350
†Hidden in a Heartbeat #1355
**Almost a Bride #1404

*Wedding Series
†A Place Called Home
**Wyoming Wildflowers

Harlequin Historicals

Widow Woman #417

PATRICIA McLINN

finds great satisfaction in transferring the characters crowded in her head onto paper to be enjoyed by readers. "Writing", she says, "is the hardest work I'd never give up." Writing has brought her new experiences, places and friends—especially friends. After degrees from North-western University, newspaper jobs have taken her from Illinois to North Carolina to Washington, D.C. Patricia now lives in Virginia, in a house that grows piles of paper, books and dog hair at an alarming rate. The paper and books are her own fault, but the dog hair comes from a charismatic collie, who helps put things in perspective when neighborhood kids refer to Patricia as "the lady who lives in Riley's house." Friends, family, books, travel, gardening and sitting on her porch are among her joys. She would love to hear from readers at P.O. Box 7052, Arlington, VA 22207.

SILHOUETTE MAKES YOU A STAR!
Feel like a star with Silhouette.
Look for the exciting details of our new contest inside all of these fabulous Silhouette novels:

Chapter One

Matty Brennan's plan to save the Flying W Ranch started forming even before she charged out of her lawyer's office, but it exploded into full bloom in the instant her nose collided with Dave Currick's collarbone.

A lot was jammed into that instant, since a particular corner of her mind also was registering that the hands she'd instinctively put up to brace herself had discovered that Dave had an even nicer chest than she'd remembered.

"Off to a fire, Matty?"

Running into him had to be an omen, she thought as she recovered her equilibrium, straightened away from his chest and rubbed her nose.

After the dire legal news Taylor Anne Larsen had just given her on top of the financial mess Matty had discovered, there'd been one throat-closing, stomach-grinding moment when Matty had feared there might not be any way out.

Taylor had suggested selling some of the ranch—as if Matty would ever do that. She was the last of the Brennans, and she would *not* be the one who shredded the Flying W into splinters and flakes.

But it wasn't the lawyer's fault—she'd been raised in some suburb in Ohio, so she didn't understand. Of course, even some people right here in Knighton, Wyoming, didn't share Matty's feeling. There was only one person she knew for certain would understand, and that was Dave—as soon as that thought surfaced, she'd veered away from it like a rattlesnake in the middle of the room.

"I truly am sorry about the grant, Matty," Taylor had said. "And I'm afraid there are more papers to sign for the estate now, too."

If Great-Uncle Henry had had a grain of sense, the Flying W wouldn't be encumbered with exorbitant inheritance taxes, not to mention the bank note coming due in two years. But the same optimism that had persuaded him no caution was needed in running a cattle ranch had also convinced him he had no need to bother with estate planning.

As Matty prepared to leave after her signing duties, Taylor held out a sheaf of papers. "These are the grant regulations. Maybe you'll see something that will help for next year, if…"

If Matty Brennan still owned the Flying W. The thought her attorney refrained from voicing dropped a sour lump into Matty's stomach as she flipped through the papers while crossing the empty reception area toward the outside door.

She *had* to find a way out. Any way out. Whatever it took.

That's when she saw it—the one loophole that might let her save the Flying W. She needed just one thing…

The next moment she'd flung open the door and started across the board sidewalk that lined the string of pseudo-frontier-town offices, only to run nose-to-chest into David Edward Currick.

Exactly the person she needed.

Definitely an omen.

She shrugged off the hands he'd cupped around her shoulders to steady her.

"Fire? No, there's no fire. I was—I was going to look for you," she improvised.

"Me?" His deep voice edged toward uncharacteristic astonishment. Usually his Western drawl stayed unhurried, unfazed and with a hint of dry amusement. He had the kind of deep, faintly raspy tone that often came from a few decades spent smoking too many cigarettes and drinking too much whiskey. But she'd been around when his voice had shifted from a childish soprano to this sexy register, and she knew it was all nature's doing.

Sometimes Mother Nature didn't play fair.

"Yes. I have something to talk to you about."

"Now, that's nice to hear, Matty. Seems like you've spent these past weeks avoidin' talkin' to me." His voice was back to normal, and that irked her.

"I have not."

"If I recall, the phrase you used when I called to ask you to dinner a few weeks back was *Don't call me again unless it's to tell me you're dead.* The logic was a shade hazy, but I got your drift. No dinner dates."

She recalled the phone call vividly. Six years after leaving for what she'd vowed would be forever, she'd arrived late the night before Great-Uncle Henry's funeral, which entailed an exhausting day-long series of condolences, ceremony and casseroles. The next day, she'd decided that before she did anything else, she needed to know how the ranch stood. So she'd tackled Henry Brennan's business affairs, now hers since she was the only one left to inherit the Flying W.

She'd spent the entire morning opening Past Due and Final Warning notices that had filled the bottom two drawers of Great-Uncle Henry's desk.

Still reeling from the knowledge that she was totally alone in the world now, with not another living relative, she had been left almost numb by the reality of the mess she'd inherited.

That's when the phone rang. She'd answered automatically.

And there had been Dave's voice. Assured. Familiar. Once loved. Asking her to dinner as if nothing had changed in all the years since their last date.

Not a "sorry," not a "we should talk," not a "life hasn't been the same without you," much less a "I'll crawl across every inch of rock, creek and prickly pear between my place and yours if you'll only smile at me once more."

Goaded by despair over the Flying W and the jumble of emotions his voice stirred, she'd lashed out. Acted on impulse, she supposed. Which should have come as no surprise to him, considering the number of times he'd criticized her for doing that very thing when they were growing up.

And then he'd never called back. Since then, whenever their paths crossed in the tiny community of Knighton, he'd acted like he was an amused older brother and she was an idiot child.

"This is business," she informed him now with every scrap of dignity she could muster. "Sort of a…a business proposition."

"Well, I'd be happy to talk to you about business, but I'm heading for an appointment right now. To see Ms. Larsen."

"Why?" she demanded, then caught herself. Despite the late April chill, he wore no jacket—Dave rarely got cold as fast as normal people—so she could see every detail of his outfit. He was wearing new jeans and a crisp white shirt with the cuffs rolled back and a black cowboy hat atop his neatly trimmed saddle-brown hair. It was a nice compromise between his more formal lawyer attire and his ranch clothes. Just right for a casual date. Taylor Anne Larsen was very attractive. Single and unattached. Intelligent. And they had lawyer stuff in common. *Why* was pretty damned obvious.

"Not that it's my business," Matty added hurriedly.

"No, it's not."

She scowled at his equable agreement.

Three years her senior, Dave had been her measuring stick all through childhood—learn to read like Dave, to ride like Dave, to rope like Dave, to get good grades like Dave. Constantly trying to catch up, and never quite making it.

He'd been the first to kiss her, of course. The first to hold her in his arms. The first to make her blood feel like it was melting. The first to make love to her.

And the only one to break her heart.

Now, of course, she could see what children they'd been then, with him still in law school and her still in college. But at the time, his ending their romance had been a heartbreaking, soul-wrenching tragedy.

She'd left vowing to make him sorry. To make him rue the day he'd let the dazzling Matty Brennan get away.

She'd been a little hazy on exactly *how* she was going to dazzle him. But it didn't matter in what arena—dancer, actress, financial whiz, literary genius or married-into-royalty—she dazzled him, as long as he was dazzled within a hairbreadth of his Wyoming's-good-enough-for-me life.

It didn't help that he'd gone on to get his law degree with ease, passed the bar on the first try, then settled down to a thriving law practice. And since his parents retired to indulge a yen for adventurous travel a few years back, he'd combined that with successfully running his family's ranch.

He was living exactly the life he'd always wanted, the life she'd once dreamed of sharing with him. And doing it right next door to the Flying W...which she would lose if she couldn't pull this off.

That was what mattered, she reminded herself.

"It's just that my business is important," she said stiffly. "Very important."

"I could come see you tomorrow—"

"No!" Twenty-four hours? No way. If she thought about this too much—if she thought about it at *all*—she'd lose her nerve. Or regain her pride. "It's, well, it's real important to me, Dave. It's urgent."

"Urgent?" Now he was frowning. "Are you okay, Matty? Is something wrong?"

"No. I mean, yes, but not the way you mean."

She took a deep breath and looked around. A young couple was coming up the steps at one end of the sidewalk, probably heading toward the real estate office next to Taylor's. Matty grabbed the rolled back cuff of Dave's white shirt and tugged him toward the opposite end, where they'd have more privacy.

"What is it, Matty? You're worrying me. Is it that Cal Ruskoff you've got working for you?"

She stared up into his narrowed hazel eyes in astonishment. "Cal? No. Why would you think that? He's great. Works like five men and never complains."

Dave's frown didn't ease, but some of the tension went out of his broad shoulders. "Then what is it?"

"Give me a second here," she said irritably.

She tried to think of a way to say this, a way to make it more palatable, and couldn't. It was like going into the swimming hole on a spring day when they were kids. There was no edging into it, inch by inch, or you'd never do it. The only way to go was to take the plunge.

She took a breath and leaped.

"I want to marry you."

For a second, she could almost believe she'd really jumped into the swimming hole. She felt the same shock of cold surround her and the same sensation that all sound in the world was muffled and distant. The only thing she could hear clearly was the beating of her own heart.

Then a single word from Dave brought her back.

"Pardon?"

He hadn't moved an inch and his expression hadn't changed. He sounded as if he was certain—as only Dave could be certain—that he'd heard wrong.

Of course he was going to make her repeat it. Dave had never made anything easy on her. Not since he'd told her, then all of five years old, that if she couldn't keep up, she should go back and play with dolls.

"I want to marry you. In fact, I *have* to marry you."

He seemed to come out of a trance. He pushed his cowboy hat back off his forehead, and leaned against the pole that held up the roof over the sidewalk, crossing one ankle over the other with an air of total nonchalance.

"Have to? You sure it was me you were thinking of?" The amusement was back in his voice. At least she thought it was amusement. It had an edge to it and the look he was giving her didn't strike her as a laughing matter, but maybe that's how he showed amusement these days. After all, she hadn't been around him for years. "Darlin', either I missed something in the past few weeks that I'd truly hate to think I'd missed or you're setting to make medical history. Unless there's someone else more, let's say, recent?"

"Don't be an idiot, Dave. I'm not pregnant."

"That's a relief. I'd hate to have you be the subject of all those tabloid newspapers for bearing a child six years after the fact. As for the more usual time frame, well a gentleman doesn't like to think he's forgotten things like that. And if someone else—"

"Oh, shut up, Dave. It's nothing like that."

"Nothing to do with oh, say, an affair of the heart?"

"Why would it have to do with an affair of the heart?"

"Well," he drawled, "marriage sometimes does."

"Not this time. I told you, it's business."

"Business?" he asked politely. "I'm sorry. I'm not following this. Call me stupid, but I associate marriage with romance, not business."

"Yeah, right. You've had enough romances to make Don Juan look like Barney Fife, and I've never heard anything about you getting married."

"Been paying attention to my social life, have you?"

"It's like the wind around here—it's only remarkable when it's not making its presence felt."

"Matty, if this is the way you ask all the men to marry you, I can see why you're still single. I thought I taught you better than that."

"*You* taught— Why you…"

She swallowed the words with the greatest of effort. He'd gotten under her skin from their earliest days. Even when she'd thought she was in love with him, he'd been able to yank her chain with the flick of his finger. But no more. And certainly not now. She couldn't afford it. The Flying W couldn't afford it.

"This is all beside the point." She barely gritted her teeth at all, she was proud of that.

"And what is the point, Matty?" His mouth twitched.

"The point—" she figured she couldn't be blamed for a little teeth-gritting now "—is that I want us to get married. Right away. But only temporarily."

"Temporarily?"

"Of course, temporarily." She was miffed. "You don't think I'd ask you to get married for good, do you?"

"I didn't mean any disrespect, ma'am. But not having been proposed to before, at least not by you—" She glared at him. Because of the mock-humble tone; not, of course, because of his intimation that he might have been proposed to by other women. "I want to keep this all straight. Orderly. Since it's business. Isn't that what you said?"

"That's what I said. We'd get married, then after a while, we'd get divorced. Uncontested. Nice and clean."

He raised one eyebrow. "Not sure I've ever heard of a clean divorce, much less a nice one."

"That's because all those other divorces were between people who were married."

"You got me there, Matty, That's a fact."

"Oh, quit with the Gary Cooper act, Currick. You know what I mean. We would be *pretending* to be married. I mean, we'd *get* married, but we wouldn't *be* married. We wouldn't—'' she shot him a glowering look to be sure he got her point ''—do *things* married couples do. So the divorce would be no big deal.''

He rubbed his chin. God, he'd gone from Gary Cooper to Gabby Hayes. If he said *Well, goooollllleeee,* she'd belt him.

''Uh-huh. Okay, so we get married—without really *being* married—and then we get divorced. I have that right?''

''Yes.''

''How long?''

''How long what?''

''Before we get divorced?''

She hadn't thought that out yet. If the Flying W didn't get the grant this year or if one year's grant wasn't enough to get it back on its feet, she'd be back where she'd started. Better give herself some leeway.

''Five years.''

He jerked up from the pole as if it had caught fire. ''Five years!''

She crossed her arms and braced her legs. ''Five years isn't a life sentence, you know. It's not like we'd have to be together all the time. We'd only have to make it look like we were married.''

He rested back against the pole. ''So it would be okay if I fooled around on the side?''

''No!'' She would have taken that back if she could, especially when he got smug. ''We have to keep up proper appearances. That's part of the deal.''

''Matty, honey, be reasonable. Unless you're going to rethink your position on conjugal rights—''

''No!''

''—and you don't want me running around on you, five years is definitely out of the question.''

She gave in with ill grace. ''Four years, then.''

''Six months.''

''No way. Three years.''

"One year."

"Two years."

"Eighteen months."

She figured furiously in her head. She'd just *have* to get the grant this year. Surely she could turn the Flying W around with two years' worth of grants. And paperwork for a divorce would take time, so with some luck... "Twenty-two months before we start the divorce proceedings."

"Done."

He stuck out his hand. She put hers in it. He wrapped his big hand around hers, the calluses slightly abrading the tender skin across the back of her hand and the strength of his fingers pressing against hers. You'd think a lawyer would have soft skin and strength only in the muscles used for endorsing checks.

"So twenty-two months from now we get divorced. When do we get married?"

Still holding her hand, he leaned back against the pole, unbalancing her enough that she had to take a step toward him to keep from falling over. She yanked her hand free.

"As fast as we can." The application deadline for this year's grant was in three and a half weeks.

For a long moment, he stared at her from the shadow cast by his hat—able to see out so much better than she could see in. "Okay," he said at last.

Matty let out a breath—and an instant later realized she'd relaxed too soon.

"Now, what do I get out of this deal?"

"You?" she blurted.

"Only seems fair, Matty, You're obviously getting something out of it. I should, too. That's what makes the best business deals. Win-win, they call it. So, I'd like to win something, too."

She couldn't argue with that. It was only fair. It was also galling as hell. "I can't afford to pay you anything." Her stiff dignity crumpled with her next words. "And you have plenty enough money as it is, so I don't know why you'd want more from me.''

"It's not money I want from you."

"Then what? You've got your law practice and the Slash-C is doing good business and you had the house renovated— so what could you possibly want from me?"

The question hung in the air between them for a moment, then turned around and slapped her in the face, stinging her cheeks with heat. What Dave had once wanted from her was her heart and body and soul. Which she had been more than willing to give him. And then he'd given them all back.

"Peace of mind and something to look forward to.''

Still smarting from her own thoughts, she snapped, "What's that supposed to mean?''

"Well, peace of mind means I want to know what you're up to. Why would you suddenly want to marry?''

She looked away, pulling the inside of her cheek in between her back teeth. "I can't tell you. Not until we're married.''

He closed his eyes as if in pain. "Is that because I can't testify against you if we're married?''

"I hadn't thought of that, but that's true, too.''

"Matty, for God's sake— I'm a lawyer, an officer of the court, I can't—''

"I know! That's why I'm not telling you. I don't want to bother your conscience.''

"Thank you for your consideration, but—''

"You don't have to get all sarcastic, Currick. It's not anything terrible. It's getting around a technicality. Honest.'' She looked up into his face, letting hurt show at his lack of faith. How much of it was real, she didn't want to know herself. "I wouldn't ask you to do something that was really wrong.''

The taut line of his shoulders eased. He believed her, and knowing that almost led her into saying something more— probably something stupid. But when he opened his mouth

and that lightly mocking tone came out, the danger of con-
fiding in him was over in a flash.

"So you can assure me that this matter would never be
handled by, oh, say, the FBI, the CIA, or the Wyoming Bu-
reau of Investigation?"

"Of course not. You know me better than that."

He held up his hands in a placating gesture. "All right.
All right. I can see that's the best I'm going to get as far as
peace of mind where you're concerned. But at least give me
something to look forward to."

"Like what?" Suspicion weighted her question and narrowed her eyes.

To her annoyance, his eyes abruptly lightened—he was
enjoying himself. "Let me think…" He stared out toward
where snow-tipped peaks met blue sky. "Got it. We breed
Brandeis to that mare of Walker's that Henry bought out
from under me a while back for the next three years and I
get any foals."

"What? No way. I'm not having Juno in foal to Brandeis
three years running, and I'm sure as hell not giving you three
of her foals. We'll breed them once, and if there's a foal,
we'll toss for it."

"We breed them until there's a foal I want."

"We breed them until there's a live foal, and you get it."

"Done."

He stuck out his hand again. After an instant's hesitation,
she grasped it, gave it one firm shake and released it before
his long fingers even finished wrapping around hers.

"I'll look into what we have to do to get a license and
such—"

"It's customary for the man to do that. Besides," he went
on as she prepared to protest, "I can do it when I'm at the
county courthouse on business and save you a trip to Jefferson."

She did have better things to do than traipse to the county
seat. As it was, she'd have to be back here in Knighton get-

ting her official residence changed as quickly as possible. "Okay, as long as you do it as soon as possible. I don't want any delays."

"We'll get married as fast as I can put it together."

"That's it then. I'll expect to hear from you soon."

"Aren't you forgetting something? How about the rest of the wedding arrangements?"

"Wed— Uh, arrangements?" Odd how she'd talked of getting married so calmly, but her tongue stuck on "wedding." "I thought…uh, I thought we'd get married before whatever judge we can find."

Actually she hadn't thought of that at all, but it sounded good now.

"That might cause questions, what with both of us being from such old Knighton families. And I don't suppose questions being asked about this marriage right from the start is something you want, is it? Now a church—"

"No. No church. I, uh, I don't have time to be messing around with a fancy we—uh, with a church and all."

"No, I suppose not. Just seems a shame to open ourselves up to questions…"

"Then you take care of the arrangements." As soon as she said them, she felt a sinking certainty that those were exactly the words he'd been angling for.

"Okay. I will."

Oh, hell, she had more important things to worry about than whatever Dave Currick had in mind. "Fine. No church, and nothing fancy, understand?"

"Nothing fancy," he agreed.

Certifiable.

He'd always been that way about one Matilda Jeanette Brennan, and it looked as if he always would be.

From the time she'd toddled after him declaring, "Me fish, too!" through the years of her being his best rough and tumble buddy, to the stunning recognition that, not only was there something to this boy-girl stuff, but *the* girl was Matty of all people, and into that all too brief period when making a life with her had seemed inevitable.

Sitting on his porch, Dave Currick rocked back on the rear legs of the worn wooden chair that had just the right balance for this maneuver and put one booted foot on the railing as he contemplated the half-moon.

So what the hell was she up to now?

She was in trouble, that was for sure. He just thanked God she'd turned to him. It slid a warmth under his rib cage to know she had come to him. A warmth that had been missing from his life for a long time. Six years.

If he'd been asked twenty-four hours ago who he thought Matty would turn to if she was in trouble, he'd have said Cal Ruskoff, that hand Henry Brennan had hired out of nowhere a couple of years back. He'd have hated the taste of the words in his mouth and he'd have hated the truth of them even more, but he'd have said them.

In the few times he'd seen Matty and Ruskoff together— at Henry's funeral or on some errand in town these past weeks—he'd seen the easy way Matty treated Ruskoff, like she was comfortable with him, at home with him, trusted him. Like he was a man she would turn to if she was in trouble. It was quite a contrast to the arctic shoulder she'd been giving Dave.

Still, she'd come to *him*.

She needed *him*. God, it felt good to know that.

When she'd first said she had to get married, fears had knotted his stomach so tight he didn't think he could talk. But she'd been so clearly incensed that he might think she was pregnant, and even more clearly at sea about his hints that Ruskoff or someone else might have broken her heart, that the knot had quickly eased.

There had been a time he could have asked Matty straight out what the problem was. Hell, he'd have known without her saying. Now, all he could do was guess that it had to be something with the Flying W.

Under Matty's grandfather, the spread was as good acre for acre as any around. After Grandpa Jules's death it had slipped, even though Matty's grandmother had done her best to keep after her brother-in-law, Henry Brennan. But Grams had died nearly four years ago now. Left on his own, Henry had never kept the spread in top order, and there had been rumblings that the elderly man had really run it down in the last year of his life. Dave had tried to check out the situation through his contacts, with no luck. He'd stopped by twice—and both times Henry Brennan had met him with a shotgun and cutting comments about how Dave Currick wasn't welcomed on Brennan land.

He'd known Matty's great-uncle must have left a legal tangle—one he'd hoped she would ask him to help her with. Instead she'd turned immediately to newcomer Taylor Anne Larsen. Another lesson to him not to hope.

But this afternoon's amazing encounter with Matty changed everything.

Maybe there was hope after all. Not of really getting married. No, she'd back out of this crazy idea soon enough. He'd seen her leap into things too many times not to know that this had been one of her classic spur-of-the-moment decisions.

But even if she called in the morning and said to forget the whole thing, it gave him an opening back into her life. And that gave him hope.

Hope after all the years, months, days—and especially all the nights—of convincing himself he had no hope.

Chapter Two

Two days after proposing to Dave Currick, Matty exited the bank with more speed than finesse. Who would have thought that a little thing like changing her official residence could cause such a hubbub?

It had been a snap at the post office—fill out a form and hand it in before anyone could comment. And she would check with Taylor on the other official documents during their meeting later.

But when Matty announced her soon-to-be address for the bank's records, Joyce Arbedick had looked up as if a firecracker had gone off under her chair, her eyes bugging out and her mouth formed into a perfect O while visions of sin obviously danced in her head.

"We're getting married," Matty had said in her own defense.

And that's when things really got crazy. All of a sudden she was surrounded where she sat at the assistant manager's desk by customers, tellers and probably passersby dragged in from the street by the noise, all wishing her happiness and a long marriage, and saying they'd always known she and Dave would end up together.

Matty shuddered now in the quiet of her truck parked alongside the bank, trying to reconstruct what had happened.

This morning, Taylor had called while Matty was out watering and feeding the four ailing cows in the barn corral, and had left a message saying she'd like to see her this afternoon. Taylor didn't say what about, but from her rather stilted voice, it wasn't good news.

'Course, Matty couldn't remember the last time any news had been good.

And that realization brought all the reasons for this temporary marriage rushing back to the front of her mind.

Each time over these past two days that she'd just about decided to call Dave and tell him the whole thing was a joke—another of her *impulses*—some reminder of what was at stake, of what would happen if she didn't take this step rushed in. Just like this call from Taylor.

Matty had called back and left a message that she'd be in to see Taylor about three, then she'd finished some chores, showered and changed, gathered her paperwork and headed into town to take care of address changes. The sooner she did, the sooner she could apply for the grant. Maybe she could ask Taylor to start—

"Matty?"

Matty gasped—not sure if the knock on the truck window next to her head or Dave's voice practically in her ear made her jolt so.

"Good Lord! Don't sneak up on someone that way!" Her heart felt as if it could beat right through her ribs.

"I didn't sneak up on anyone—" Dave gestured for her to open the window, and his voice lowered along with the window. "You were so busy chewing on your thumbnail you would have been down to your knuckle before you noticed anyone coming."

Matty hid her ragged nail by balling her hand into a fist. Just like Dave to remind her any time she slipped back into that childhood bad habit. "What do you want?"

"You."

She blinked, while heat bloomed in her chest like a time-elapse movie of a flower on high speed. Then it sizzled through nerve endings alive with the memory of what it meant to be wanted by Dave.

"Why?" It came out a croak.

"We have time to get blood tests before your three o'clock with Taylor."

Her mind sent an immediate cease-and-desist order to all nerve endings, but it took the heat a while to evaporate. Was he so tight with Taylor that he knew her entire schedule? But that wasn't the question Matty voiced. "Blood tests?"

"You're not still afraid of needles are you?"

"Of course not," she lied. "But you didn't tell me we had an appointment."

"It's not a real appointment. When I mentioned to Doc you were in town this afternoon, he said he could fit us in if we came by before three."

"How'd you know—"

"Taylor called me, too."

"That wasn't what I was going to ask," she said with a fair assumption of dignity. "I wondered how you knew I'd come into town early."

"Elementary, my dear." He opened the truck door and gestured for her to get out. He had on old jeans, worn to a faded blue that she knew would be as a soft as their color. The material molded around the muscled length of his thighs, and other lengths she forced her gaze away from. "I tried to call the Flying W, got no answer. I deduced you'd headed into town early."

"That's kind of a stretch, Sherlock," she scoffed as they headed up the block toward the small clinic that served the south end of Lewis County and the north end of Clark County.

"Ah, but it was confirmed about fifteen minutes ago when all three lines on my office phone lit up simultaneously and two friends stopped by my office."

"How does that confirm I'd come to town?"

"They'd all heard about your public announcement at the bank that we're getting married. I thought a notice in the paper was how these things are done. Guess the bridegroom's the last to know."

She halted before they stepped up to the sidewalk and met his eyes. She'd been avoiding doing too much of that, because Dave's darkly fringed hazel eyes had always packed quite a wallop where she was concerned. But she owed him a direct look while she said this.

"I'm sorry, Dave. I didn't mean for it to get out this way, but when I told Joyce my new address and she goggled at me like we'd not only be living in sin but had invented the concept, I blurted it out. But I should have warned you somehow. I'm sorry they blindsided you like that."

He looked back at her for a long moment. His expression gradually shifted from surprise to disconcertingly assessing. Then one side of his mouth lifted in a wry smile. "No problem. I'm getting used to having things sprung on me this week. Compared to an offer of marriage this was pretty minor. Besides, you did tell me that public appearances were part of this package deal."

"Yeah, I did," she said, feeling lightened. She started along the sidewalk, but Dave's hand on her arm stopped her.

"There's one thing I wondered about, Matty,"

"What?"

"You're awfully eager to get your address changed, aren't you? Not even waiting until we're married."

"Just want to keep things straight," she mumbled. "C'mon, let's go get those blood tests. Doc won't wait all day."

* * *

"You don't have to walk me all the way inside," Matty protested twenty minutes later as Dave ushered her into Taylor Larsen's reception area. "I'm perfectly all right and you can go about your business now."

"You still look pale."

She glared at him. "I am not pale and I wasn't going to faint. I was fine until you shoved my head down between my knees. *Then* I was dizzy."

Which had nothing at all to do with the sensation of his hand against the back of her neck, slowly stroking into her hair, then down inside the collar of her sweater.

"Uh-huh," he murmured, falsely soothing. "Afternoon, Lisa."

"Dave, Matty." The tone of voice used by Lisa Currick—Dave's younger sister and Taylor's office manager—immediately announced she was miffed. "I hear congratulations are in order."

Matty's heart sank under a load of guilt. She hadn't given a thought to how this might affect Lisa.

Some in town still clucked about Lisa having moved into her own small house on the edge of town when she'd returned from New York City a few years back instead of living on the ranch. But Matty had figured that had to do with Lisa's need for independence, not any bad blood between the siblings. The gap of six years between brother and sister had meant they weren't buddies as kids, not the way she and Dave had been buddies. But the Currick family was close and loyal.

"Or maybe," Lisa continued. "I should make that I-told-you-so. Half the town's been telling me they always knew you two would get together if you'd stop squabbling long enough to listen to your pheromones. They all seemed to think that as your sister, I'd already know about this."

Of course Lisa was hurt that she hadn't been told first.

Especially since she didn't know this wasn't going to be a real marriage.

"Oh, Lisa, I'm so sorry—but, honestly, it's not what you think—"

"Sorry, Lees," Dave interrupted firmly at the same time he squeezed so tightly around Matty's waist that she almost yelped. "We'd intended to tell you first. Word kind of leaked out about a half hour ago, and you know how this town is. I'll explain it all to you over dinner in Jefferson, how's that? You have time before class tonight?"

"Not tonight. Tomorrow." She waved toward an interior door, clearly well on her way to being mollified. "Taylor's waiting for you both, so go in."

"Both of us? Wait a minute, why would Taylor—"

Dave interrupted again. "Tell Lisa thanks for the congratulations, Matty, and let's go in." He gave Taylor's office door a quick knock before opening it.

"Thanks, Lisa," she said hurriedly as he guided her into the inner office, "but I don't see why you—"

"Hello, Matty, David." With an air of formality, Taylor stood behind her desk. "I'm glad you both could come this afternoon to discuss this."

Her gesture indicated documents on her desk. They bore Dave's letterhead.

"Discuss what?" Matty asked.

Taylor sat, looking at the pages as she flipped through them, and they took the twin chairs across the desk from her. "You're right, Matty, there isn't much to discuss. Dave did an excellent job drafting it."

"Drafting what—?"

"I took the liberty of sending this to Taylor yesterday, so she could look it over on your behalf beforehand. Thought that would be better than springing it on you, Taylor," he added, looking across the desk.

"I appreciate that, Dave. It—"

Matty had had enough of these lawyerly courtesies. Spacing each word, she demanded, "What is it?"

Dave gave a fair portrayal of surprise that she would have to ask, but when he turned to her she recognized the glint in his eyes. "Our prenuptial agreement, dear."

"Our prenup—?" Matty glared at him. "You worried I'm going to try to rob you, Currick?"

Taylor looked up quickly.

"No, of course not, dear." Dave reached across the narrow chasm between their chairs and took her hand. She tried to snatch it back. His hold tightened enough to make her wince.

"You must have jumped right on this. You had it drafted by yesterday afternoon? And it was only two days ago that we—"

"I know it was only two days ago that we set the date for sure," he interrupted with a warning in his eyes. And he was right—another half sentence and she would have given it away. "But since we'd been talking about marriage for so long, I'd had it on my mind. With land holdings like ours it's best to set everything out beforehand."

"That's true, Matty," Taylor added earnestly. "And this agreement safeguards the Flying W as thoroughly as the Slash-C. The boundaries would revert to what they are now, and the income generated, plus equipment or stock bought during the period of the marriage would be divided fifty-fifty."

"Oh."

Dave gave her an ironic little nod at her deflated tone, which Taylor didn't see because she was looking at the papers again. It was beyond equal, since the Slash-C would no doubt generate more income and buy more equipment than the Flying W would.

"In fact, it's an extremely fair document. The only thing is…"

"What?" Matty demanded, suspicions aroused again.

"There's a rather odd clause about if you should divorce,

you both agree to breed Brandeis and Juno, with Dave getting first live foal.''

''Oh, that. That's okay.''

Taylor's frown deepened. ''Then it says that if you initiate divorce proceedings any time after two years of marriage, Dave gets Juno outright.''

''What!''

''Now, Matty,'' Dave said in a mockingly soothing rumble. ''It's only fair. I was thinking and thinking about it, and it seems to me that getting a divorce within the first two years shows the marriage was just a pure mistake—the kind anybody can make. But after that, it starts to look like carelessness to pull apart a marriage.''

Matty opened her mouth, but Dave kept on talking. '''Course, if I initiate divorce proceedings any time after two years, then I don't get a thing. And it's not like it's a life sentence. After all, nobody can expect Juno to live more than another, oh, fifteen years, twenty at the most. After that you could divorce me and walk away free.''

Oh, he was clever, Mr. Attorney Currick. She saw clear as day that the clause was to make sure she didn't hold him to the marriage longer than the twenty-two months they'd agreed on, with two months thrown in like a sale on doughnuts.

''It's all right, Taylor. I'll accept that clause. After all, we won't be using it, will we, dear?'' She gazed into his face, a small smile pulling at her lips, and had the pleasure of seeing wariness skim across his eyes.

''Of course, we're all optimistic that none of these clauses will ever be used,'' said Taylor, though her reasons for that expectation were probably quite different from Matty's. Matty intended to end the mock marriage right on schedule, while Taylor was probably romantically thinking the marriage would never end— *Hah!*

''But just in case…'' Matty put a finger to her chin as if suddenly struck by a thought. ''It only seems right that we have a clause that if you initiate divorce proceedings after two years, I get Brandeis free and clear. To keep things even."

Dave gave a strangled cough, which Matty was fairly certain had started as a laugh.

"Well done," he murmured just loud enough for her to hear. Then he added at regular volume. "Matty's got a point, Taylor. If you insert the clause, I'll initial it and we can sign right now."

"Well, that's done," Matty said, pulling the short tail of straight hair at the end of her braid free from her collar.

Dave knew that it used to drive her nuts in high school that she had straight hair. After he and Matty had shifted from buddies to dating, he'd probably spent a thousand hours in the Flying W's kitchen talking with Grams, waiting for Matty to do something or other to her hair that would make it curl...until the first lick of Wyoming wind got to it.

She didn't even seem to notice now.

He'd always liked it straight. Straight and silky, and with a thousand colors streaked into the natural light brown by days in the sun. He could spend the rest of his life cataloging the different colors there.

"Yup, it's done."

"What next?"

"Want some ice cream?"

She frowned at him fiercely. "I meant what other stuff do we have to get out of the way before we get married?"

"Oh. Not much."

He fought a grin. Wait until she found out that they could have gone and gotten married that first day—no blood test, no waiting period, fill out the form at the county courthouse, find a judge, then back to the courthouse to register the marriage certificate.

Except he hadn't been willing to take that risk. If he'd gone along with Matty's rush to marry, she'd have either gone running or she'd have clamped down hard on her stubbornness to see this through—whatever the hell *this* was—and he'd never know what was really behind this move. This way, with time to think things over, she'd eventually back out. But with some luck, they would have mended enough bridges by then to at least keep talking to each other.

That was a lot after more than six years of pretending that their lifetime of friendship, infatuation and love hadn't existed. An awful lot. Though he had a feeling it might not be enough.

"Let's see, this is Friday. Doc said he'd hurry the blood tests for us and the prenup's all signed, so…I'd say we could get married Tuesday."

"Tuesday?" She sounded as if someone had his hands around her throat, cutting off her air.

"Wednesday better for you?"

She'd caught the glint of laughter in his eyes. He knew that when she snapped, "Tuesday will do fine."

"Tuesday it is then. I'll come by Monday morning and pick up your things."

"My things?"

"Clothes and such. If you want to bring some furniture to the Slash-C, we can arrange that later on."

He could read her face so easily—she hadn't thought about moving in with him being one of the results of saying she wanted to marry him. But she recovered quickly, his Matty did. Quickly enough to rap out a terse, "Fine."

"'Bout nine o'clock, say?"

"Fine."

"Fine," he echoed. "How 'bout getting ice cream before you head back to the ranch?"

"Uh, no. No thanks. I— There's something else I need to talk to Taylor about."

She was gone in a second, and he was left contemplating the closed door, wondering if that had been the truth or if the reality of what she'd signed on to do was finally starting to penetrate her stubborn head.

When you'd had as bad a weekend as Matty had had, Monday ought to be different. No such luck.

First, the ranch pickup's transmission seized up Saturday morning as Cal was heading out to check stock in the west range. Cal did what he could, but it was going to need to go to the shop. And they were funny about wanting money for the parts and labor the old heap kept sucking up.

Then, a pair of late-calving heifers started having trouble. The first finally gave birth to a sickly calf. They'd done what they could for mother and calf, and were heading in for coffee when the second heifer started calving. As thanks for their troubles, the animal had kicked Matty in the hip. At least her calf survived. The first one died as the moon rose.

Even allowing themselves only a few hours of sleep, they got a late start Sunday when they both finally rode out to the west range in a chilling rain. They found a section of fence down and Flying W head thoroughly intermingled with Bert Watson's Diamond D brand. Straightening that out and getting up a temporary fix on the fence ate the rest of daylight.

Some day of rest.

But of the whole miserable weekend, last night, when she'd told Cal Ruskoff about what the week ahead held, was the worst.

He'd come into the main house after supper to talk about what he would work on the next day over a cup of coffee, a custom he'd started with Great-Uncle Henry and continued with her.

She'd debated not telling him at all. But that didn't seem fair—after all, it would affect his job. Besides, even a recluse like Cal would hear the talk from town eventually, and it might not make things look too good if her top hand didn't know she was married.

She hadn't told him before that moment because…well,

she didn't know precisely why. Maybe she'd needed to sleep on it. Or maybe she'd needed to give Dave a couple days to back out.

But by last night, she'd known Dave wasn't going to change his mind. He was not the sort to leave a woman at the altar. *No, he was the sort to take her out for a ride and tell her breaking up was for her own good.*

But this time, she hadn't heard from him since leaving him outside Taylor's office. So he wasn't backing out. And that meant she had to tell Cal.

She'd taken a deep breath and said, as casually as she could, "Cal, I have something to tell you... I'm getting married. Tuesday. To Dave Currick."

First he'd gone silent. Then he'd commented that Henry had told him not to let Dave Currick set foot on the Flying W.

"Oh, that. Great-Uncle Henry got it into his head that he hated Dave because Dave broke up with me back when we were kids. You know how Henry was."

"He broke up with you. You've been gone years. Been working too hard to see anybody these weeks you've been back. And now you're getting married. What's going on, Matty?"

She'd started explaining. Mostly explaining why she couldn't explain. At least not the whole thing. Not right now. But that when she *did* explain the whole thing, he'd see that it was really the best thing for the ranch. And how it wasn't hurting anyone.

It was a little disjointed as explanations went, but it made sense, she knew it did. The more she'd talked, however, the more he'd gotten all stiff-jawed. And when she'd finished, he'd slammed his fist against her kitchen table, told her she was a fool and walked out. She'd been too stunned to do any more than sit there.

She'd spent a restless night, arguing with that word "fool"—without even knowing how he meant it. Jealousy didn't enter into it, because there wasn't that kind of feeling between her and Cal.

This morning, she hadn't seen so much as Cal's shadow... not until Dave pulled up by the back door in his midnight-blue pickup that hummed like a barbershop quartet. Of course, a Slash-C pickup's transmission wouldn't even *think* of seizing up.

Dave stepped out of the truck, wearing the snug, worn jeans and faded shirt that proclaimed that this day he was working as ranch owner and not lawyer. And Matty was suddenly deeply grateful for her rotten weekend and for Cal's strange reaction to her announcement. They'd kept her too busy to think of Dave as anything other than a means to her end.

Because with him right in front of her, the movement of his thighs as he got out of the truck, the flex of his shoulders as he gave the door a push to close it, the turn of his head as his gaze zeroed in on her, the *end* she found her thoughts drifting to was the taut one encased in his jeans.

To her relief, Cal came sauntering out of the barn, as if she hadn't just been in there calling his name. She glared at him—that way she couldn't stare at Dave.

"Morning, Matty. You got your things ready?" When she didn't answer right away, Dave turned, looking over his shoulder, probably to see what she was looking at. "Morning, Cal," he added in a neutral voice. "I suppose you've heard that congratulations are in order?"

By this time Cal had come up even with Dave, and she'd advanced so the three of them stood in a loose triangle.

"Yeah? Do you love her?"

"Cal—!" she started.

Dave cut her off. His easy smile was gone, but his voice was nearly as unhurried as ever. "You don't know me well enough to be asking me that, Ruskoff." He settled his hat lower, shadowing his eyes. "Why don't you ask her?"

"All right, I will." Cal stepped toward her. "Do you, Matty? Do you love him?"

Her eyes flicked to Dave, then away.

Love him? The phrase seemed to reverberate in her head and her heart, picking up an echo of Grams's voice.

Do you love him, girl? Truly love him? Or are you set on him because that's what you've always expected of yourself. Think about it hard, Matty. Do you love him?

"Well, Matty?" Cal insisted. "Are you marrying Currick because you love him?"

Almost grateful, she looked fully at him. "Cal, I told you last night, there're other things involved. Besides—" she added strongly as he opened his mouth, "it's between Dave and me. Whatever we do shouldn't matter to anyone else."

"She's got you there, Ruskoff," Dave murmured. And even without looking at him, Matty was certain his lips were twitching.

Cal paid him no heed, continuing to stare at her. "You can't do this, Matty."

"Cal, don't go making a tragedy out of something that's no big deal. Dave and I worked it out. It'll all be fine. You'll see. I'll go get my stuff."

She turned on her heel and didn't look back.

It was really kind of sweet of Cal, she thought as she opened the screen door to the back hall. She never would have expected the silent ranch hand to worry about such things as love.

As the door swung closed behind her, she heard Dave's voice from outside, and stopped.

"You obviously don't know your employer well, Ruskoff."

She looked back in time to see Cal spin around and face Dave. "Are you saying you think she should do this—marry you, in some damned fool scheme to help the ranch?"

"She told you that's why she's marrying me?"

"Not in so many words," he snapped.

"But still, you think she's after my money?" Dave sounded only mildly interested.

"No. Matty wouldn't— Besides, she told me about that prenup."

"I'd give her money, if that's what she wanted. And she knows it."

"That's not the question. The question is if you're saying you think she should really go through with this harebrained scheme."

"I'm not putting forward an opinion one way or the other on whether she can or she should. But I *am* saying that the surest way of making damned sure that Matilda Brennan— soon to be Matilda Brennan Currick," he inserted with emphasis, "will try something is to tell her she *can't* do it. The second surest way is to tell her she *shouldn't* do it."

When Matty swung open the screen door, she had a moment's view of the two men looking at each other hard, nearly nose to nose, before they turned their heads toward her.

This concern stuff was sweet, but it could get out of hand.

"If you two are done acting like a couple of bull moose and talking about me like I'm not here, you could help me bring my things out instead of leaving me to do all the lugging."

She had the satisfaction of seeing both men meekly turn and head into the house. Dave let Cal precede him. Cal shot her a look from the corner of his eye as she stood in the hallway with her arms crossed under her breasts, then kept moving.

"Currick! Just for the record," she said as he reached her and stopped, "I don't want your money, and I wouldn't take it if you offered."

Dave leaned one hand on the wall above her shoulder, crowding her in the narrow space. She could feel the warmth of his body, smell the breeze and sun on him. He had dropped his chin to look at her; she stared back with her chin raised.

If he simply bent his elbow, his mouth would meet hers and his body would press against hers. Would they fit together as well as they had from the first? Would his taste and feel be the same. Would the sensations—?

No! All that was past. Long gone. Part of her childhood.

She refused to move, but she won herself some mental space by asking, "Are you going to help or are you going to stand here all day, Currick?"

He smiled down at her. "Wanted to point out that we were talking about you like you weren't there, because you *weren't* there." He straightened away from the wall and headed down the hallway in the direction Cal had disappeared in. "You were in here, listening through the door."

"I was not! I was..." Well, come to think of it she was.

Just before he turned the corner to the stairs Dave looked back; he was grinning.

"I had every right to listen— You were talking about me and you're on my property!"

All she heard was his chuckle.

Dave came out of the courthouse in Jefferson late that afternoon whistling a song from the old movies his mother loved, and headed to where he'd parked his car.

Things were as set for tomorrow as they could be. He couldn't pin everything down because a lot depended on exactly how and when Matty backed out of this.

He'd had to line up a judge in case they made it that far, but he'd selected a longtime friend of the family. He'd even dropped a couple subtle hints to Judge Halloran, though the older man hadn't seemed to pick them up. But Dave hadn't wanted to be any more forthcoming. Judge Halloran had a habit of being forthright, and the last thing Dave wanted was for Halloran to say anything along the lines of "Dave thought you'd chicken out" to Matty tomorrow morning.

No, he wanted her to have no excuses to find fault with him at all. Because after she backed out, he intended to keep seeing her. At the very least, she'd have to come over to get her clothes and other personal effects back.

A new store's sign caught his eye and he stopped whistling in the middle of "Pick Yourself Up, Dust Yourself Off and Start All Over Again."

The flower shop sign advertised that it did weddings.

Well, why not? A bride should have a bouquet, even one who wasn't going to go through with the ceremony. Besides, maybe giving Matty flowers would soften her up some more about agreeing to keep seeing him afterward.

Five minutes after he'd pushed open the door he was regretting this decision.

"A regular bunch of wedding flowers" hadn't satisfied the clerk with the T-shirt that read True Flower Power. She'd barely contained her shock that he was doing the ordering—"And so late!"—instead of the bride. His not knowing anything about what Matty intended to wear also earned a disapproving stare.

By the time she was reeling off a list of possibilities that had his head swimming, a trickle of sweat had worked down the center of his back.

"Look," he said, breaking into a discourse on pink roses compared to peach roses, "do up something nice. Simple, but nice, okay?"

"Surely you want something that has special meaning for you and your bride, something that signifies your relationship?"

Prickly pear? He didn't think this woman would understand that request.

"Regular flowers will— No, wait. I know something. Indian Paintbrush."

"Indian Paintbrush?"

"It's a wildflower. Has bright red flowers." Whose vibrancy had always reminded him of Matty.

"Actually its flowers are small and greenish." Her voice broke. "It's the bracts that are red."

"If you can't get any—"

"I can. It's not something I would usually have from suppliers, but some is growing in my yard. It's…I'm so moved." She had a hand to her heart and was blinking back tears. "So touched. It's perfect, just perfect. No one ever thinks of it for a wedding bouquet, but nothing could be more perfect. How did you know that Indian Paintbrush's essence makes dreams come true?"

"Is that a fact? Uh, look, I really got to go now, so if you'll bill me like we talked about, and have the flowers delivered to the courthouse in the morning, I'm sure you'll make them look fine."

"Oh, I will, I will," she vowed. "With Indian Paintbrush as the base flower and then complemented by other elements that will enhance its ability to balance polarities. It's really all about yin and yang. Of course, this mountain-grown plant is more subtle, has a stronger element of yin than the desert's yang—"

Dave closed the door on yin and yang, and breathed a sigh of relief.

The bride looked thunderous.

Knowing Matty as he did, Dave preferred that to the pinched, white expression she'd worn on the drive to the county courthouse this morning. When he'd picked her up at the Flying W an hour and a half ago, she'd looked like a bull-rider who'd taken a fall and broken a few vital bones. Now she looked like the bull—about to charge.

When he'd stepped into the empty kitchen at the appointed time, he'd fought off a wave of missing Grams, then called out to Matty that he was there. He'd been fully prepared to wait like he used to, but she'd come downstairs almost immediately.

He'd like to think the tightness in his chest and throat was at the surprise, but it seemed doubtful.

She wore a suit, but not like any of the suits he'd seen

women wear in the courthouse. And not like anything he'd ever seen Matty in before.

It had just enough color to not be off-white. Not pink, not peach, either, but something in between. The skirt was straight and stopped above her knees, leaving a nice length of curve before reaching some strappy black shoes with a heel a little bigger than on her cowboy boots. He could tell that because her eyes were about two inches below his instead of their usual three. The jacket was molded to her curves like a caress. As far as he could tell, from the faint curve and hint of shadow that showed at the point of the V opening, she wore no blouse under it.

He could imagine his hand stroking down into that shadow, to the smooth heat and curves he remembered so well.

A couple of buttons slipped loose, and—

Jerking his mind away from that, he looked up. Her hair was pulled back from her face in a sleek line that twisted somehow at the back of her head, leaving a few tendrils at her nape. She wore drop pearl earrings he remembered his parents giving her for her eighteenth birthday.

She moistened her lips with her tongue and his mind started down another familiar, hot path. This time, when he looked up, he met her eyes.

Defiant vulnerability.

"Now I know how the cattle feel when they're being auctioned off," she muttered. Her voice sounded strained, and she cleared her throat.

Odd, he had to clear his throat, too.

He'd pushed aside a temptation to ease his own reaction by teasing her, and said simply, "You look beautiful, Matty."

She'd flushed fast and bright, and then she'd gone pale. And she'd stayed pale and silent throughout the trip to Jefferson.

He was tempted to touch her. Hell, he was tempted to draw

her into his arms and explore the soft lips she'd wetted until she opened them and let him inside to the warmth and sweetness of her mouth. To explore that shadow where her jacket buttoned until she opened even more to him.

Clamping down on his thoughts, he turned the truck's heater on instead.

The change in her from nervous to furious had occurred at the courthouse. They'd filled in all the blanks of the license form and handed it over to the motherly looking clerk with the permanent smile lines etched at her eyes.

"What about the blood tests?" Matty had suddenly asked.

Dave had been surprised she'd been paying that much attention to the process of form-filling and such.

"What about them?"

"Don't you have to show her the results?"

He opened his mouth, but before he could answer, the clerk announced, "Don't need blood tests here, honey. Not to get a license."

Matty spun on him. "You said we needed blood tests!"

"I never said that." He was glad to again be on this familiar—and safe—footing with Matty. "I simply got us in to see Doc and you assumed it was because the blood tests were a requirement."

"Why you—"

"Now, honey..." He got out the traditional phrase of the placating male without laughing, but barely. "Doc said you hadn't been in for a checkup in ages and you looked a little rundown, but knowing how you felt about needles, he didn't think you'd come in on your own, so..."

"Are you saying you tricked me into having a blood test under false pretenses for my *health,* you lying, no-good—?"

"I think it's a good idea," interrupted the woman behind the desk, apparently unperturbed by Matty's flaring anger at her intended groom. Chances were she'd seen it before. "No matter what the state says. You can't be too sure these days. And it lets a couple start married life without one more worry hanging over their heads. They have enough things to fret about. Money and a place to live and in-laws and then when the little ones start coming… Well, I say it's one less thing to worry about, knowing that neither of you is bringing in something to the marriage that nobody should have to deal with.''

''We don't need to be tested for that,'' Matty said curtly. ''We're not—''

He jogged her elbow hard to remind her not to say too much. It might not have been necessary, because the clerk was going on, and it was unlikely Matty could have stemmed that flow.

''Oh, I know every young couple thinks that, but if they were all right, there wouldn't be this terrible disease around the way it is, now would there? So, I say, better safe than sorry. Yes, sir, you get that test and then you know for sure. And that way—'' she finished off the form with a flourish and handed it to Dave ''—you start your marriage with a clean slate. Now, you bring that back to me with the signatures after you've seen the preacher and we'll see that you're officially married in the eyes of Clark County and the state of Wyoming.''

Matty blinked at her. ''Just like that?''

The woman beamed back. ''Just like that.''

''No waiting period?''

''No, not here in Clark County. Fill out the form, pay your fee, get your license and find a judge or a preacher and you can be married in half an hour.''

''Thank you.'' From the way those words came out, Matty was grinding her teeth. She glared at him. ''Let's go.''

''Congratulations, you two! Hope the wedding's beautiful.''

Out in the hallway, Dave simply nodded toward the stairs and said, ''Judge Halloran's office is upstairs.''

But she must have heard something in his voice, because she hissed at him, ''If you laugh, David Edward Currick, I will string you up to a tree where nobody'll ever find you, smear you with honey and leave you for the buzzards.''

He wasn't sure he would have laughed—he was expecting the reference to the judge's office to be the final straw that prompted Matty to end this. It had already progressed a lot farther than he'd expected. But at her response a chuckle escaped. ''Well, the honey part sounds fine, but I'm not partial to the rest of it.''

She spun on him a third of the way up the stairs, unmindful of the two men forced to detour around them.

''You knew I wanted to get married right away—the sooner the better—and you delayed it for a week. A whole week! If you didn't want to do this, why didn't you tell me?''

''I wanted to give you time to change your mind.''

Her wrath faded abruptly, and the look she gave him was searching.

''I'm not going to change my mind, Dave. But I can see why you might think that. If you want to back out, I'd understand. It's…'' She swallowed, clearly not able or not willing to say more.

It had to be something pretty damned big pushing her toward wanting to—*needing* to—marry him so suddenly.

There was nothing sudden about his wanting to marry Matty. But he'd given up on the dream a long time ago. He'd even tried his damnedest to find someone else who gave him that until-death-do-us-part feeling. It hadn't worked. He'd pretty much figured on being alone.

And now Matty was standing in front of him saying she wasn't going to call off this crazy plan of hers to get married—for reasons unspecified, and with no pretense that she was in love with him.

He felt like a man awaking from a dream to find himself standing in front of an open airplane door, and facing the decision of whether to jump or not.

A wise man would be sure he wore a parachute before he faced that choice.

A wise man would know there had to be safer ways to test a hope that there might still be something between old lovers than by getting married.

A wise man would turn tail and run.

Who had ever said he was wise when it came to Matilda Jeanette Brennan?

"I'm not backing out." He took her elbow and started her up the stairs again. "Judge Halloran's waiting for us."

So were Taylor Anne Larsen and Cal Ruskoff.

Matty balked at the sight of them. "What—?"

"We need witnesses, I thought you'd rather have friends than a couple of strangers from the clerk's office." He didn't say that he'd also thought it would be a good idea to have witnesses that *she'd* been the one to back out. And that he'd chosen the two people available who he'd thought would be most protective of her. That's why he'd passed up Lisa— If worse came to worse, and an outsider was looking over the situation, his sister might be considered biased.

Matty made no other protest, even docilely took the bright bouquet Taylor handed her with only a quick glance at him. He returned a faint shrug. Someday he'd have to tell Matty the story of his ordering the Indian Paintbrush for her wedding bouquet, she'd get a kick out of it, especially the part where he'd fled the store. He almost laughed aloud when he remembered what had prompted him to order the flowers in the first place—marrying her was a darn sight more likely to ensure he got to see her again than a few flowers!

After being introduced to Matty and Cal, and saying hello to the two lawyers, whom he already knew, Judge Halloran got right to business.

The ceremony went fast. At least it felt that way to Dave. The whole thing seemed to take place in a sort of fog, where sounds irrationally shifted from louder to fainter than normal, and faces slipped in and out of focus.

A couple of ominous moments stood out clear and stark.

The first came when Judge Halloran asked if anyone knew a reason these two should not be married.

There'd been a creak of boot leather, like Ruskoff had shifted his weight. Dave turned to the other man. Cal wore an expression that promised retribution if harm came to Matty. Dave simply looked back. Cal remained silent and in another second, the judge was rolling along with the familiar words that somehow sounded so odd.

The second worrisome moment came in the silence of waiting for Matty's "I do." She cleared her throat, and Dave didn't breathe. She could still back out. Now, right this second. Did he want her to?

"I do." Her voice came clear and strong and determined.

After that, it was still misty, but fairly easy. He'd even gotten a kick out of Matty's look of panic when the rings were mentioned, and her flicker of relief when he held up the ring for her hand, then surprise when Taylor handed over the ring Matty was to put on his hand.

He'd bought them as a kind of insurance against her saying he hadn't taken her seriously.

Then it came to, "You may kiss the bride."

Dave gave her no time to think—or himself—but placed a hand to each side of her face to draw her toward him and kissed her...hard. She grabbed his arms, apparently to steady herself, and gasped. Their mouths opened to each other, and his tongue found hers.

The heat and rhythm were instant and powerful.

He stroked his tongue inside her mouth, and hers twined against it. He took in the taste of her like a starving man. He shifted the angle to take it deeper, and she met him. It was what he'd imagined. It was much more.

The kiss ended only because they had to breathe. And that let in just enough common sense to remind him where they were and what was happening.

"I now pronounce you man and wife." Judge Halloran gave a laugh. "And from the looks of it, just in time."

Chapter Three

"I've got one more stop to make before we head to the ranch," Dave announced as he pulled into the Methodist Church parking lot where the exterior lights were starting to show against the shadows of dusk. "Promised Ervin I'd drop something by."

Matty moaned, but it seemed churlish to object too strenuously to someone doing a favor for a man of the cloth.

"Hurry up, then. I can't wait to get out of these clothes." She thought she caught a flicker across Dave's face, and wanted to kick herself for mentioning taking off her clothes. Ever since that kiss, she'd been trying her damnedest to keep the mood light and casual, and to pretend as best she could that there had been nothing unusual at all in the most bizarre morning of her life. "Why'd you insist we have lunch at Trents? You know I can't resist their prime rib."

"McDonald's didn't seem the place to take our witnesses for a wedding lunch."

"That wouldn't have helped anyway. I can't resist Big

Macs, either," she said with a sigh. Though, if truth be told, the reason she'd eaten so much and so fast at lunch was nerves, not taste buds.

Why had he kissed her that way? Why had she kissed him back?

Habit? Instinct? Desire?

Not that any of that truly mattered. The only thing that mattered was the fear that Dave would think she'd asked him to marry her because she still wanted him. That he would think she'd set all this up as an elaborate ruse to get him to marry her. She'd have to make sure he understood that she still saw their marriage as strictly a business deal.

And that no strings in this deal led to the bedroom door.

As Dave closed the driver's door, she leaned back and closed her eyes, considering undoing the skirt button at her waist.

"I should have taken a doggy bag instead of finishing that whole meal," she muttered to herself.

"You're not the doggy bag sort, Matty."

Her eyes flew open to find Dave opening the passenger door, his grin faintly lopsided. "You're the I-can't-believe-I-ate-the-whole-thing type."

"I thought you had something for Ervin."

"I do. Come with me."

"You're kidding. I can hardly move. I just want to get—" She stopped herself from saying *undressed.*

"I'll carry you."

The offer, mixed with the thoughts sparked by her unspoken words, brought alive images that she dearly wished had stayed in deep hibernation. *Dave's arms around her, lifting her from the water of the swimming hole, carrying her to the blanket in the shade. His hands peeling down her wet suit—*

"What? Why would—hey! Stop that!" Matty pushed at Dave's shoulders, trying to shut out the heat that came from inside her as well as from his chest and arms surrounding her. But he already had one arm under her knees and the other circling her back. "Put me down!"

Who could have known the material of his sports jacket rubbing against the nylon-covered underside of her knees would be as disturbingly erotic a friction as bare skin...maybe more so. Any motion she made to avoid that friction brought the rest of her into firmer contact with his chest and moved their faces so close that in another second...

"Quit squirming or I'll drop you. Hang on, Matty, I've got to open the door."

He fumbled with the latch of the main church door. The movement of his hand and arm had her bobbling up and down against his chest. And apparently lunch had not only left her stuffed but a little woozy, because her stomach was doing flips. She'd never had this reaction before to prime rib.

"It would be a whole lot easier if you put me down."

Her own voice sounded oddly breathy and low.

"You know what they say—ah!—" he swung the door open triumphantly and quickly carried her inside "—about thresholds and newly married couples."

"Not the threshold of a church, for heaven's sake, Currick. That's— Oh, no, no way, you're not carrying me down those stairs."

"Scared, Matty?"

"Smart. If you fall, I go down first and you land on top of me. I'd be a pancake." He set her on her feet, and she started down the stairs that led off the main vestibule. "This is ridiculous—it's dark down here and deserted. Ervin's not even here. And I was perfectly comfortable in the truck, so why you insisted—"

"I thought you could use some exercise. Work off that prime rib," he said from directly behind.

"By carrying me? Currick, you are—"

"Surprise!"

Shouts and light jumped out at her, and Matty instinctively stepped back, directly into Dave. His arms came around her, crossing under her breasts, his chin resting against her hair. She made no effort to move.

"Surprise, Matty," he said softly as people started swarming toward them. Taylor and Lisa, Reverend Ervin Foley, Doc Johnson, Ruth and Hugh Moski, Joyce from the bank, Brandy from the post office, among a score of other familiar faces, and off to one side, standing by himself, Cal.

"What is this?"

"Your wedding reception," announced Joyce, with a satisfied smile. "We know you'd decided against a big wedding, but we had to do a little something to let you and Dave know how happy we are for you two!"

A quick glance showed that the "little something" included decorating the Methodist Church's basement meeting room with streamers and balloons, covering the folding tables with wedding-themed paper, opening a space for dancing, importing Hugh Moski's portable sound system and a white-frosted, rosette-studded, four-tiered wedding cake on a round table all its own, next to another table stacked with packages wrapped in pastel papers and bows.

"Oh, no. You shouldn't have." Matty was certain the guilt in her anguished whisper would give the whole charade away.

But judging from Taylor's wide smile, she took it for another emotion. "We wanted to."

Matty twisted to look up at Dave. "You shouldn't have let them, when…"

He gave her a squeeze to halt her words, accompanied by a philosophical shrug. "There's no stopping some folks when it comes to doing something they want to do. Not without making more of a *fuss* than I thought you'd want."

"But, you thought—"

He gave his head a slight warning shake, then shrugged. "I'd have handled it."

As their eyes held, she read the message he didn't put into words. If she'd backed out at the courthouse as he had expected her to, he would have come here and taken the brunt of the questions and confusion and gossip.

"Oh, look at that," cooed Joyce. "Just like an old married couple, telling each other secrets without saying a word. But, c'mon, now, you two, we've got some celebrating to do. First off, we'll have you cut the cake and get some pictures of you feeding each other a slice. Then we'll have the dancing."

"Cake? Oh, I couldn't eat a bite after our lunch."

"Sure you can. What you need is a little champagne to settle your stomach. Hugh! Open the champagne so we can toast the happy couple."

Matty was kissed on the cheek, shook by the hand, instructed to smile, handed champagne glasses, ordered to look at Dave and smile, given a knife, posed behind the cake, offered congratulations, told to open her mouth for cake, prompted yet again to smile and called on to kiss Dave for "just one more picture"—until her head spun.

"Okay, Dave, give Matty another bite of cake, I was out of film last time," instructed a voice from the audience.

"Oh, God," she murmured.

"Like bringing coals to Newcastle, isn't it, Matty?"

Feeling a glare would not be the best expression to have captured by the cameras clicking with unnerving frequency, Matty satisfied herself with a low-voiced, "Very funny, Currick. But I swear, if you try to feed me one more thing—"

He popped not only a morsel of white cake with a fragment of icing on it, but the tip of his index finger into her mouth. She captured it, fully intending to bite down. But somehow, as he stepped closer, with his other hand at the small of her back, and looked directly into her eyes, she couldn't make her teeth clamp down. At least she had the satisfaction of seeing the amusement in his eyes evaporate as she drew in more of the sweetness on his finger with her tongue and lips before she released it.

"Great! Great!" came the voice of their latest director.

"Now another kiss, and not a peck like last time, you two, we want a *real* kiss."

"Glad to oblige." Dave's voice seemed to rumble through her nerve endings.

Surely he wouldn't kiss her the way he had in the judge's chambers. He'd been trying to make a point then. Something to do with male pride. That was the admittedly vague conclusion she'd reached during the uneasy drive to the restaurant for lunch.

As for her response to and—*admit it, Matty*—participation in that kiss, that had happened because she hadn't expected it, hadn't prepared for it. Besides, she was tired. Not much sleep the past few nights, and a lot of worry. And on top of all that, there were those lingering responses from when she'd been a girl and Dave had been the only male in the universe to kiss her romantically.

This time would be different.

It was.

And just as unexpected.

His face lowered to hers. She closed her eyes and braced herself, but he didn't claim her, he didn't set a rhythm that reminded her of long-ago passions. Instead he kissed her softly. Sliding his lips over hers gently, kissing the corner of her mouth, then her top lip, then the bottom. She tasted the sweetness of cake and the tartness of champagne on him, and wanted more. He found an opening—or she gave him one—and he explored her mouth as if he hadn't been the first one to ever kiss her this way. With a slow, soft tenderness that brought an ache to her throat, as well as parts of her body well below her throat.

And when he ended the kiss before anyone could consider it an unseemly demonstration in the church basement, he touched his lips to her nose, then her forehead, and tucked her head under his chin, so she didn't have to look at the friends and neighbors making approving sounds around them.

"Glad to oblige," he repeated, though this time in such a low voice that only she could hear it.

For an instant, Matty panicked.

She pulled back enough to get a clear look at his face.

"Everything okay, Matty?"

He winked as he asked it, and she felt a wave of weakness rush over her. Relief. Had to be.

She straightened and found a smile. "Fine. Just fine."

And after all that, they made her dance.

At least it was fairly quiet in the middle of the floor, with only Dave for company. The fact that he had his arms around her meant she didn't have to do all the work of standing up straight.

"I think this is some form of torture society's come up with," she muttered. "It's a rite of passage to see if you really have the endurance to be married."

Dave interrupted his humming along with the song emanating from Hugh's sound system. "Quit your complaining. Look at all the presents you're getting."

"That's another thing. Dave—" she took ahold of both his shoulders to look up at him earnestly "—we can't take those things. It's not right."

"We don't have much choice."

"But—"

"Not if you want to make this look real. But that doesn't mean we have to keep them. We'll keep a list of who gave what and after…well, later, we can donate the things to charity in the names of the givers. How's that?"

"I guess that's fair."

She settled back into the usual dancing position and he resumed humming as they moved around the floor.

"Dave? This song is familiar. What is it?"

"It should be familiar, I told Hugh it's our song."

"*Our* song? We never had a song, even when there was a *we* to have a song."

"We do now. It's called 'A Fine Romance.' Mom used to sing it."

"Oh, one of your mother's songs—must be something Fred Astaire sang."

"Most likely."

"Remember on rainy days how she used to play us that music over and over, and act out the whole movie and make us and Lisa dance around with her?"

"Mm-hmm."

Letting herself relax more fully into Dave's hold, Matty smiled. She used to enjoy those rainy days, fired by Donna Currick's enthusiasm for old-fashioned musicals. Whenever any had appeared on television, it had been an event in the Currick household, with popcorn made well ahead of time and no interruptions allowed. When a particularly romantic dance ended, she could remember Mrs. Currick's soft, satisfied sigh, then the look she invariably turned toward her husband.

When Matty had gotten a little older she had wondered if Donna Currick ever regretted giving up her dreams of starring in Broadway musicals to settle down with her rancher husband in Clark County, Wyoming. When Matty had gotten older still, she'd remembered those looks, recognized what they meant and decided the answer was no.

"I don't remember the words to this one. Do you?"

Rather than answer, Dave picked up the lyrics, as if he'd been silently singing the gently sarcastic phrases about what a fine romance this was that had no kisses and no embraces, Matty didn't know whether to laugh or cry. It certainly fit the bill as "their song."

The music ended and she stepped out of his arms.

His eyes glinted with mischief and something else, not so easily identified. "Appropriate for us, don't you think?"

"You want to know what I think?" Ignoring that unidentified element, she played strictly to the mischief. "I think there is one thing absolutely certain after hearing this song. You did *not* inherit your mother's singing voice."

Dave's laughter drew smiles from all around the room.

"Sure am glad I got that dance on the camcorder," gloated Joyce. "This will be something you can look back on ten years from now and remember exactly how you felt today."

Matty met Dave's look for an instant, and she wondered if he was thinking the same thing she was—that piece of video could be around five, ten, even twenty times longer than their marriage lasted.

"Hey, Dave," came the voice of a neighboring rancher. "I wanted to ask you about that bull Terry Gatchell's selling. I don't mean to be taking you away from your bride for more than a second, whatever Betty says, but you saw it last spring, didn't you? I'm thinking of buying it and I wanted to know…"

As Fred Montress droned on, Dave quirked a fatalistic look at Matty. They both knew once Fred got into a discussion of breeding stock, it would be a spell before he'd let Dave get free.

"Sorry, Matty," he murmured as Fred wrapped a beefy arm around his shoulders and led him away.

"It's okay, I'll just…I'll…" Feeling oddly bereft alone in the middle of the dance floor, she scanned the gathering, passing over Joyce's beaming face and the beckoning finger of Mrs. Van Hopft, her second-grade teacher, before spotting Lisa in the far corner, and making a beeline for her.

"Lisa, I swear, if anyone gives me one more bite of cake," she started as she plopped down in the empty chair beside Dave's younger sister, "or one more sip of champagne, I am going to positively—" A drop of moisture splatted a spreading blot on Lisa's navy skirt. A *tear?* Lisa had been so completely self-contained since her return to Knighton that Matty almost didn't believe her own eyes. "Explode. Lisa, are you all right?"

"Haven't you ever seen anyone cry at a wedding before?" she responded blinking hard.

Matty refrained from pointing out that, first, she hadn't heard of *this* anyone crying under any circumstances for several years. And, second, that this was the reception, not the wedding.

Lisa wiped at the moisture in the corner of her eyes. "I was watching you two dance and thinking about when we were kids."

She launched into a series of reminisces about how inseparable Matty and Dave had been growing up.

"It's like you knew even then that Dave was the right man for you. A good man."

Lisa's quiet words were like hammer blows. Because he hadn't turned out to be the right man at all, and all this was a pose, a masquerade, a ruse.

Oh, God, what have I done?

Matty felt as if her head were inside one of those containers that whirled around to dry lettuce. She knew how the lettuce felt after a few too many rotations.

"And here he comes." Lisa nodded to behind Matty. She turned and saw Dave walking toward them. "I'll say one thing," Lisa added with deep affection, "he is a good man, that husband of yours."

That husband of yours.

My husband. Husband! The word slapped her, then swamped her, like storm-whipped waves. Dave was her husband.

David Edward Currick, do you take this woman...I do.

Omigod! Omigod! Omigod! *I'm married. I married Dave. Dave Currick. Married!*

Dave stood before her with his hand extended. His mouth quirked into a grin.

"C'mon, Mrs. Currick." There was something about the line from the corner of his jaw, down his neck and disappearing under the collar of his shirt that made her catch her breath. Something of power that she was certain hadn't been there before. Something that said he was no longer a boy.

She'd married this…this *man*. Not the boy she'd once known better even than her own heart, but a man who was a mystery to her. Six years had made him a stranger.

What have I done? Oh, Lord, what have I done?

His grin faded and something else came into his eyes. "Let's go home."

Maybe it was natural for the bride to turn so pale that her eyes looked huge and terrified when she first heard herself addressed as *Mrs*.

And maybe not, Dave thought grimly as he drove through the darkness toward the ranch. Maybe Matty hadn't thought about the Slash-C being her home now. For someone as attached to her land, as wrapped up with the Flying W as she was, that might come as a shock.

She'd made it through the wedding ceremony and the wedding lunch and even the hours of the reception, so what was left to be afraid of?

Surely she wasn't afraid of him. Wasn't afraid of their…wedding night.

It wasn't even going to be a true wedding night. She had to know he would live up to his bargain. But even if it were going to be a true wedding night…

Matty, this might hurt you.

You'd never hurt me, Dave.

It's not that I'd want to, sweetheart, but what I read says a girl's first time—

I know. I read those books, too. But I know something no book does. I know you could never hurt me.

I'll try not to, but…I'll go slow. Matty, don't! If you do that—

It's all right, Dave. I want this. I want you… You won't hurt me.

But he had. That first time for both of them, when she'd

smiled through her tears, and he'd thought his heart might explode with what he felt for her.

And he'd hurt her again later, when he'd said they should part and there had been no smile and hardly any tears. Just a shocked, void look of despair.

That was the last he'd seen of her for more than six years except a couple glimpses during her flying visits to her grandmother, followed by standing across Grams's grave from the moving statue that had hardly resembled his Matty at all. And then not even glimpses of her. He'd heard about a couple more visits she'd made to the Flying W, but apparently she'd become better at avoiding him.

Until Henry Brennan died suddenly, and Matty had returned to Wyoming.

He glanced at his passenger, sitting so still beside him as they turned into Slash-C land.

You'd never hurt me, Dave.

She wasn't saying that this time, not with words and not with attitude. She no longer had that faith in him.

Still, when she'd run into trouble, she'd turned to him. He was still unclear on what the trouble was. But no matter what, he'd get her out of it.

I'll do my best not to hurt you, Matty, but we both know now that nobody can live up to that kind of faith all the time.

Chapter Four

By the time she stood on the lit porch of the Slash-C home ranch while Dave unlocked the door, Matty had quelled the panic she'd experienced at the moment of understanding that to the world, Dave Currick was, indeed, her husband.

At least she'd pushed it to a back room of her mind.

All she wanted now was to take this darned skirt off, wash her face, brush her teeth and sleep for about a thousand hours.

The lock clicked open, and Dave turned to her with a small smile. "Suppose we should play it safe and follow all the traditions."

She hadn't sorted out what that meant when he reached toward her with both arms. She stepped back so fast she only saved herself from falling off the porch by grabbing the railing.

"What do you think you're doing?"

"For God's sake, Matty, I wasn't going to attack you. I was going to carry you over the threshold."

Her stomach flipped the way it had when he'd picked her

up at the church, and panic broke down the door of its back room with one mighty thud. No way was she going to let Dave put his arms around her again. No way was she going to let him hold her against his chest, so her arms naturally went around his neck and his face was so close that his mouth...

"Don't be an idiot!" she snapped. *To him or herself?* "We've done enough playacting already today. There's no sense pretending when it's the two of us."

He pushed open the door, and gestured, wide and mocking, for her to precede him into the house.

"No pretending then. Don't worry, Matty, I'm real clear this isn't supposed to be a real marriage. And that it's no love match."

The sting to his voice made her face hot as she marched purposefully past him.

"I'm glad you do. It's strictly a business proposition."

"Ah, yes, a business proposition," he said in that cool, amused way that could make her see red faster than a regiment of Santa Clauses. He followed her in and closed the door behind him with enough force to make her flinch. "Would you like to tell me now what exactly that business is? And what the real reason is behind this abrupt urge to marry me?"

Her legs demonstrated a sudden tenuency to tremble, as if she'd been on horseback for too many hours. In defiance of their weakness, she marched down the front hall of the rambling house to the archway that led to the family room.

But when she got there, she had to prop herself up against the back of the couch that faced the stone fireplace to keep from crumbling to the hardwood floor.

Dave didn't seem to notice. He stopped in the archway and crossed his arms over his chest. Maybe it was the pose, but she didn't think she'd ever seen him look more intimidating. The soft glow from the lamp on the hall table backlit his large frame. A light left on in the kitchen cut across his features in stark relief and black shadows.

"Well?"

For an instant, she glimpsed in his eyes what looked to be pain and something a voice in the back of her head called longing. When the expression disappeared, she almost reached out to try to grab it back. How stupid was that? Sure as hell, she was wrong. And, even surer, she didn't *want* those emotions to exist.

She just wanted to save her ranch.

She drew in a breath, and pushed out words.

"I needed a Clark County address. Legally, and fast. It's the only way I can get an Irrigation Commission grant. With most of the Flying W in Lewis County, my percentage of Clark County acreage isn't enough to qualify—two percentage points, but they said no exceptions. And without that money for new irrigation equipment, the Flying W…" She couldn't say the words. "We need that money. The way it is now, I couldn't even sell it for enough to cover the debts."

He stared at her with no expression, and she kept explaining, telling him about the difference it made being in Clark County over being in Lewis County, about Taylor's efforts to get an exception, about thinking her last chance was gone, about coming across a phrase about "official residency" and thinking maybe, just maybe, she didn't have to give up hope. Of running into him like fate had put him outside Taylor's office door on that day at that time, with her having that very specific need to keep her ranch going. A need he could fill. Layer after layer of words.

He cut through them with one sentence.

"You married me for my damned address."

He sounded absolutely calm, though his voice might have been a bit harsher than usual. But she didn't like the way he said that. Still, she was surprised into a flinch when he let loose with a string of uncharacteristic curses.

"I knew you'd think it was impulsive, but—"

"*Impulsive?* Matty Brennan you don't satisfy yourself with rushing in where angels fear to tread, you pass up even the fools who are hanging back because they can see this is a damned bad idea!"

He took a step toward her, then seemed to think *that* might be a bad idea, and swung away to face out the dark window.

"You don't have to be insulting, Currick. If it hadn't been the only hope I could see of saving the Flying W, I never would have..."

"Your only hope?" He had that mocking note back in his voice, which made her glad she'd stopped herself before saying that she never would have thrown herself on his mercy this way.

Despite that note, though, she believed his next words. That's why they bothered her. "I would have given you the money, Matty—"

"I told you, I don't want your money."

"—Hell, I would have given you enough acres so you'd qualify for the grant. Why go through—" two strides brought him back to her, he pulled her left hand away from the top of the couch and held it up in front of her face along with his left hand, so the pair of gold rings winked at her "—all this?"

"I didn't want your charity, Currick. All I needed was a Clark County address, but I couldn't afford to wait, and the only way to avoid that was marrying a Clark County resident. It should have been simple."

"Simple," he repeated, flat, yet as sharp as a knife.

She defended herself against the cut of it. "You're the one who made it all this fancy stuff. I thought it could be quiet, between the two of us. I thought—"

"No you didn't. You didn't think at all."

"I did, too! And you said you supposed it was a good thing you *didn't* know what I was planning, and I thought that was a good idea, because then you couldn't be accused of having any part of it. Deniability—that's what Taylor said it was called when I asked her about a hypothetical situation sort of simi—''

He was not listening, and he was not cool or emotionless anymore. ''You saw what you wanted and you took the most direct path to it, and it didn't matter who you ran over on your way. The way you always have.''

There was no protecting herself from the cut of that. But with an effort of will, Matty gathered her dignity. ''I'm sorry, Dave. I regret involving you in this. I presumed on our old friendship. If you'll drive me to the Flying W…or I'll take a truck and return it in the morning.''

''The hell you will. This is our wedding night—'' He gave the words a twist that tightened the knot in her stomach. ''And I'll be damned if I'm going to let you rush back home to the Flying W and raise all sorts of questions.'' He cursed again in the same deadly tone. ''I'm in it now. We're committed to this farce, because if we don't make it look good, everyone will know it's a fraud.''

''Fraud?'' People went to jail for fraud. But she'd checked those papers Taylor had given her and all they mentioned was a fine. She'd never have exposed Dave to something that could get him put in jail.

Or maybe it wasn't the word fraud that cut so deep. Maybe it was *farce.*

''Take the west room for tonight. I'll figure out the details in the morning.''

''*You'll* figure out—''

He whirled around to face her. Automatically she straightened, bringing them almost nose to nose.

''Yes, dammit, I'll figure it out. In…the…morning.''

''I'm not staying here. I'm—''

He grabbed her wrist and jerked her toward the hallway that led to the bedrooms. ''You're not going anywhere. You're dead on your feet. You're going to the west room. And you're going to bed. I'm going to bed, too—in my *own* bed.''

He released her wrist at the open door to the guest room where she'd spent a good number of nights in her girlhood. Without looking back, he strode down the hall and closed the door to the master bedroom.

Only he didn't go to bed. As she lay in the wide bed in the guest room, she could hear him pacing, the faint sounds reaching her from the wall by her head all night long, until she finally dozed off as the sky started to lighten from pitch to smoke.

The worst moment for Dave, even worse than the fighting or the long hours of mentally beating himself up for being fool enough to hope, was waking up to full sun late the next morning and finding her gone.

For long enough for it to hurt he held his breath and thought maybe he'd dreamt the whole thing. But his dreams were never quite as weird or wonderful as real life with Matty Brennan.

Or as painful.

He knew immediately that she was gone. Probably the quiet, he told himself.

Still, he rolled out of bed and methodically checked first the guest room, then the hall bathroom, then the kitchen.

She'd slept in the bed, and he saw signs she'd used the other two rooms, though she'd tidied up after herself. So, he hadn't dreamt this, and she surely was gone. But he wasn't going to do any wider searching in his all-together. He headed for a shower in the master bathroom, where, twenty-four hours earlier, he'd prepared for his wedding to Matty.

Considering the kick in the teeth his ego had taken last night, he supposed he should be glad he still had some teeth to brush, he told his reflection in the mirror.

He'd known from the start that she'd come to him only because she was in a bind of some kind. And it hadn't taken a genius to guess it had to do with the Flying W. Still, he'd been fool enough to let himself think her coming to him had something to do with him as a *person*. He'd never figured on it being what address his mail came to.

Or maybe he hadn't wanted to see. He'd known the Flying W was in trouble. He'd even wondered about her quick action in changing her address.

We need that money.

The Flying W was her birthright. For damn sure it was her only inheritance.

The way it is now, I couldn't even sell it for enough to cover the debts.

Sell it. Sell it and leave.

To go back to the life she'd created away from Wyoming, away from him. But in order to do that, first she had to get the place into order and retire some of the debts. To do that, she needed this grant. And to get the grant, she needed a Clark County address.

Enter one David Edward Currick.

Not as the companion of her childhood. Not as the boy who had courted her. Not as the young man she'd first loved and had been ready to marry. Not as the man who had been more than ready to step back into her life.

But as a convenience with the necessary address, who was a big enough fool to agree to marry her. And as the tool she would use to open the door so she could walk out of his life for good.

The hell of it was, he couldn't even deny her that. He'd help her get the Flying W back to where it was, with this marriage or with anything else that needed doing. Because he'd always looked out for Matty, and he always would.

Maybe he could argue she'd used him. But he'd more than cooperated.

That should teach him for having a big head about himself. Or for hoping there might be something between him and Matty again.

And none of that, not even all of it taken together, changed that he was still certifiable about her.

Just a lot more cautious.

* * *

"Rider coming in."

Cal made the laconic announcement from where he stood propped against the door frame of the lean-to where they kept shoeing supplies and salves, ointments, vaccines and medicines that didn't need special handling.

"Who?" She stopped packing the items she'd need for the afternoon's planned checkup on the head in the south section, and raised her head.

"Too far to tell."

She went to the doorway beside him, shading her eyes. Distance, sun glaring down, it made no difference. She instantly recognized the way Dave Currick sat a horse.

Cal, apparently divining the identity of the rider from her expression, said, "You don't have to see him. I'll get rid of him."

Without answering, she retreated into the shed. She could go from here, through the barn, out the corral, behind the string of buildings at its other side. In two minutes she could be as lost as she needed to be. She remained in the deep shadow, looking out.

Cal had moved beyond the doorway by the time Dave rode in on Brandeis.

"Currick," Cal said with little welcome in his voice.

"Ruskoff. Where's Matty?"

"Matty? You expecting her to be here?"

"You could say that," Dave drawled, dismounting.

Most men of her acquaintance would have stayed astride, preserving the body-language advantage of the greater height. And she wouldn't be at all surprised if that show of "sportsmanship" was what prompted Cal to drop any pose of not knowing something was seriously wrong. Not that he'd asked her anything when she rode in. He'd looked at her and shook his head.

"What the hell's going on with you two, Currick?"

"The fact that you have to ask me means either you didn't want to ask Matty or you asked her and she told you it was none of your damned business. Either way, it's none of your damned business."

Dave said the words without heat, but Matty half expected Cal to fire up. Instead, when he responded, he sounded solemn.

"It's my business as far as caring about Matty goes. And it's my business as far as putting my name on that piece of paper as witness to you two getting married yesterday. I had my doubts, but in that judge's chambers, when he said the new couple could kiss—"

She stepped to the doorway. "I wish you two would break this habit of talking about me behind my back."

Dave turned toward her, unhurried and unsurprised. "My first choice, Matty, would be to talk to you, not about you."

Cal gave her a long, searching stare before grunting something and walking away.

She gestured toward a bench outside the lean-to. She and Dave took seats in heavy silence, leaving two feet of empty bench between them. Without turning her head, she cut a look at Dave, hoping for a clue to how to begin saying all the contradictory things whipping through her brain.

Trying to sort through them had been her reason for leaving at first light. She sure hadn't made any progress tossing and turning in that bed last night.

I'll figure out the details in the morning.

That's what he'd said last night, and that's probably what he intended now. Dave had always been the one who figured things out for the both of them. It had never bothered her when they were growing up; that's just the way things were. But when she'd fled Wyoming and heartbreak six years ago there had been no one but her to figure things out. She'd been too determined at first to show Dave a thing or two to be scared. And then she discovered she wasn't half bad at this figuring out. She'd been out on her own, running her own life for six years now. She didn't think she could go back to how she used to be. She didn't want to.

On the other hand, she couldn't argue with his right to make this particular decision. She'd had her chance to back out of it before. It was only fair now that he had all the information, that he have a chance to back out.

He was working a piece of straw between the pads of his thumb and first finger. A fidgety sort of action for the most unfidgety person she'd ever known.

Odd. She'd forgotten this about Dave Currick. He seldom got angry—*long fuse on that one,* Grams used to say—but when he did reach his boiling point, he didn't come down from it fast. And when he was done being angry he didn't know what to do with himself and the head of steam he'd built up.

"I'm sorry, Matty. I'm sorry I lit into you like that last night."

She hadn't expected that. Hadn't considered he'd apologize. Her first words came out strained and awkward. "Okay. You had reason. And…"

"And what?" he prodded.

She slanted a look at him. Her stumbling words had carried her toward one facet of honesty, she might as well go all the way. "It's kind of, uh, interesting to see that famed Dave Currick cool slip."

His mouth twisted. "That's how you saw it, huh?"

"Yeah, that's how I saw it."

Her smile at his wry discomfort over his reaction last night faded as she remembered its cause. She drew a deep breath.

"I shouldn't have taken off this morning without letting you know. But I needed to think, and I do my best thinking working." She thought he tensed, but when she looked at him, she saw no sign of added tension. "Dave, I truly didn't mean for this to cause you harm. If there's really fraud to be dealt with, I'll be sure it comes on me and not you. But I swear I looked over those papers, and it said nothing about that. I know I'm not a lawyer, but... Well, I'd understand if you back out—I hope you won't, but I'd understand. And if there's trouble—"

"Our deal on trouble still holds, Matty."

"Deal?" She didn't remember negotiating about trouble when they concocted this agreement. But he sounded so solemn, there must have been something.

"If one of us is going to get in trouble, we both get in trouble. I'd hold you to that bargain, so my honor requires I live up to it now."

A spurt of laughter escaped her, and she spotted the answering twinkle in his eyes. "That was when we were kids— six years old. That's fine for having to answer to Grams or your mom and dad for mischief. This is a lot more serious, even though I'm sure fraud's not involved."

He looked at her then, searching, serious.

"It's that bad, Matty?"

She met his gaze long enough for him to see the truth, but had to look away before admitting, "It's that bad."

He slowly surveyed the area around them. He would see where Cal had used old timber to repair a break in the corral. He'd see the rutted road that cried out for grading and gravel. He'd see the flaking paint on the barn. If he got up and walked a few feet, he'd see they'd used up all their back stock of hay this past winter.

He'd see it, and draw the right conclusions.

Oh, he'd no doubt heard rumors of hard times at the Flying W, but, being Dave, he wouldn't have relied on rumors to make a judgment. And he hadn't been around the Flying W to see for himself before now, except for Monday when he'd come to get her stuff and yesterday when he'd picked her up for the trip to Jefferson. But if he'd been half as nervous as she'd been, he'd been in no state to notice things like peeling paint.

"You could let the creditors take it over, Matty. You could

walk away. You wouldn't have anything out of the ranch, but it would save you a lot of work.''

It was like a kick to her gut. Dave thought she would walk away from the Flying W? She'd figured he was the one person who'd understand, and now to hear him suggest she sell like it was worth seriously considering felt like someone had yanked a good hunk of the earth out from under her feet.

"Have you ever known me to be afraid of hard work?''

"A lot can change in six years.''

"Not that. Besides, I owe the Flying W more than that. I owe Grams and Gramps more than that.'' Her voice sounded as if she'd swallowed something that now blocked her throat—maybe the same something that had suddenly stuck a pole down her backbone. "I'm going to get it back to where it was if it's the last thing I do.''

He stuck the twist of straw in his mouth and chewed on it before saying, "If you're planning to stick around to do that, that's all the more reason to stick to our tried and true deal.''

The pole down her back collapsed abruptly. He might not understand her, but he was willing to stick by her. She twisted to stare at his profile, to be certain she hadn't misunderstood him. "You'd still go through with this?''

"If you think this grant will make the difference.''

"It can make all the difference, Dave. That money will let us drill a well and keep it operating in the Dry Creek section, and that will mean I can increase the herd by six percent, maybe do more selective breeding—when I have the capital, of course. And, with better irrigation I can plant hay on the flat behind the Three Widows hills, which would cut my winter feed bills by up to twenty percent. Twenty percent!''

She'd started cautiously, but as she went on her enthusiasm took over. She even loosened up enough to tell him her opinion of the boneheaded eligibility restrictions the grant carried.

"I truly did try every other way Taylor and I could think of,'' she continued. "And don't think I'm taking it away from anyone else. They've got enough money to give away four more grants than they've got applications for. So, it would go to waste otherwise. And marrying you was the only way I could see to get that grant. If there'd been any other way, believe me, I never would have married you or—''

"You wouldn't have let the villain tie you to the railroad track.''

"What? What are you laughing at?''

"Trying to see you in the role of Sweet Young Thing in this melodrama, willing to sacrifice herself in marriage to save the old homestead.''

The echo of her own words came back to her: *If there'd been any other way, believe me, I never would have married you—*

If he'd said those words, she doubted she'd be laughing. But Dave had always had the ability to laugh at himself. Of course, it was easy to laugh if the words held no sting for him.

"I never meant to imply—'' she started stiffly. But, with Dave laughing beside her, stiffness gave way to a chuckle. "I wouldn't exactly call it getting tied to the railroad track.''

"Worse, much worse. You're going to be living with me. What do they say about a fate worse than death?''

"You know, I was thinking about that—that living together stuff.''

"Oh?''

"I don't have to move to the Slash-C. I could stay here and go over to the Slash-C now and then. It would be a lot less disruptive for you.''

"Don't you think people would wonder why my bride was always driving up to the front door of her supposed new home?''

"I wouldn't drive, I'd ride—the back way like I always used to. Just like this morning. Nobody'd ever see me, especially if I did it at night.''

"That can be a dangerous ride at night.''

She snorted. "I can do that ride in my sleep.''

"Setting that issue aside for a moment, and even setting aside the blow to my ego when it got out that my bride preferred to ride back to her old bed each night instead of staying under my roof—"

"How would it get out?"

"Your hands, my—"

"Most are just here now and then, and Cal wouldn't say anything."

"Such loyalty. That's rare in a mere employee." His good humor had developed a dent. "But, even if Ruskoff kept his mouth shut, I doubt all my hands would be so noble. Starting with Jack at foreman, and right on down to Bryan, who comes in after high school. Not to mention Pamela Dobson, who cleans the house twice a week. If you don't think she'll be able to tell whether you're living there or not, you sadly underestimate her."

She hadn't considered Pamela. She wasn't a gossip per se, but she treasured her reputation for knowing the best dirt in two counties. And if others got wind that Pamela thought something was strange in this marriage, those with no scruples about gossip and nosiness would dig like starving dogs after a bone.

"If we're going to make this work, appearances are going to count a lot, Matty." Dave sounded every bit the respected lawyer now. "We don't want to give anyone cause to start doubting or they might see things we can't afford to have them see."

We. Such a small word, but so warming. Even in such a businesslike tone. For so many years, she and Dave had always been *we.* When that had ended, there'd been a gap in her heart. There'd been other *we's*—some of a romantic nature and some not—but it wasn't the same.

"Maybe so," she said reluctantly. "You've got a point that some nights I should be at the Slash-C. But there's no reason—"

"Every night."

Every night. The clutch at the pit of her stomach forced her to admit to herself that Dave's convenience had not been her only consideration in proposing that she be a commuter rather than a resident at the Slash-C. She had her own efficiency to consider, after all. And if, maybe, there was still a touch, a lingering reminder of what had once been between them…well, some old habits were hard to break, even if they were bad for your morale.

"I'll need to be here at the Flying W every day, and some mornings so early that it would make better sense for me to start off here."

"As you said, it's not a long ride—"

"If I see the need to spend the night at the Flying W, I'm going to do it, Currick. I'm not promising to spend every night at the Slash-C."

"Most nights," he proposed.

He'd made valid points. "Okay, most nights."

"And you'll move into the master bedroom."

"Hey!"

He raised his hands in a gesture of innocence. "Your things, I meant. Remember Pamela."

"Then you have to make room for me."

"Some closet space, sure—"

She narrowed her eyes. *Okay, Currick, you mean to dicker? Then I mean to get the best deal possible.* "Closet, dresser and bathroom drawers—and if you have that ratty bear rug in your bedroom, you have to get rid of it."

"Ratty? Hey, I bagged that bear when I was eleven years old and—"

"Don't get me started, Currick. I still think that bear was already dead when you shot it." She held up her hand to stop his protest in that old argument. "But either way, no one would believe I'd moved into that room if that thing was still on the wall."

"All right, all right. I'll put it in the ranch office. Jack likes it."

"Fine. And, another thing, you have to clear out when I'm getting dressed or in the shower and such."

"You're a hard woman, Matty, but all right."

"And I'll sleep in the guest room when I'm there."

"That's up to you."

"I'll sleep in the guest room," she repeated.

"You'll have to make real sure to make the bed like Pamela does or she'll spot it in a split second."

"Fine, so that's it, now—"

"And we should find Juno a stall in the Slash-C stable for when you don't want to leave her out."

She eyed him; the bland look he returned didn't calm her suspicions. "Don't go counting your foals before they're conceived, Currick."

He repeated his hands-up gesture of innocence. "Purely being practical, that's all."

"I get to pick which stall."

"Not Brandeis'."

How did he know she'd considered that disruptive move? "Okay, any stall except Brandeis'. Deal."

She put out her hand but he didn't meet it.

"Isn't binding with a glove on," he said, as if giving a legal opinion. But she suspected it was a dare.

Without a word, she stripped the work glove from her right hand. He wrapped his hand around hers, the warmth and friction both comforting and unsettling as they shook three times. For another few beats she stared down at her hand enclosed in his. With her first move to end the clasp, he released her hand.

"So, is tonight a good night for you to move into my room?" A flicker of his grin appeared. "Your things in, I mean."

"I've got a long day ahead—"

"I've got a pretty full day myself. Got to ride sections with Jack when I get back, then I've got appointments in town till seven. Thought I'd pick up supper at Chicken Little.

I could pick up a double order. That way I don't have to cook, you don't have to cook."

"Only Chicken Little has to cook," she filled in from the slogan with a smile.

"Right. So?"

"Okay. Sounds good. See you tonight, then."

He nodded and stood. "See you tonight."

He was about four yards away when she called after him, "Hey, Currick."

He turned part way back toward her. "Yeah?"

"If I'm sacrificing myself to save the old homestead by marrying you, you know what that makes your role in this melodrama?"

"Dudley Do-Right?" he suggested hopefully.

She shook her head. "Dastardly ol' Snively Whiplash."

A couple times during the rest of that long workday, she caught herself smiling at the memory of his answering laughter.

Chapter Five

Matty dropped her pencil as she grabbed a fistful of hair over each ear and let loose with a primal scream. The pencil hit the wood surface of the table, bounced on its abused eraser end, flipped and broke off its point, then dribbled off the end of the table to the family room floor.

"That's the sound I always imagined Charlie Brown made when Lucy pulled away the football right before he was going to kick it, and he fell to the turf."

Dave's calm voice from the couch did not soothe her in the least.

And you'd think after two weeks she'd be accustomed to being around him. Not that things hadn't gotten more comfortable between the two of them. It had really gone much smoother than she would have thought. Or than she'd expected after those first two nights.

Oh, he was all cooperation the night she moved her things into his room. That was the problem. It had been unnerving, somehow, to have Dave handling her clothes.

He'd asked if he could help. She couldn't think of a good reason to turn him down. But at least she'd had the sense to make sure he didn't put away her things in the dresser. Sure, there were innocent items like T-shirts and sweaters and shorts. But there were also underwear and nightgowns.

When she'd left Wyoming, she'd been strictly a white cotton girl. But her first roommate at Tulane had introduced her to the wonders of lingerie. Now she had both utilitarian and indulgent. And she didn't want to have to think about Dave's hands the next time she wore either kind. So she'd asked him to put her hanging clothes into the closet in the cleared-out space beside his. She wouldn't be wearing her city clothes much anyhow.

The whole process should have been innocuous.

Somehow it hadn't been. It started when Dave hung the silk suit she'd worn for the wedding as the first item of hers to go in. It was right next to a dark suit of his that looked like the deep charcoal one he'd worn Tuesday. It had emphasized the straight, broad line of his shoulders nearly as well as his work shirts did. And it fit him to perfection.

She shook her head to dislodge the vision.

Dave was partway in the closet now, screwing in hooks along the sidewall to hold a rack for her belts and scarves. His backside brushed against the suit, setting it in motion. The skirt swung up against the trousers of his suit, wrapping around them the way it would if a wearer's thigh had wrapped around the powerful male leg inside the trousers. His suit jacket responded to the motion, moving forward, with one sleeve slipping against her jacket, like a man wrapping his arms around his lover, so that her breasts would press against his chest. The pressure a pure pleasure. The way it had been when Dave had held her and kissed her at their wedding.

Dave twisted around just then, reaching toward her suit.

She'd dropped the handful of socks she'd been holding, letting them fall on the dresser top and floor, and dived to reach the suit first. If he'd put his hands on that suit she might have burst into flames.

"I'll take that." She'd snatched it away from him, and watched his brows rise.

"I was going to get it out of the way, so it didn't get messed up. I'll put it right back."

"Don't bother." She was pulling it off the hanger, unhooking the skirt. "It needs to go to the dry cleaners next time I'm in town."

"I can take it in. I'm going to Jefferson tomo—"

"No!" A vision of Dave with the suit on the truck seat next to him had flashed into her brain, and the damned suit was climbing all over him.

"Okay," he'd said slowly, giving her a bemused look.

"But thanks," she'd added.

"You're welcome."

She'd felt him looking at her now and then, but after that she had carefully not looked at what he was doing. By the time they finished he hadn't done a single thing she could call him to account over. He hadn't even argued about the bearskin. He'd simply moved it to his office, which was why she'd taken to doing the books in the family room.

"Charlie Brown had it easy," she told him now. "He should try doing the Flying W's books. Especially trying to figure out what on earth Great-Uncle Henry did with money."

Doing the books wasn't her favorite thing. Trying to untangle Great-Uncle Henry's mishmash didn't help. And even if she got the numbers to come out anywhere in the same neighborhood two times running, they came out in such a deep red that it seemed as if she was being punished for her hard work.

The fact that with a little bit of capital she had ideas that she knew she could make work, tripled the frustration.

And all the while she'd been conscious of Dave reading behind her—with absolutely no good reason to be conscious of him, which was really irritating. It wasn't as if he'd made any sounds or anything. He sat there quietly reading. Totally calm, totally at peace, while she tried hard not to pull her hair out.

"May I make two suggestions without you jumping down my throat?"

She pivoted in her chair to look at him. "Depends on the suggestions."

He smiled. "That's honest. Okay, here goes nothing. The first one is come over here and have some cashews. They're still chilled."

Grams used to keep cashews in the freezer to keep Matty from eating up her supply. Instead she'd developed a taste for them cold. She didn't quite smile as she went to the old chest used as a coffee table in front of the couch, but she felt some of the tension easing out of her shoulders.

"Well, that one won't cause any throat-jumping."

He held up the dish to her and she took four cashews. As soon as those were gone, she plunked down on the chest next to the dish and took some more.

Without thinking, she picked up his glass of ginger ale to take a swig. But as soon as her lips touched the rim, she realized what she'd done. From childhood on, they'd shared without asking or thinking—whatever one had the other was welcomed to.

Returning that glass to its coaster seemed like the most complicated procedure she had ever performed.

Only when it was back in place, did she mutter, "Sorry. I wasn't thinking."

"It's okay. Old habits are bound to crop up."

"It won't again," she said stiffly. That easy-sharing habit was from a time long gone. "Okay, that suggestion wasn't so bad. What's the other suggestion?"

"Why not get a computer for your books, Matty. It might not straighten out Henry's records, but it would make it a lot easier to deal with what's going on now."

"Yeah, like I can afford one."

"You could use mine. And after—later, you can get one for the Flying W. It does help a lot."

"I suppose it would."

"I could show you. It's not that hard."

She wasn't quite ready to respond to that offer. "How'd you learn?"

"Read a couple of books. Looked at the manual."

"Oh, yeah, *everything* comes easy for you." She'd noticed before that working on the Flying W's books engendered a dour mood in her.

"Not everything."

"Yeah? Name one thing."

"I could do that."

"Right. School? Family? Friends? You were born knowing where you wanted to be and how to get there. Each step neatly followed the other, with nary a mis-step. While I staggered around from job to job and city to city like the ball in a pinball machine."

"Would you say pinball machine balls stagger?"

She laughed, totally deflating her attempt at put-upon tragedy. "Oh, shut up Currick. You know what I mean."

"Actually I don't. You've never told me anything about your time away from here. Was stagger a fittin' word?"

She chuckled. "A time or two. Oh, not to the point of debauchery or anything—"

"That's good to hear." His tone was beyond dry to dusty.

"But, there were times... God, some of those warm spring nights in New Orleans after I transferred to Tulane—you could get drunk just on the air and the flowers. But we seldom were satisfied with that. And at Mardi Gras, it was really wild. I danced in fountains and had a man pay five hundred dollars for my shoes so he could drink champagne from one." She sighed. "I do love New Orleans."

"But you didn't stay there."

She wasn't sure if it was a statement or question. How

much did he know of what she'd done after she'd packed up her broken heart and struck out into the wide world?

"No. A job took me to San Antonio."

"What kind of job?"

"The lucky kind. My last summer in college, I was working at a store that rented party equipment, and I fell into organizing events. One company had its regional branch in San Antonio, and they liked my work, so I went there. I know you can't imagine anyone getting paid for organizing parties, but it takes a lot of work to get a party to come off like it was no work at all."

"So you've been organizing parties since then?"

She examined his face, but saw no sign that he was laughing at her.

"No. After a few months in San Antonio, I started doing public relations for the firm. At first releases and information on the parties, then it branched out. After about a year of that, I shifted to PR full-time."

"But you didn't stay there."

"No. Then I went to Atlanta for a while."

"Why?"

She hesitated before answering. "I followed a man there."

That was absolutely true. If Dave took it to mean it had been a romantic involvement instead of the purely professional relationship that had had her boss in San Antonio taking her along when he got promoted, that was a conclusion he'd be responsible for jumping to, as he was always criticizing her for doing.

"It didn't last?"

"I moved on." When she'd realized the man she'd thought would be her mentor was more interested in his own comfort by keeping her right where she was, making him look better, rather than in helping her up the next rung in the ladder.

"Where to?"

"Chicago. First, I did PR for another corporation, but then I moved to a big university hospital. That was amazing—

seeing a little girl smile for the first time in the morning, doing releases on groundbreaking research in the afternoon, and taking a date to a fund-raiser that night. It wasn't just about a company trying to have a better image, it was about letting people know about some terrific work being done— so more money would come in so more terrific work could be done.''

''No wonder you didn't want to come back.''

''Didn't want to—?'' Meeting his eyes she saw a vulnerability there that she knew she wasn't imagining. It seemed only fair to put some of her own vulnerability chips on the table. ''You're wrong, Dave. I wanted to come back. I couldn't. It wasn't all fun and games.''

''I don't suppose it was,'' he said in an impossibly neutral tone. ''Those were responsible jobs. Must have had a lot stress and— Hey, wait a minute.'' He sounded more like himself now. ''How'd you do all those jobs dealing with money, if you don't know how to do books and don't know how to use a computer?''

''Never said I didn't know how. I said it was impossible to figure out Henry's supposed system. As for the computer, I said I couldn't afford one. You assumed I didn't know how to use one.''

He spent a lot longer looking at his nearly empty ginger ale glass than it seemed to deserve. ''I suppose I did. Sorry.''

And she'd let him think it, just to back him into this kind of apology. How come it didn't feel better than this?

''No problem.'' She brushed the last of the cashew crumbs from her hands and stood. ''Well, I better get to bed now, or I won't be worth anything in the morning.''

''Yeah, time for bed for me, too.''

But after Matty gathered the papers and headed to her room, Dave remained. Not looking at his book, not really looking at anything.

So it didn't matter when the timer turned the lights out and he continued to sit in the dark.

Sounds of her activities reached him. A drawer opened, then closed. The syncopated beat of boots hitting the floor. By now she'd be at the side of the bed, pulling the covers back, wearing…what? Black negligee? He'd seen some of the sexy lingerie she'd hurried into drawers the night she'd unpacked. Had the men she'd mentioned so casually seen her in black lace? Had they loved her? Had she left any of them wondering how they could ever hope to fill the hole in their life? Had leaving any of them caused her pain?

You're wrong, Dave. I wanted to come back. I couldn't.

Why couldn't she? And was the wanting all in the past tense?

The abrupt opening of her bedroom door had him blinking into a slice of light that cut across the hall and family room, the tip finding him still in the leather chair.

"Hey, Currick, you said you could name one thing that didn't come easy to you, let's hear it."

She stood with one hand propped on a hip clad not in black lace, but what looked to be green flannel. He'd bet she felt soft and warm.

"C'mon, Currick, no stalling."

"I didn't think you even heard me say that, you were so involved in telling me what came easy to me and that you had to work for."

"Oh, no you don't—you do that all the time, changing the subject like that. You're not going to lead me off the subject by baiting me this time. I challenged you to name one thing that didn't come easy for you. And you said you could, but then you—"

"You."

"—got me started on… What?"

"I said you."

"Me? Me what?"

"You didn't come easy for me, Matty."

He'd stunned her. Even if it hadn't shown in her wide eyes and open mouth, the fact that she had no retort said it all.

"Never," he said quietly. "Not even when we were kids. I never understood the restlessness in you, that energy that pushed you into leaping into things. I had a lot of time to think about it, and I think we were on different schedules, I guess you could say.

She was still goggling at him, but he could see the quick, smooth wheels of her mind taking in what he was saying.

"While you were off exploring the world and finding yourself like a normal person, in college and beyond, I stayed at home and wondered what was wrong with me that I didn't want to." He tried for a grin, and got about halfway. "People that age are supposed to be finding themselves. Supposed to be struggling to find an identity. Not me." This grin was better, maybe it even qualified as wry. "I had to face it—I lack the emotional imagination for an identity crisis."

"You? You were always so damned *perfect*—"

"No, don't try to make me feel better about this, Matty," he said dryly. Her tone had been disgusted, not complimentary. "I accepted it a while back that I'm that sort of person. Boring, bland and settled. All along, I knew where I wanted to be, and I'm here. I knew what I wanted to do, and I'm doing it. I knew how I wanted to fit into the world, and I'm comfortable as I am. Multiple choice just isn't my style, I suppose. But you—"

"Now wait a minute, Currick. That's going too far. I'd say you had plenty of multiple choice with all the women I hear you've dated."

"You ever hear of safety in numbers?"

"Afraid one of 'em would catch you, and then you wouldn't be the swinging bachelor of the Slash-C?"

He let out a deep, weary sigh. "I know I'm going to pay for this in gettin' the rough side of your tongue about my ego, but it was their safety, not mine I was thinking of. I didn't want any of them to think I was going to give more than I knew I could. Maybe I had the feeling the best I'd ever have was already given out, and I hadn't gotten it back. Careless of me, maybe, but that's how it was."

Looking at each other in the murky shadows, he could see the question of whether he was saying what she thought he might be saying—*worried* he might be saying?—spark across her eyes.

The question never came. Instead she abruptly straightened, and the spark in her eyes changed to a different kind of heat.

"Oh, of course, chivalrous Dave Currick, protector of womankind wasn't looking out for himself. Just safeguarding the hearts of all the foolish females who threw themselves at him. I should have realized."

She spun on one bare heel, and marched back to the bedroom. She didn't slam the door, but the sound of it still echoed in his ears as, once more in the dark, he pushed his hands through his hair in frustration.

Matty was nearer the phone when it rang just after breakfast so she automatically picked up the receiver.

"Slash-C."

"Matty! Oh, Matty, dear, it's Donna Currick."

The first sound of that warm voice and memories flooded through Matty. Grams had raised her, had been her anchor and her support from the time a drunken driver left her as the only survivor in a car accident that made her an orphan when she was still a toddler. But it was Donna Currick who had helped ease her through so many of the terrors of growing from a child to a woman, from her first bra and heels, to hairstyles and hormone swings.

Tears pricked at the back of her eyes in an instant, unexpected and completely inconvenient—just the way they used to during those unsettling times when she'd so often relied on Dave's mother for understanding. *Dave's mother*, now her mother-in-law. Oh, Lord…

"Mrs. Currick," she managed to say through numb lips

as she flashed Dave a look. She hoped it didn't show outright panic, especially since things had been polite but cool between them this morning.

That's the way she intended to keep it. It would be much safer that way. She'd been all too ready last night to not only accept what he said, but to read all sorts of meanings into it. It was too easy to fall back into old, bad habits with Dave. She'd let herself say too much, telling him that she couldn't come back. And then, when she'd gone back to the living room and tried to be more in control of the conversation, she'd nearly fallen to pieces over that outrageous statement of his that she hadn't come easy for him. If there was one thing she'd been in her entire life it was easy for Dave Currick.

Not that it did her pride any good to admit it, but even uncomfortable truths were still the truth.

Still, pride or no pride, at this moment, she couldn't regret it if her look across the kitchen to him resembled an SOS sign, because he immediately came to her side.

"My mother?"

She nodded, even as she said into the mouthpiece, "Where are you and Mr. Currick now?"

Dave mouthed the word "office," placed one large hand on her shoulder and patted it twice in a gesture of encouragement that warmed her skin, then he headed down the hall.

"Bangkok. We just returned, back from the most wonderful expedition into the backcountry. You wouldn't believe how different it is from Wyoming! I rode an elephant. And— What? Oh, yes, Ed says I shouldn't get sidetracked when it's your news that—"

A click sounded, then Dave's voice came on, sounding amplified and loud to Matty. "Mom? It's Dave. I'm on the speakerphone in the office. Matty? Why don't you hang up there and come back here with me so we can talk to them together?"

He emphasized the word "together" enough to indicate it

was also so they could exchange visual signals. Dave Currick was no dummy.

"Good idea."

As she hung up the kitchen receiver, she heard Dave asking where his parents were and Mrs. Currick starting on the same answer.

When she realized she was dawdling down the hall like a chickenhearted coward, she forced herself to pick up her pace. As she headed for a chair near the door to the back porch that gave the office direct access to outdoors, Dave motioned her to come over to where he was sitting behind the desk, not far from the phone, set on speaker.

Ed Currick was talking. "We came back to our hotel from this excursion to a garbled message from Lisa—interference on the phone lines I suppose. Although we're paying an arm and a leg for a hotel that's supposed to have all the modern conveniences."

Matty pushed a pile of papers back, preparing to lean against the edge of the desk, even though that would leave her staring at the bearskin on the wall. But Dave wrapped his hand around her arm and drew her toward the big leather chair he was seated in. For one mind-emptying second she thought he was going to pull her down to his lap. Instead he patted the padded arm and steered her toward it. When she didn't immediately comply, he touched her lips with one hand and his with the other, then drew imaginary lines in the air that converged at the speakerphone. For good measure, he cupped his hands behind his ears and flapped them.

She got it. His parents would be able to tell how far apart they were sitting by their voices, and they would read a great deal into that. Especially his mother.

She perched sidesaddle on the chair arm, balancing precariously, and turned more away from Dave than toward him.

"All we could make out was something about you, Dave, and a judge. Wouldn't have known what was going on at all if I hadn't received an e-mail from Herm Halloran. Could have knocked me over with a feather.''

''I'm sorry if our getting married surprised you, Dad—''

Mr. Currick gave a bark of laughter. ''Oh, it's no surprise about you two— I meant Herm knowing how to e-mail. No, only thing about you two getting married is, we wish we could have been there to see it.''

Hot, moist pressure filled Matty's eyes. She bobbled on her narrow seat and Dave gripped her arm, steadying her and also sliding her around so she straddled the arm, a much more secure seat, and one that let them look at each other.

''I didn't think…'' she said to him. She felt stricken at the sudden recognition of what their son's wedding might have meant to his parents.

''*We* didn't think,'' he amended firmly, but also giving a slight shrug, dismissing her worry.

A mellower chuckle came from halfway around the world this time. ''No, I don't suppose you two did think much about that sort of thing. Not after all the time you waited to get married.''

After a faint shuffling sound, Donna Currick came back on. ''Oh, yes, I do wish we could have been there to see you two finally get married. And to give you a beautiful wedding. Getting married in the courthouse—oh, Dave, how could you do that?''

Dave rolled his eyes in amusement, but Matty felt an obligation to come to his defense. Only from a sense of fairness, of course, because she'd gotten him into this.

''It was my idea, Mrs. Currick. I thought—''

''Oh, Matty, dear, *Mrs.* sounds so formal. I think you should call me Mom Currick now, don't you? Or Donna if you're not comfortable yet with Mom.''

Matty couldn't speak. She feared that if she tried to form words the lump in her throat would dissolve into tears. Was this what guilt tasted like?

Dave obviously didn't share her guilt. He quirked a grin

at her as he diverted his mother's attention. "We had a very nice reception."

"That's what Lisa said in her message. And something about it being a surprise?"

"Yeah, it was a surprise—practically knocked the bride right off her feet," he added with a slow smile that had Matty reliving the sensation of being swung up into his arms and carried into the church.

A muffled sound came across the wire. "I don't know what your father was talking about, that Lisa's message was garbled. I understood it perfectly." Her voice faded a bit as she apparently faced her husband, "You just couldn't believe your ears, Ed." Then came back in full force. "And she said she'd never seen a couple better suited to each other. I wish I could have seen you." The sniffle reached them loud and clear. "I always dreamed of the day I'd see you two walk down the aisle together."

Matty stared at Dave and saw her disbelief mirrored back to her. Well before Dave broke up with her six years ago, Donna Currick had made it quite plain that, while she loved Matty as a daughter and didn't mind their dating, she'd thoroughly disapproved of their becoming what she considered too serious.

"You could've fooled me," Dave murmured.

"Don't be disrespectful, David. I thought you were too young then, but now... Oh, this is wonderful! We'll have to give you a *real* reception when we get home. We can be back in a week—"

"No!"

Matty and Dave were in perfect unison—for once.

He was laughing, and showed no sign of taking matters in hand.

"That's so nice of you Mrs.—uh, Donna. But, please, don't even think about cutting your trip short. I mean, I know—we *both* know how long you've dreamed about this trip and how much planning it took. That's the reason we

didn't tell you ahead of time,'' she added with a flash of
brilliance. ''In fact, that's the reason we tried to keep the
whole thing quiet. We didn't want to wait, but we didn't want
to interrupt your trip, so we thought if we went and quietly
got married by the judge, we could be married and you could
continue your trip.''

''That's right,'' Dave said, and Matty smiled at him in
appreciation of his support. ''In fact, Matty didn't want to
have a reception at all. So two would be terrible.''

Her smile plummeted to a frown as she swatted his arm.

''Ouch!'' he yelped for effect, and pretended to cower into
the chair, all the while grinning at her.

''Dave, stop that,'' Donna said automatically.

''Me? I didn't do a thing.'' An evil chuckle badly dented
his protest of innocence.

But his mother wasn't listening anyway. ''Oh, but, Matty,
dear, you must do all the lovely wedding things. I know you
don't think so now, but you'll regret it later if you don't.''

''But we *did* have a reception,'' she reminded the older
woman. ''And truly, it was great. They decorated, and had
music and dancing and a cake and—''

''We did the cake-cutting tradition of feeding each other
a piece,'' Dave inserted.

His expression was bland, but his eyes radiated heat. A
heat that ignited a sensory memory of the taste of his fingers
against her tongue. A heat that must have been contagious
because it centered low in her belly.

''—and everything,'' she finished lamely.

But it seemed to satisfy Donna. ''Well, I'm glad to hear
that. And to hear that you enjoyed it so much. Lisa said folks
took lots of pictures.''

''Hundreds,'' Matty confirmed.

''So at least we'll get to see those when we get back. And
I suppose it wouldn't make much sense to have a second
reception so soon after the first.''

"Right," Dave finally contributed. "Besides, we have a lot to do right now—we're awfully busy."

"I'm sure you are," Donna said with a little chuckle. Her voice grew slightly fainter as if she'd turned away from the mouthpiece again. "They say they're awfully busy right now, Ed. Apparently they don't want a couple of old fogies around to cramp their style."

"Mother," Dave said in the long-suffering tone of children—adult and otherwise—but with a smile lurking in his eyes.

Only then did Matty realize what Donna Currick thought was keeping the newlyweds busy.

"Around the ranches," she blurted out. "You know, spring work."

"Of course, of course, dear," soothed Donna. "And I know those early days of marriage can take a lot of adjustment. Be patient with each other. And don't be fooled into thinking that because you knew each other so long growing up that you know everything about each other now. Not only will there be changes from these past six years, but there will be changes all along, each day of your married life—if you're lucky. And, Matty?"

"Yes—I'm here."

Dave winked at her, easing some of her renewed guilt at receiving these words of wisdom under false pretenses.

"One more thing, and I mean this very seriously. Don't let Dave browbeat you, Matty, dear. He's gotten too accustomed to running everything and everyone."

"Hey!" Dave protested, no longer looking quite so amused.

Matty smirked at him. "No, I won't let him browbeat me, Donna."

"I know you won't. You're such a strong woman now. That's why you two are so good for each other. What? Oh, your father says we should let you two young people go now so you can start your day."

A flurry of good wishes and goodbyes followed before Dave leaned forward and punched the speakerphone button to disconnect.

"Well, I think that went pretty well."

"Do you?" Matty rose from the chair arm, wrapping her arms around her waist, hands cupping her elbows, and moving across the room to the battered leather couch under the windows. She sank into the cushions with her chin dropped down.

Dave watched her warily. He wasn't big on body language, but that message came through loud and clear.

"Don't you?" he finally asked.

Her only answer was a gesture consisting of half a head shake and half a shrug.

"I don't think they saw through our pose at all," he pursued, "so what's worrying you, Matty?"

She looked up at him and her eyes were pained. "Maybe it's because they didn't see through it. They took it all as truth and they were so happy. What's going to happen when we…when it ends? How're they going to feel then?"

He came around the desk and sat on the couch beside her, propping one foot up on the scarred wooden table. "They'll get over it. We'll make sure it's a friendly divorce. Give 'em visiting rights to their ex-daughter-in-law." He grinned wickedly. "And give you visiting rights to Juno's foal."

"You can't shrug and say *They'll get over it,* Dave. They'll be hurt."

"Well, they *will* get over it, Matty. People do get over things. Even being hurt."

She looked at him for a long, serious moment. "You were right, Dave."

"I was?"

"I didn't think this through. I was so intent on what's good for the Flying W, I didn't think about the other people who might be hurt by this. Not only the people who gave us presents, but people who are emotionally involved. People like your parents and Lisa. Your mother and father were always so good to me... I didn't think about how they'd feel about this. If I had thought about it, I never would have put them in the position they're going to be in when this ends.''

Dave stared at her.

And don't be fooled into thinking that because you knew each other so long growing up that you know everything about each other now.

He slid back on the couch, and took it in. Sometimes his mother was downright spooky.

He'd accused Matty of not thinking it through? How about him? He was always supposed to be the sensible one of the pair of them, but when it came right down to it, Matty— whom he had accused more than once of being selfish and shortsighted and a fool—had seen farther and more sympathetically into the hearts of his mother and father than he had.

''Maybe I should stop this now,'' she said while she chewed on her thumbnail. ''Before I do any more damage.''

She was ready to call it off, no matter what the cost to her or her ranch. He could see it in her eyes, in the decided line of her jaw. End the whole charade now. Give up a near-certain shot at the grant money. Give up the renewed hope of turning around the Flying W. Give up living here at the Slash-C. Give up being his wife.

In that instant, Dave knew that if he'd been selfish in plunging into this escapade with Matty, he was prepared to be a damned sight more selfish.

He slid his hand around hers, and drew it into the space between them.

''You're not doing this alone, Matty. It's *we*—''

''Dave—'' she was shaking her head ''—this is no time for that one for all and all for one motto from our childhood. I was the one who came up with the scheme, and—''

''And I was the one who went along with it. We made the

same vows in front of Judge Halloran, remember? We signed the same marriage certificate.''

She looked away from him at those words and tugged her hand free. He didn't let it stop him.

''Being brutally honest here, Matty. I never gave a thought to how my folks would react.''

She didn't turn all the way toward him, but her gaze slanted back to his face.

''It wasn't exactly out of sight out of mind, but they might not see it that way,'' he admitted.

He ran his hand through his hair, wondering how he had managed to put his parents so thoroughly out of his mind. It wasn't as if they were the shy, retiring types who were easy to forget. And it wasn't that he didn't care about them. He'd known from a pretty early age that whatever their differences, he was damned lucky to have parents who loved him the way they did. And he loved them back, even when they drove him nuts. So, how come he hadn't given them a thought?

''Look, Matty, I'm not meaning to sound harsh or uncaring in saying, *They'll get over it.* But they truly will. Eventually.'' She winced at that word, and he hurried on. ''On the other hand, the damage has been done. Telling them now won't make it any better than if we play this out the way we'd planned and let them think in the end that the marriage just didn't work out.''

She faced him, but her eyes were full of doubt. ''That's true, but still—''

''Look at it this way, if we tell them now, they've only had a couple days of being happy about it before they know the truth. If we go ahead like we'd planned, they'll have a couple of good years they wouldn't have had otherwise.''

She giggled.

It wasn't the response he'd expected. Matty could be darned hard on a guy's ego. Here he'd been all earnest and trying to think of his parents and she's giggling.

''Now what?'' he asked in resignation. ''I didn't say a

single word that could make you think of me as Snidely Whiplash.''

"No, but you make your parents sound like a pair of old cowponies you've turned out to pasture to enjoy their twilight years.''

He chuckled. "If that image works for you.''

"They'd hate it.'' She was trying to stifle her amusement, without much success.

"Yeah, they would.'' He grinned unrepentantly, partly because he knew his parents wouldn't mind the teasing even if they knew about it and mostly because it eased the knot in his gut to see the pain lift from Matty's eyes.

Chapter Six

"Morning." Dave's voice rumbled at her.

Matty stopped dead in the small hallway between the guest room and the closed door to the master bedroom, missing another nose-to-collarbone encounter with him by less than an inch.

Only this time the collarbone was naked.

She'd gotten up earlier than usual this morning because they'd agreed last night that they would both prefer to be out of the house before Pamela Dobson arrived for her first tour of cleaning duty since the wedding.

But she hadn't counted on how long it would take her to make the bed so its appearance would match Pamela's precision corners.

Instead of scooting to the bathroom past a sleeping Dave with most of a good-size room between them, she was trying to ease past the upright version in a hallway about the size of a closet. An upright version that had tousled hair, a dark shadow of beard stubble and wore only navy-blue boxer shorts.

At least she wore pajamas of jersey knit that couldn't be seen through and that covered her from a decorous V-neck of the cap-sleeve top to her bare feet.

"Morning." At least that's what she'd intended to say. She cleared her throat and tried it again, this time with passable success.

"You headin' to the bathroom now?"

"Yeah, yeah, I am."

She turned sideways, trying to avoid contact with him. But he stood there, looking as if he might be about to fall asleep again. How could he manage to make her think of both a dangerous bandito and an oversize sleepy toddler simultaneously?

"Uh, Dave?"

"Hmm?"

"Are you going to move so I can use the bathroom? And maybe you should go make the coffee now? Strong coffee?"

"Huh? Oh, yeah, coffee." He gave her a sleepy smile, rubbed one palm against his chest absently and turned partway to the side to let her pass.

Only his coordination or his depth perception or something seemed to be off, because instead of clearing each other, his naked chest rubbed across the entire length of her right arm, from shoulder to elbow, and most of it along bare skin.

It felt exactly the way a jalapeño pepper tasted. An explosion of hot and spicy, yet somehow, for all that heat, a trace underneath of something impossibly sweet.

She fled.

It wasn't graceful and it wasn't particularly dignified, but it was necessary. She hoped he was too sleepy to recognize her flight for what it was.

She half sprinted to the bathroom, and slammed the door behind her, dumping the clothes she'd been carrying clutched to her chest onto the counter.

And in the mirror she saw the evidence of what she'd already felt—the tips of her breasts tightening to telltale points. From the time she'd recognized desire for Dave, her breasts had always responded this way. Even before they'd made love for the first time, he'd taught her both torment and pleasure by his attentions to that sensitive flesh.

She locked the door. Not against him—Dave would never intrude that way. Maybe she locked it against her own irresponsible thoughts.

She sat on the edge of the tub, and avoided looking at herself in the mirror, rubbing her opposite hand over the tingling skin of her arm, and drew in a deep breath.

Trouble was, that breath seemed to pull into her senses the musky scent of Dave that she'd first inhaled when they'd nearly collided in the hall.

The scent of a warm, vital male, newly awakened. Just the way he would smell if a woman woke up with her head on his bare, broad chest. Hair tousled and cheeks roughened by sleep, while his eyes were soft and lazy. Just the way he would look if he rolled over in bed to rumble that "Morning."

She'd never had those experiences.

Six years ago, with both of them living at home, the acres of their two ranches had offered privacy and protection to intimacy. But they had never had an opportunity to spend a whole night together. When he'd gone off to college, Grams had refused to let Matty visit him on campus. And when Matty had started college herself—at a different school, and several hundred miles apart—he'd been awash in studying as he'd started law school and her money had been too tight to allow for road trips.

She used to daydream about what it would be like to spend an entire night with Dave. To wake up together in the morning. To have his arms around her. To watch those long, thick lashes flicker up, and see those hazel eyes sleepy and relaxed.

Then to start the day together. Maybe watch him shave.

Certainly to take a shower together. And then go back to bed and spend an entire day on a firm mattress and soft sheets.

"Matty?"

She jumped, more at his voice than the knock at the door. "What?"

"How much longer you going to be? Pamela's going to be here in twenty minutes."

Matty mumbled a curse, looked at her watch and repeated it louder. Where had the last half hour gone? Only her rear end, now numb, seemed to have sensed the passage of time.

"You better use the hall bathroom."

"Jeez, what have you been doing in there?"

Fear swept through her that somehow he might be able to read her thoughts through the door. She knew it was irrational, but knowing didn't stop it.

"None of your business," she snapped. "The deal was I got the bathroom first. No time limit. You agreed, so there's no sense—"

"All right, all right. I'll use the hall bathroom. Boy, sounds like someone woke up on the wrong side of the bed."

She refused to consider what side of what bed would have put her in an entirely different frame of mind this morning.

"Hey, Matty!"

For a moment he thought she was going to keep going. She must have set a speed record for eating breakfast and some other sort of record for escaping Pamela Dobson without the other woman spending at least an hour unearthing any secrets she might be harboring.

After he'd given up on getting into his own bathroom and used the hall bathroom, he'd rushed. But he still hadn't beaten Pamela's arrival. Or her eagle eye.

That's why he wanted to talk to Matty. But when he came out of the office's exterior door, she already had Juno roped up and was leading her to the barn where Matty's rig was stored. In a matter of minutes she'd have Juno bridled and saddled, and would be on her way.

"Wait up. I need to talk to you."

He could almost hear her exasperated sigh, but at least she stood still and waited until he reached her in the open area between the corral gate and the barn doors.

"What do you want?"

"You can start by quitting directing that lethal frown at me."

"Why?"

"General principle? Peace on earth, goodwill toward men?"

"Dave, I have too much to do today—"

"Want to tell me about it?"

"No." She glanced at him, bit her lip and softened that some. "At least not yet. If the grant comes through and some other things work out...but there's no chance of that happening if I stand around wasting time on this nonsense—"

"Peace on earth nonsense? No, wait—" He snagged her arm as she started to turn away at his teasing. "How about because we have an audience— Don't look. That's right, look at me. Pamela's watching us from the kitchen window. And she could give a hawk lessons."

If anything, Matty's frown deepened. "So? That's pretty much standard operating procedure for Pamela."

"Right. So's adding two and two and coming up with twenty-two."

He shifted so he blocked the kitchen window's view of Matty's all too revealing face. Loosening his grip on her, he ran his hand up and down her upper arm.

"Dave, I really have a lot to do today, so if you could hurry this up, I'd—"

When she tried to pull back, he held on to her arm, hoping it still looked like a gesture of affection instead of a wrestling hold.

"Pamela got here early—which we probably should have

figured on—and she saw me coming out of the hall bathroom with my shaving kit. She didn't hesitate to ask why I was using that bathroom instead of mine. I said you were in there, and you liked your privacy. She harrumphed, and said if we'd wanted privacy we shouldn't have gotten married. And then she gave me one of those two-plus-two-equals-twenty-two looks.''

''Are you telling me that from seeing you come out of the bathroom, Pamela Dobson's concocting…'' She'd started off scoffing, but by the time her words trailed off, she sounded worried. ''Maybe we should go back in and, uh, say something. You know, call each other darling and stuff.''

She made it sound like such an extreme measure that he found himself grinning.

''You think your acting skills are up to it, Matty?''

''I can do anything I have to do.'' He wondered if she had any idea that she'd squared up to him like a patriot facing a firing squad when she said those words.

''How about a little pantomime?''

Wariness was in her eyes, in the tilt of her head and in her voice as she asked, ''What do you have in mind?''

''Giving Pamela an explanation she'll believe—and all without saying a word.''

''You've clearly got an idea, so spill it, Currick.''

''If she thinks we've had a fight, that would explain your desire for privacy and my using the other bathroom—might even explain it if you didn't do a perfect job of making the guest bed.''

''Great idea!''

''Except, since you just sent me a thousand-watt smile—'' one that had threatened to melt his backbone ''—it's going to be obvious the fight's over. And you know what the other half of making up is.''

''I don't—''

''You did say that keeping up appearances was part of our deal.''

"Sure, but—"

"Well, this is one way to make sure word gets around that we're a normal, newlywed couple. Having spats, and then making up. For appearances' sake, of course. Unless—" he paused artfully "—you're scared or maybe you're afraid you can't handle kissing—"

"Can't handle it? That's ridiculous. I have no reason to be scared. It was no big deal at the reception and it's no big deal now. It's exactly the same thing. A necessity."

Necessity? That's all she'd considered those kisses? Okay, she didn't love him anymore, but that was going too far.

He'd been treating her with kid gloves, but maybe it was time to make her admit that she'd responded as strongly to their kisses the day they got married as he had.

"You know what they say about necessity," he started in a husky murmur as he stepped in, crowding her. He could see her urge to back away in the faint tensing of her muscles, but she stood her ground. To make sure that didn't change he cupped his palms gently around her head.

"No, I don't know—what do they say about necessity?" It was a dare.

"It's the mother of invention."

He curved his palms closer to her skull, drawing her toward him. He wanted to read what was in her eyes, but her lashes dropped over them.

He expected resistance, or at least reluctance, as he brushed his lips across hers.

Then Matty moved.

She put her hands over his—and still he didn't know which way this would go.

She dropped Juno's reins and came toward him.

Their mouths flirted with kissing, brushing and teasing without pattern or intent. A touch to her top lip, a whisper at the corner of his mouth, a hint of invasion at the seam of her lips.

Then she angled her head and the kiss shifted from a butterfly to a dragon. With heat and claws and power.

Without volition his hands tightened on her, needing to be closer, wanting to be deeper. The invasion became real as his tongue demanded entrance. She hesitated only long enough to make him sweat, then her lips parted.

Oh, the taste of Matty. A sound came from him, a sort of growl, and he didn't care.

It was different from their you-may-now-kiss-the-bride kiss. This wasn't impulse and instinct. This time he'd intended to kiss her and she'd known it was coming. It was no accident.

She couldn't pretend this didn't exist. She couldn't ignore the dragon that kept roaring to life when they touched.

With the combustion gobbling up their oxygen, he broke the kiss only enough to drag in two lungfuls. Then he took her mouth again.

With his body rioting to lie her down on the ground and make this real, the unraveling ropes of his discipline could be trusted only enough to have his hands cupping her head and his mouth mating with hers. Her hair pulled loose from the braid to slide silk over his fingers. Her mouth drew him into a universe of hot, damp satin.

Then her tongue stroked into his mouth, and the blast of heat that coursed through him was like being incinerated from the inside out. He'd have no complaint for the rest of his life if he could experience that feeling, oh, say, twenty times a day.

Another sensation tapped at his consciousness, but it was outside the haze of desire so it took an extra minute for it to penetrate.

Matty's touch had changed. Her hands no longer simply covered his, but had slid to his wrists and were exerting pressure to release herself from him. He delved hungrily deep into her mouth once more before easing his grip enough for her pressure to have effect, but he cooperated no more than that, and he made no effort to untangle her hair where it snagged around his fingers, pulling more from the braid.

She drew back, as if she hated to leave him, smoothed his hair back at his temple, then glided her palm down his cheek, his throat and to his chest, which was rising and falling in fast, heavy breaths. She smiled at him, mistily, besottedly.

"That should take care of the necessity of satisfying Pamela," she said in a voice that should have been reserved for the most private of endearances.

Then she turned and continued toward the corral.

Dave stayed where he was.

Sure, he didn't want to face Pamela yet. Besides, it wouldn't hurt any to let her think he wanted to watch Matty's jeans-clad rear end as she grabbed Juno's reins and headed for the barn. He'd simply look like a new husband who was waiting for the opportunity to wave goodbye to his wife. Instead of a man who was in no condition to walk.

You know what they say about necessity.

No, I don't know—what do they say about necessity?

It's the mother of invention.

He'd intended to push her. He'd intended to prove to her that she wasn't as immune as she wanted to think.

Instead it had been Matty who had invented a new form of torture.

And then she'd walked away as if it was all acting.

Was he totally wrong? Was he the only one who felt this? If so, he'd agreed to two years of hell on earth.

Feeling the burn of Dave's eyes on her back—no, throughout her whole body—Matty used all her stubbornness to walk normally until she was well inside the dim barn.

She ducked into the empty stall where she'd been storing her saddle and other gear and, now out of his sight, sank back against the rough wall with a hand spread wide over her abdomen—as if that would stop the somersaults or put out the fire.

And fire was exactly what she'd been playing with.

If she hadn't ended that kiss when she had...well, Pamela would have had plenty to talk about in town, and most of it X-rated.

He'd been goading her, and she'd intended to let him know she wasn't afraid of him, wasn't afraid of any lingering...*whatever* between them. She could handle it. She was no longer the young girl who had never kissed anyone other than him, much less any more intimate activities. She'd lived in the world for six years, and she'd experienced it. She'd had romances. Not as many as he had, but a few.

Definitely not as many as he'd had, because he'd learned some things she'd swear he hadn't known before—and that she still didn't know. Like that kiss.

None of her romances had kissed her like that. None of them had made her feel as if his mouth on hers was the most important thing in the world, and answered every question she'd ever had.

She hadn't bargained for that when they'd entered into this deal. She'd been thinking strictly about the Flying W's welfare. Hadn't she?

She shook her head. It didn't matter now. She'd asked for this token marriage and he'd agreed. How and why were far less important than the facts of the matter.

She'd wanted to teach him a lesson. But she was the one who had flunked.

She couldn't pretend there wasn't still chemistry between them. But chemistry had never been the problem. There had been plenty of chemistry between them right to the end; a sizzling kiss that would have gone a lot farther if he hadn't backed away and told her he thought it would be a good idea to see other people.

So chemistry clearly hadn't been enough for him then, and she'd be a fool to think that might have changed. Because one thing *had* changed in the past six years—she was no longer a lovesick fool.

* * *

They had the morning routine down by now. Dave got up first, started the coffee and read the paper, leaving Matty the bathroom. Since she often showered at night after working all day at the Flying W, she was quick in the mornings. He headed into the bathroom as soon as she got out.

There had been no more kisses.

That was probably for the best. It certainly seemed to suit Matty, who had taken to treating him with absent cordiality, as if she had her mind filled with other things. She worked long hours at the Flying W. At least from her comments it seemed her work was beginning to pay off—not financially yet, but in improved efficiency around her ranch.

And it was definitely best for his peace of mind, too. He couldn't think of much worse than living with Matty over the next two years with it clear that he wanted more and just as clear that she didn't—unless it was not seeing her at all.

So he'd accepted the status quo.

There was one snag. When he went in, the bathroom would still have that Matty smell in it. Even without the steam from a shower, the enclosed area was redolent with her soap, her lotion. Oh, he knew they weren't anything special, but they seemed to mix with an essence of Matty, and become something entirely different. Entirely impossible for his body to ignore, no matter what his mind said.

He was finding that it took him longer to get ready himself than it ever had before.

He also found that a lot of his showers were tending toward the chilly side.

Those two factors had combined to make him short on time and temper most mornings.

Maybe Matty took pity on him. Or maybe it really was what she said—that it was as easy to fix breakfast for one as two. But either way, the other part of their morning routine was that Matty would cook a real ranch breakfast—some combination of eggs, bacon, sausage, ham, cheese, biscuits, toast and various kinds of jams and jellies.

He'd eat till he thought he might bust out of his clothes—lawyer clothes or ranch clothes depending on the day—and then his duty was to clean up, while Matty rode to the Flying W.

Only this day, instead of heading toward the corral where she'd left Juno out overnight, she started poking in cabinets and jotting notes on a sheet of paper. He twisted around to watch her while he loaded the dishwasher.

"Taking inventory, Matty?"

"Sort of. We're running low on some things. I'm making a list, and thought you could swing by the store on your way back to the ranch tonight. I thought about pancakes this morning, but you don't have the makings for them."

"Never knew you could make pancakes."

"You never knew a lot of things I can make now."

If she'd said those words before she'd gone off to the wide world, it would have been in a sticking-out-her-tongue-at-him tone. But now it was matter-of-fact. So, why did that get under his skin more than the other?

He had no answer, but the fact that it did get under his skin was the reason he gave her a certain kind of look and used a certain kind of tone when he said, "Yeah? You gonna show me more of those things you learned, or you gonna stop at pancakes?"

Her gaze snapped to him, color sparked across her cheeks, and he even thought something hotter than a spark showed deep in her eyes in the second before she looked away.

"Oh," she started, so laid-back she should have fallen over, "I might stretch it as far as waffles. If you're good."

"I'm very good."

But now she wasn't listening to his certain tone or paying attention to his certain look. Matty had opened the cupboard by the back door, and after a low whistle, she was too busy gawking.

"Marriage driving you to drink, Currick?"

Wiping his wet hands on a dish towel, he moved next to her to peer around the edge of the cupboard door. His arm brushed hers. He felt the response in the fine hairs exposed by the rolled-back cuff of his shirt. Maybe he wasn't entirely alone; she stepped back and put her opposite hand over the patch of skin where he could see goose bumps blooming.

He bit back the pleasure, because goose bumps didn't prove anything, and drawled, "Oh, that. Beer was on sale. Thought I'd stock up."

"For what? A year? Or are you planning a party I don't know about?"

"Not exactly a party."

She looked up, a flash of something vulnerable in her face making him want to touch her. But he held off, because she crossed her arms over her waist in a definite don't-touch message and asked, "What exactly, then?"

"A bunch of lawyers getting together to talk shop. It's our answer to the good old boy network that was in place when we started practicing around here."

"And you supply the beer?"

"Yup. The beer and the place. They come here because I'm—because I *was*—unattached. Most of the rest of 'em have families who'd object to having their place taken over for a full day by a horde of ravenous lawyers. This year's date was already set, and you usually work every day, so I decided to go ahead and have it here."

"A full day? That's a lot of shop you guys talk."

"Well, we do a project, too." She'd relaxed, all sign of that vulnerability long gone and her crossed arms easing from their clench. But he could no more figure why she'd relaxed than he'd known why she'd gone tense.

"A project? Like a legal project? That you all work on?"

Now, *this* reaction he recognized from the Matty of old. She had a scheme going. He could practically see the wheels turning in her head, though what they were chewing over, he had absolutely no idea.

"Yeah, a legal project. We work up a paper or prepare a brief on a hot new topic—or an old cold one—then we send it off to the bar association. They make us show up in Cheyenne for their recertification rigmarole now and then, but this keeps 'em off our back in between."

"Oh. Something theoretical?"

"Most times. There aren't a lot of hot new legal topics with practical applications around here."

He grinned, and the ends of her mouth tilted up, too. But he had the feeling it was automatic. So, when she abruptly asked, "Who all comes?" he wasn't that surprised.

He reeled off about a dozen names from the surrounding three counties, most of whom she knew of.

"Bob Brathenwaite?" she repeated absently. "He's in the state house now, isn't he?"

"Yeah, elected year before last. But he's still practicing regularly. Why the interest in—?"

"And Taylor, will she come?"

"She came last year for the first time...I expect she'll come again."

"You know, Dave—" Matty turned to him with an earnest expression "—this is a great opportunity. I mean for me to really play the role of wife. I think you should let me make all the arrangements. Give me the date and a list of who to ask and I'll do the inviting, the food and all the rest."

"It's not anything fancy. There's no need—"

"It's like you said before, Dave. We've got to pay attention to appearances if we want people to believe this. And wouldn't people expect a new bride to want to make something special of the first time she entertained guests?"

"Not the ones who've known you since you were a kid—" He stepped back from the not entirely playful punch she'd aimed at his stomach.

He supposed her interest in this was Matty wanting to keep

up the illusion that they were a normal newly married couple. That's what he'd agreed to, and he couldn't see any possible harm.

"All right, all right. If you want to do this, great. Saves me having to remember to cool down all this beer."

Dave had just come out of the Knighton Bank safe-deposit box vault when Joyce Arbedick waylaid him. He'd stopped by the bank before lunch to put his and Matty's marriage certificate in the safe-deposit box.

He'd found himself looking at it a couple of times a day when he began to doubt this whole thing was real, so he decided that before he wore the thing to tatters he better put it somewhere safe.

"Oh, Dave, it's good to finally see you! I've been keeping an eye out, but I guess you've been keeping close to the ranch."

Her obvious visions of continuous connubial bliss must have been contagious, because Dave felt a heat pulsing through his body as if it had immediate memories of things that hadn't happened in more than half a decade. Worse, the heat must have been visible somehow, because Joyce grinned and rapped him on the arm with a thick wad of something in a bag.

"I didn't mean to make you blush, Dave. No need now— you're legal, remember?" She gave a tinkling laugh.

Dave produced a passable smile and ignored everything except her first comment.

"Was there something you needed to see me about, Joyce?"

"Oh, yes, I want to give you copies of these pictures I took at the reception. I know you didn't have a professional photographer or anything, so I thought you might like them. Not that there are any prize winners." She giggled. "But at least you'll have a few memories."

She held out the bag. From the impact it had had against

his arm, he knew it was a darn sight more than "a few" photos. As it was, he already had enough pictures in his head of Matty on that day to ensure he'd never run out of memories. But Joyce meant well.

He took the bag and thanked her, including Matty in the thanks.

"Oh, yes, I'm sure she'll like having them," Joyce said. "A girl likes to have photos from her wedding, no matter how fast it happens. And here's something else I'm sure Matty will be glad to see."

He automatically accepted the manila envelope she handed to him.

"What's this?"

"The confirmations on her closing out her retirement accounts and the papers showing the money's in the ranch account now. Just a minute," she told another employee who had called her name. "I do wish she'd kept at least one IRA, but you know Matty—when she makes her mind up, there's no budging her."

Joyce laughed gaily at that and waved goodbye as she headed toward her co-worker. Dave mumbled a farewell and left the bank.

The path back to his office, on the second floor above the Van Hopft Pharmacy, was so familiar he didn't have to think about where he was going. So he could set his entire mind on what Matty had done. Someone who had known her most of her life should have expected this: She'd sunk every last bit of her savings into running the ranch.

What if she didn't get the grant? What if she did but it wasn't enough to turn around the Flying W?

She'd lose not only her sole inheritance, but whatever nest egg she'd built up working away from the ranch.

Then she'd have to stay married to him.

The thought stopped him dead on the second step of the narrow stairway to his office.

Disgust hit him first. What sort of man would want to win a woman that way—by default, by destitution?

Practicality came second, and in the form of an answer to his first question: Not the kind of man who loved a woman like Matty. Because it wouldn't work. Destitution would drive her away. She'd stand on her own two feet if she had to crawl.

He half smiled at that phrase—it sounded just like Matty—as he continued up the stairs toward the old-fashioned wooden and frosted-glass door with David E. Currick, Attorney At Law painted on it.

No, Matty losing the Flying W wasn't an option. Because if she did, he'd lose her.

He didn't know yet what he would do, but he'd do something to make sure this turned out right for her. Only then would there be any chance that things could turn out right for *them.*

As he passed the desk of Ruth Moski, his longtime office manager, he automatically asked, "Ruth, would you get me a burger and fries from the café for lunch?"

"No."

He'd taken two more steps before her answer sank in. He turned back to the white-haired woman who could have been a TV ad exec's image of a cozy grandmother type except for her penchant for wearing dangly earrings with feathers, rocks, lacquered leaves and other bits of nature.

"No?"

"No. You've hidden in your office long enough."

This was the downside of having someone who has known you since you were a baby—and had the embarrassing pictures to prove it—as your office manager. It had taken him a couple years to get over his mother's training and feel comfortable calling her Ruth instead of Mrs. Moski. But it could have been worse: he could have had the only other qualified person around as his office assistant—his sister, Lisa. She had even less compunction about telling him her opinion than Ruth did.

"I'm not hiding, Ruth," he said with great reasonableness. "I have a lot of work to do and—"

"Baloney. You don't want to face the joshin' you know you're going to get from that crew at the café, startin' with my Hugh. It's childish, but it's their way of saying you're important to 'em, part of the group. Bonding. Sort of like a bunch of athletes patting each other on the butt, only with words."

He closed his eyes. Lord, he wished Lisa hadn't talked Ruth into taking that sociology class with her last semester.

"As much as I appreciate—"

"It's the God's honest truth and you know it. And it's high time you stopped hidin' in here. You're going to have to face up to it sooner or later. The longer you wait, the worse it's going to be."

"Ruth, I appreciate your good intentions," he tried again, "but I don't think the joshing from the Counter Crew is going to reach some critical mass if I eat lunch at my desk and catch up on work today."

"I meant your stomach. I'm not getting your lunch anymore, and last I heard the café's not deliverin', so the longer you wait the hungrier you're going to get."

Chapter Seven

Dave had a big grin ready to go when he stepped into the Knighton Café, and he produced it as soon as the first voice called out to him.

"So, how's married life treating you, Dave?"

"Just fine."

"Early days yet," said one wag from the counter.

"Yeah, it's still the *honeeeymooooon*," crooned another.

"Surprised you made it to town at all, what with all the things you got to tend to at the Slash-C," said Hugh with a lascivious grin.

"Dave! Over here. Come sit here."

It was Lisa. She was sitting at her usual booth in the back corner—the quietest spot—with her usual set of books fanned around her.

He supposed he should be honored. Lisa rarely allowed anyone to interrupt her lunchtime study routine.

But instead of honored, he felt wary. Of all the people in Knighton, Lisa posed the most danger to this charade with

Matty. With his parents away, Lisa knew him and Matty better than anybody else. She'd always been sharper than any tack he'd ever come across, and since she'd returned after attending college in New York, she stood for no nonsense from anyone. Add that to her no-holds-barred tendency to tell him what she thought, and this could spell trouble.

"How's Matty?"

"Oh, you know Matty. Just like she's always been. She'll never change."

"Don't be an idiot, of course she's changed. Nobody can leave a place to go to college, come back years later to find themselves facing the task of digging their way out of a mudslide with a teaspoon and not change. Good Lord, I thought you had more sense than that. I guess that was too much to hope for from a man."

"You don't think much of men, do you, Lisa? How come? What happened to give you such a poor opinion of half the human race? Something in New York?" He'd asked this before, and she'd never given him a real answer. And he knew perfectly well that she wouldn't answer now. So the question was actually a diversionary tactic, a fact he wasn't too proud to admit—to himself.

"Less than half the human race," she corrected immediately. "And I'm openminded enough to see there might be exceptions. Are you going to straighten up and prove to be one of those exceptions?"

He held his hands up in surrender, bestowing on her his most successful smile.

"Don't shoot, Lisa, I'm unarmed."

"Hmmph. That might work on Judge Halloran, but it won't work on me, big brother."

"How did this shooting war start, anyway?"

"I asked a straightforward question about Matty and you gave an inane answer. There's something strange about all this. I saw how you looked at Matty at Henry Brennan's funeral, and I how she *didn't* look at you. And then before a month's passed, you up and get married—practically in secret, in front of a judge, without a real wedding.''

Lisa's eyes bored into him, and he used all his discipline to return her look without squirming.

"If I hadn't seen how the two of you were together at the reception," she added, "I'd *really* be suspicious."

Heaven protect him from *really* suspicious Currick females!

"But what I want to know now," his sister continued, "is what's this I heard about Matty handling the arrangements for your get-together of the tricounty's legal brain trust?"

"Matty wanted to do a little entertaining."

Lisa snorted. "Entertaining? With most of that group, tearing open the bag of chips before tossing it on a table could pass as fine dining. Did you talk her into this, Dave?"

He laughed at the idea. "Lisa, you malign the both of us—me that I'd be dumb enough to try to talk Matty into anything and her that she'd ever listen if I tried."

"You wouldn't come at it direct, I'll give you that much, but you always were leading Matty to do things your way."

His laugh faded as her expression remained serious. "You're kidding, right?"

She shook her head. "You got so used to being the leader and having her as your faithful follower when you were little kids that you never adjusted when she caught up to you."

"When did you add psychology to your degrees?" he grumbled.

She ignored that. "You're more subtle, but you still do a lot of bossing. Don't look like I've popped your last balloon, Dave. The way things were doesn't mean they have to stay that way now. As long as you've grown up, and have the smarts to see that she has, too."

He had nothing to say to that—there was nothing he *could* say to it. The usually acute Lisa was so far off on this one, he couldn't respond without hurting her feelings.

But Lisa continued studying him as if he had words printed

across his forehead. He wasn't uncomfortable, just ready for a new topic, that's all, so he said, "So, you're closing in on another degree, aren't you, Lisa?"

She waited while he ate two French fries from her plate, then looked down at the spread of books as if she'd forgotten about them.

"MBA. Finish next June."

He shook his head in admiration. "That's terrific, Lisa. What are you going to do with the MBA? You going to stay working for Taylor?"

"Maybe." She slanted a look at him. "Maybe I'll start on a law degree, so I can join that legal brain trust of yours."

He laughed. "It would be a major step down in class for you, Lisa. A major step down."

Cal, on foot, nodded into the milling congregation of heifers and calves. "Red with the white slash."

Matty spotted the one he meant and maneuvered old Reve into position. Juno was just learning to work cattle, so among the nervous first-time mothers, she preferred riding an old hand like Reve. He wasn't fast, but he was sure and steady.

They'd been working steadily, down to the last few now. Cal would spot one that needed doctoring, she'd rope the calf, he'd administer the vaccine, loose her rope and they were on to the next one. A chute would have made this easier, but building chutes cost money.

As always, the thought of what wasn't being done at the Flying W because of money brought her back around to the grant. She should have heard by now. She'd been so sure that with the Slash-C being her official address it would all be routine. It had seemed a sure thing from reading the regulations or she never would have swallowed her pride and asked Dave to marry her.

Although she had to admit that her pride hadn't felt nearly as prickly lately.

You didn't come easy for me, Matty... I never understood

the restlessness in you, that energy that pushed you into leap-
ing into things… While you were off exploring the world and
finding yourself like a normal person, in college and beyond,
I stayed at home and wondered what was wrong with me that
I didn't want to.

She'd scoffed at his words then, but they hadn't left her.
The stuff about her not being easy for him, no, that couldn't
be true. But maybe things hadn't been as perfect for Dave
these past six years as they'd seemed from the outside.
Maybe he had hurt some, too. Maybe he even—

"Hey, you gonna rope that critter or stare at him till he
dies?"

Matty jolted at Cal's call. "Sorry."

She adjusted the coil in her left hand, guided Reve into
position and started the loop in her right hand on the clock-
wise rotation of a houlihan catch. The rope settled securely
over the neck of the red calf with the narrow white stripe on
his face. And Reve planted his feet to keep the rope taut so
Cal could go to work.

How many thousands of times had she done this in her
life? It didn't matter. Every time the rope went true and taut
she felt the twang of pleasure at doing it well.

If there was one thing she'd known how to do growing
up, it was how to throw a rope.

If there was one thing she'd learned as an adult, it was
how to throw a party.

Especially throwing the kind of party meant to put people
in the mood to give you something you wanted. Mostly that
was money, but sometimes it was something else. This was
one of the *sometimes*.

The idea had come to her full-blown in that instant yesterday after she'd realized it wasn't a regular party Dave had
planned without telling her.

She wouldn't lie to herself; she'd been relieved to hear it
was a work session for a group of his lawyer cronies. *Re-*
lieved—how stupid was that? What difference would it have

made if he *had* planned to have a real party—even the social event of the decade—without telling her? It wasn't like they were a real couple who would make decisions together.

Just because they'd done okay in the mornings didn't make them a team.

Just because he'd made room for her in bureaus and closets, just because he kept his word about giving her first shot at the bathroom in the mornings, just because he pitched in and put some dishes in the dishwasher, didn't mean they were a real couple.

And just because he'd gone along with this marriage didn't mean that she wasn't on her own when it came to making sure there were changes made.

No, she'd do this herself, with some help from Taylor, who had loved the idea as soon as she heard it. She'd make this work for her. Make it work for the Flying W. By herself. She'd needed Dave for his address, but that was only for the short run. Not the way she'd once thought she needed him. Not the kind of need that had to be filled so your heart could keep pumping and your lungs could keep pushing out and pulling in. No, not that kind of need at all.

And once she got the Flying W back on its feet, she'd make up for leaning on him even temporarily. A lot of that depended on getting the grant and hopefully putting through the other project she had her eye on. But she couldn't control those things; she *could* make sure she made a success of this legal gathering. It would help future people who might need the grant. And maybe it would be a little bit of a thank-you to Dave, too.

Dave heard Matty ride in well after dark, and went out to the barn to meet her. He'd been waiting nearly two hours for her return. For most of that time, the envelope he'd picked up from the mailbox when he drove in had stared at him from the family room mantel where he'd propped it. Now it rested in his shirt pocket like a rock against his chest.

"Hey there, Matty." He patted Juno's neck.

"Oh." Matty's eyes popped open. "Hi. I didn't see you standing there."

"Tough to see me with your eyes closed."

"I was just resting them."

"Hard day." He didn't make it a question.

"Yeah."

"Want to tell me about it?"

"Not particularly."

He hesitated, both because of that answer and because he saw that her weariness was more than a long day in the saddle and physical labor. Maybe he should wait. If it was bad news, she'd deal with it better after a good night's sleep...

As long as you've grown up, and have the smarts to see that she has, too.

Lisa's remembered words rattled sharply in his head. But dammit, Matty looked so tired...was it so wrong to want to protect her, to want to smooth the way for her?

You got so used to being the leader and her your faithful follower when you were little kids that you never adjusted when she caught up to you...

He shook his head to himself. That was nonsense; he knew Matty's strength.

"No what?" she asked, tipping her head, as if trying to read him better.

He pushed out the first thought that came to mind. "Thinking about you riding in the dark. You shouldn't do that, Matty. It can be dangerous."

She snorted. "I can do that ride with my eyes closed. I did it a thousand times as a kid and nothing ever happened."

"That was on horses who knew the trail. Juno doesn't."

"She doesn't need to—" her voice sounded a little strange and the muscles of her face seemed to be fighting some urge "—because I do."

The last word came out half strangled.

"Matty, are you okay?"

His concerned question was interrupted and answered when she yawned. A huge yawn. A yawn so deep and so big that she slipped sideways in the saddle a little and he moved toward her. But she automatically righted herself. Matty hadn't changed in that way. She'd stay in the saddle if she were completely asleep instead of only three-quarters.

She'd blow her top if she recognized that he'd made a move meant to protect her from any fall. And she'd blow her top if she knew he was delaying handing over the envelope for the same reason.

"I've got something here for you. Came today."

"What?" But he was already handing up the envelope to her and she could see *what* from the official return address imprinted on it. "Oh. It's from the commission."

"I know."

"Guess I should open it."

"Guess so."

But she held each end in a gloved hand and looked at the fat envelope.

"Want me to?" he offered.

"No." She yanked off her gloves, dropping them to the V of the saddle between her legs. She tore open the envelope and skimmed across the contents. Then he watched her eyes travel back to the start of the letter and take in its contents more slowly. At the end, she sucked in a slow breath between her teeth.

He knew right then that he'd make this right for her. No matter what it took, Matty would not lose the Flying W.

When she started to read it a third time, he cuffed her on the thigh. "Matty, if you don't tell me what that letter says—"

"We've got it! We've got it! The Flying W got the grant!"

As she shouted, she started to dismount, only instead of swinging her right leg back and over Juno's rump, Matty brought her right leg forward, twisting in her left stirrup at the same time she slid her leg between her own body and the horse's neck. It was a fancier dismount, one that should have ended in her making a little hop to the ground.

But Juno wasn't used to the maneuver, and skittered to the side and back as Matty released. The horse's side bumped Matty's back as she came down, and she stumbled forward.

Right into Dave's open arms.

Closing his arms around her was as right as breathing. She was laughing, interrupted by little huffs from being first knocked by a thousand pounds of horseflesh, then having her momentum stopped by his body. Still holding her, he tried to ease the force of the impact by retreating two steps, until his back met a solid surface.

She threw her arms around his neck, her grin masking any signs of her earlier exhaustion.

"The Flying W's got a reprieve!"

She was so close, so warm, so alive, so familiar and so…Matty. There was no planning, no consideration of pushing her, no thought of how she might react or what the consequences might be. He kissed her.

And she kissed him back. As she had in front of the judge. As she had in front of Pamela Dobson. As naturally as if the years apart had evaporated. But this time it couldn't be a performance, because they had no audience. Just the two of them, the way it used to be.

Her mouth moved against his in a joyful glide that made him want to howl.

"I am so excited, Dave!"

She tightened her arms around his neck in a spasm of joy, and he used the opportunity to bow his head and come back to her mouth.

"I got that feeling," he murmured against her lips. "In fact, I could say the same."

He kissed the corner of her mouth, then caught her bottom lip and tugged it gently between his teeth. Her lips parted and she made a little sound that he caught in his mouth, swallowing it like a shot of the smoothest whiskey, hot and sweet intoxication speeding directly into his bloodstream. He flicked his tongue in once, darted out, then came back again, repeating the dance until he thought his veins might explode.

And then she pushed him even further with an answering touch of her tongue against his. Slight at first, then stronger. A slow glide that grew more eager.

Ah, Matty. The taste and feel of her.

He slid one hand down her back, holding their positions, with her right leg tucked between his two. Then he turned them, pivoting so her back would be against the wall, to have his body pressed against her curves, to feel the sensations of her body against his, but to still have his hands free.

But somehow their legs tangled and they made another half turn, his left shoulder coming up against the unlatched door of a stall. The door gave way, and so did he, with Matty tumbling right along with him.

He twisted as they went down, so she landed mostly on top of him. But they didn't come down square, and the momentum kept them rolling.

They came to rest against the far stall wall, shadows and the smell of fresh, clean hay blanketing them like fine-spun silk.

"Are you okay?"

"Yes."

She didn't look away from him. He felt a tremor through his arms at the effort of holding his upper body away from her, though it was definitely a tremor of willpower, not muscles.

"Matty?"

She didn't say no.

He bent his elbows and felt the sweet cushion of her breasts against his chest as his mouth found hers again. Her leg was still between his, riding high enough to bring a pressure that made him crave more. Better yet, their tumble had left one of his legs between hers, too, and he drew it up to give her the same sensations. She gave a breathy moan into his mouth, and her hips rocked.

He swore that despite the layers of clothing he could feel the tightening points of her breasts against his chest. From the first time he'd dared a fleeting brush against her breasts, her responsiveness had brought him such satisfaction.

He shifted to slide his hand up her side, under where her shirt had worked free from her jeans. His palm against her skin was like a rocket going off inside him. A rocket given a power boost by the quick, soft intake of her breath. He wanted to savor every second of her skin under his hand, but some instinct even deeper pushed him. He found the silky edge of her bra, found the texture of lace, then where the lace and silkiness met he found what he'd been seeking, the tight nub of her nipple. He circled it, then brushed across the tip. Her hips came off the ground, and he met the cradle between her legs with the weight of his arousal.

He heard the hard, sharp knocking of what must have been his heart. If he touched her lips again or brought his mouth to her breast now, with the two of them in this position, with the heat and weight of his wanting growing more palpable each second, he didn't know how he'd stop.

"Dave?"

Breathing burned his lungs, all because the air tasted of Matty. And the knocking never quit.

"Are you okay?" Okay with letting this take them where it would lead—where he desperately wanted it to lead, where it had so often led before.

But she seemed to take it more prosaically.

"I...I'm fine, but..."

"But?" he prompted, his voice rasping, his eyes on her lips.

"But I don't think Brandeis is—okay, I mean."

Her words snapped the knocking he'd heard from metaphor into reality. It wasn't his heart. It was Brandeis' hoofs.

Kicking at the wall that separated them from his stall next door with all the power of an irked stallion.

"He sounds upset."

"Jealous," he managed to say with a grin.

It was the wrong thing to say.

Matty's expression stiffened, leaching out the joy, and returning all the signs of tiredness.

"He doesn't need to be," she said lightly, shifting her hips to the side that would get her free of him the fastest. "You're still all his."

He'd meant that Brandeis would be jealous because he wasn't having the pleasure Dave was having, but it would do no good to explain. It never had done any good to try to explain things to Matty. She got something in her head and that was it.

Ignoring the discomfort, he jackknifed his body up and offered her a hand. She ignored it, and started getting up on her own. He reached down and grabbed her hand, tugging her to her feet with more force than finesse.

Her gaze, wider now, came up to his face, but he had himself back under control.

"Glad to hear it," he said, with his usual calm. "Tell you what, you go take a shower and I'll fix dinner, and we'll celebrate this grant, and you can tell me what it all means for the Flying W."

She knew perfectly well what Dave was doing getting her to talk about what the grant meant for the Flying W.

The moment she emerged in clean jeans, a big, soft sweater and her hair slicked back to find him setting the small table, he'd asked about the grant. That led to talk of well-drilling techniques and irrigation theories. Anytime the conversation threatened to flag, he'd ask another of his calm questions, and they'd be off again, talking about ranches in general, and theirs in particular.

He was trying to spare her embarrassment for throwing
herself at him. And she let him. At least for a while.

But how long could a reasonable person ignore the gorilla
in the middle of the room? Even with the cooperation of her
dinner companion. It wasn't like talking about the grant kept
her from thinking—or remembering.

They'd finished the grilled steaks, microwaved potatoes
and broccoli and salad before she brought it up, however.
But finally, she started clearing the table—that was the deal,
one cooked, the other cleaned—and also cleared her throat.

"Dave, there's something…I think we should clear this
up."

"Clear what up?"

"What happened earlier." He gave her no help, and as she
started toward the sink with the stack of dishes, she added,
"In the barn."

"I thought what happened was pretty obvious."

He hooked the fingers of one hand into their empty water
glasses and picked up the butter dish with his other hand.
The look he gave her as he deposited the glasses by the sink
had her blood heating, or maybe it was the raspy note in his
voice. Either way, it was because those signs of his made her
embarrassed about her behavior. Yes, it was definitely embarrassment warming her insides, she told herself as she
quickly deposited the dishes in the dishwasher.

"What was obvious was that I should have stopped it."

He turned from the open refrigerator door and studied her
before inquiring, "So you see me as the poor male, unable
to control the primitive desires that drive him?"

"Of course not."

"Then why should *you* have stopped it?" He closed the
fridge door with more muscle than necessary.

"Because I'm the one who started the whole thing."

"That's true."

And the way he was eyeing her, he was remembering her

throwing herself at him, wrapping her arms around his neck and plastering her body to his.

"I didn't kiss you first." As soon as she'd made the protest, she realized that was opening a door to dangerous territory. Because she *had* kissed him back. She slammed it closed as fast as she could. "But that's not what I was talking about, anyhow. I was talking about the whole...whole, uh..."

"Charade? Masquerade? Con game?"

She glared at him, liking each of his suggestions less than the previous one. "This temporary marriage. So, I have the responsibility for keeping things on an even keel. And for not letting things get, uh, complicated. *That's* why I should have stopped it. Plus, I was the one who stated clearly, upfront, that there would be no...:uh, physical expressions of... of a...an intimate nature."

He raised his brows at that but said nothing at first, leaning back and watching her. She closed her mouth firmly, refusing to be drawn into saying anymore until he responded.

His eyes glinted, though she didn't think he was amused. "So, why didn't you?"

"Why didn't I what?"

"Stop it."

"I got carried away by the moment. It didn't mean anything. That happens to people sometimes, like that famous *Life Magazine* picture of the sailor kissing the woman on V-J Day."

"Okay," he snapped, and walked away, heading toward the family room.

"*Okay?*" she demanded, following him.

"Yes, okay. No harm done. No apology necessary. You've made it clear it was a celebration and I happened to be handy. Fine. As long as you don't get carried away like that with anyone else while we're married. I don't think my reputation could take it."

"Oh, that's so damned male possessive, Currick." Even

as she flared up, a voice in the back of her head noted that she might be a tad eager to embrace a nice, clear-cut reaction like anger. "Like you're worried people will think you can't control the little wife, and you couldn't take the ribbing."

"No," he said calmly as he sat in his usual spot on the sofa next to the end table stacked with a jumble of ranching and law journals. "I couldn't take the sympathy."

"Sympathy? You mean for being married to me?" she started indignantly, hands on her hips as she glared at him from across the trunk coffee table.

"No, I mean everybody thinking there goes that poor bastard Dave Currick, who got his heart broken twice by Matty Brennan."

She stopped dead. She felt as if she was lost in a maze and every path was blocked by a wall of evergreens. Her heartbeat picked up a quicker cadence.

"Of course," continued Dave in that maddeningly calm way of his, "they wouldn't know they were wrong this time."

"This time? *Both* times. They'd be wrong *both* times."

"This time."

"Are you trying to make out that you were heartbroken six years ago?"

"You find that hard to believe? Why? Are you doubting I have a heart?"

She ignored the last part. "Hard to believe? Yeah, I find it hard to believe, since you *dumped* me!"

"Dumped you? I did not dump you, I—"

"The hell you didn't! You broke it off."

"I did not break it off. I said—"

"You did, too. You said we should—"

"We should take a break from each other and see other people."

"—see other people," she repeated bitterly. "The international code for get lost."

Take a break from each other. God, she could still feel the pain of those words from him. She'd been so in love. All her life she'd been in love with him. She would have followed him anywhere, lived any sort of life as long as they were together.

"I said we should see other people for a while, and that's what I meant." His calm tone from the start of the sentence was slipping away with each word. *Good.* "You're the one who bolted away like all you'd been waiting for was for someone to open the cage a crack."

"Cage? I never said anything about a cage. You were the one who kicked me out. Like I was a baby bird in the nest and you were the mother bird and you wanted to see if I'd go *splat* on the ground."

"I have never felt the least like a mother bird toward you, Matilda Brennan!"

She opened her mouth for a hot retort, but before she could form one, the image of Dave outfitted in feathers and sitting in a huge nest took hold of her mind. Instead of words, a chortle came out of her mouth. Then a full-blown laugh.

Dave put his hands on his hips, and asked in resignation, "All right, Matty, what's so funny?"

"You...feathers...nest...mother bird!"

And she was gone, laughing so hard, she had to sit down. Dave eased into a few chuckles, too. And soon they were seated side by side on the couch.

Dave leaned back, but she was aware he was watching her. Unable to take it any longer, she shifted around to put one arm across the couch's back and face him.

"What, Currick?"

"If you thought I was such an ogre why did you ask me to...to get into this business arrangement with you?"

"I never said you were an ogre. You simply realized we weren't meant to have a future sooner than I did. And that doesn't change that you're still probably the most honorable, responsible man I know."

"At least among the single men living in Clark County,"

he added with cool wryness. "Did you really think I'd dumped you?"

"Of course I did. I was twenty years old—a very sheltered twenty, thanks to Grams and Gramps and your parents and you—and so in love I couldn't see straight. I felt like I'd had my insides ripped out." She shifted her focus from his face to over his left shoulder, where the hazy past seemed to reside. "And I couldn't do any of the things I'd done before when I was hurting. I couldn't go to your parents. I couldn't run back to Grams without everyone around here knowing. And I sure couldn't go to you."

She blinked at the memory of those dark days that had stretched into weeks that had stretched into months. She risked a glance at him, then looked away before she was even certain the intensity of his look was real and not her imagination.

"You know, it wasn't only losing you, though that doesn't do a girl's ego any good, either," she said with a twisted smile. "I felt like I lost your family, too. And to some extent my own home. And my future. I'd always known exactly what I was going to do—be your wife and help you run the Slash-C—and all of a sudden that was gone. Just a yawning blank ahead of me."

From the corner of her eye she caught the movement of his jerky nod. "Yeah, I know. That's what my parents, even Grams, said."

"Grams? What do you mean? What did she have to say about it?"

She looked at him fully now, and saw no hint of the intensity she thought she'd seen a moment earlier. Instead his eyes were shuttered, his face expressionless.

"They all were worried you were coasting on the tail of my dreams and not bothering to find your own."

Matty stared at him. "That's why you dumped me?"

"I didn't—" he started, then stopped when he looked up, obviously recognizing her goading for what it was. "I thought I was doing the *honorable, responsible* thing, giving you some time to test your wings. I didn't know you'd forget the wings and go straight to rockets so you could blast off.''

''I came back for visits.''

''For visits.''

Maybe it was her imagination, or maybe she really did hear an element of pain in that flat echo.

She'd visited Wyoming off and on after leaving so abruptly. She'd worked hard at building a new life, but she hadn't cut all ties with the old one, especially before her grandmother's death four years ago. On those short trips she'd done her best to keep up a good front of the cosmopolitan sophisticate amusing herself in humble surroundings, like Marie Antoinette playing milkmaid. And she'd done her absolute best to not see Dave.

She'd succeeded remarkably well. Until Great-Uncle Henry's death had brought her back for good. There had been no doubt in her mind about what she'd do when she received the notification. Because the alternative was selling the Flying W, and that was no option at all.

''And I came back for good.''

''After six years. And the first thing you did was make it real clear you wanted nothing to do with me.'' His tone was so damned neutral. ''And the second thing you did was make Cal Ruskoff your foreman.''

''So? That has nothing to do with it.''

''Doesn't it?''

''Of course not,'' she said emphatically, glad to be on sure ground. ''Great-Uncle Henry should have done it a long time ago. Cal was really running the place as best he could around Henry's oddities. It's not much of a title, considering we only have a couple other hands who come in now and then. Besides, he's a top hand. And a reliable worker. And he'd been around the past two years, which I hadn't been. He knew what had been going on with the operation—and what had been going wrong.''

"I'm sure he's all that...and more."

"What's that supposed to mean?"

"What do you suppose it means?"

"Are you saying...are you trying to imply...? Good Lord, you make it sound as if Cal's my boy toy or something."

"Boy toy wouldn't have been the first phrase that came to mind," he said in his judicial voice, "but if that's what you want to use..."

"That's ridiculous. *Absurd.* In the first place, Cal Ruskoff has too much self-respect to be anybody's boy toy, and in the second—"

"Self-respect has nothing to do with it."

"—place, it's absolutely absurd to make it sound as if all I'd have to do was snap my fingers and a man—"

"Not snap your fingers. Less than that. Just the right look."

"—would...he'd..."

"Be in your bed? Be your lover? Those phrases will do if you think *boy toy* lacks dignity."

"That's...that's ridiculous."

"Is it? Did he ever kiss you, Matty?"

"No!" She said it too fast, too vehemently, and he spotted it immediately.

"Ah, you kissed him."

"It's not like you're trying to make it sound. Nothing happened."

"Your choice, I take it."

"It was mutual if you must know." She tried for dignity, then gave that up in favor of disbelief. "You make it sound as if I'm some sort of femme fatale, when it's damned obvious I'm not going to be the next supermodel. So what's this junk about every man—"

"Not every man."

"Oh, now that sounds more like the old Dave Currick talking. So you think only Cal's got weird enough taste to be attracted to me, huh? And—"

"Not that either. You don't jump to conclusions, you leap to them, girl. Weird doesn't come into this discussion. I said not every man would be attracted to you—I doubt there's a woman alive who would turn on every man—but you have your fair share. Ruskoff isn't a lone wolf when it comes to looking at you that way. You've never seen it. Maybe that's some of the appeal—you're so damned oblivious."

"Oblivious?"

"You don't like oblivious? How about obtuse, then?"

Instead of rising to that bait, she sat back and considered him. Something else she remembered about Dave—when something was cutting a little too close to the bone for him, he often resorted to word games. And they'd been talking about the possibility of her and Cal having something going on...

Interesting. Very interesting.

"Quit looking at me like that, Matty."

"Like what?"

"Like those wheels turning in your head are going to catch me up and grind me into powder."

"Oh, yeah, right, like anyone could do that to Mr. Cool Currick. And even if I could, it wouldn't come out powder, it would be shaved iced. Besides...I was just wondering..."

He closed his eyes momentarily, apparently resigned. "Wondering what, Matty?"

"What kind of man it is who finds me attractive."

"One with a lot of patience."

"Fine. I won't try your patience any longer, Currick." She got up, but he grabbed her arm as she started to pass him.

"You want to know what kind of man finds you attractive? One who finds himself reaching his hand out toward the fascinating reds and oranges and yellows, even though he knows the flames can burn him."

He's a smart one, that Dave of yours. Grams had always told Matty that, back when Dave Currick *was* hers. *A smart one, all right.*

And smart ones who thought they could get burned learned their lesson quickly, and stopped reaching for what they perceived as flames. Dave certainly had.

"Oh." She blinked at a sudden feeling of deflation that stung her eyes. "Guess I should be looking for a fireman, then."

He dropped his hand from her arm.

"Maybe so."

Lying in bed staring at the ceiling was nothing new for Matty. It was how she'd started most nights after returning to Wyoming. Always hoping the ceiling arithmetic she computed would arrive at better solutions than she'd come up with on paper for the Flying W's books.

But this time what kept her awake weren't calculations.

Odd how Dave had homed in on her relationship with Cal. Odder still that he'd asked about kissing.

The night after Great-Uncle Henry's funeral—only a few short hours after she'd discovered the financial mess, and then turned down Dave's invitation to dinner—Cal had come up to the main house to talk about what he intended to do the next day. A late-season snow had started that afternoon and hadn't let up. When Cal had prepared to follow the narrow path through the snow to his small cottage, she'd said it was plain stupid for him to leave.

People will think more's going on than's going on, he'd said.

She'd stared at him, seeing the kindness in his eyes and—to be totally honest—the muscled, hard body. At that moment it seemed like the most reasonable thing in the world. If her memories had slid to the sight of Dave at the graveside, so handsome and somehow distant, she couldn't be arrested for that. *So maybe we should prove them all right.*

Matty—

She'd given him no time to say more, putting her arms around his neck and kissing him. He'd cooperated. And there had been a spark. A genuine spark. They both agreed on that. But the spark had cooled and gentled in no time flat.

With her arms still around his neck, she'd backed off enough to look into his face. He looked shocked.

Damn, Matty, I thought when we... It's why I've held off. I never...

Well, at least that was balm for her ego. He'd expected a conflagration, too.

I guess this comes under the heading of Not Meant to Be.

She'd gotten that much out with dignity, but then she'd burst into tears.

In the end, Cal had stayed all night at the main house, but it was spent at the kitchen table over leftover brownies and hot chocolate, listening to her disjointed woes, fears and disappointments. The one area she hadn't strayed to was Dave.

Cal had been the most understanding shoulder to cry on— literally and figuratively—that she'd ever had. He'd said little about himself, but a few phrases had let her know she wasn't the only one at that table who felt life wasn't in the best shape possible. Maybe that was what had connected them— a comradeship of loneliness. And a fond protectiveness for a fellow wayfarer.

Her eyelids started to drift down.

Whatever it was, it now felt like a durable, reliable friendship, which required little conversation and raised no doubts in her mind.

She cuddled closer into the pillow.

It would have been so much easier if she'd felt with Cal the way she'd felt kissing Dave in the barn.

Her eyes popped wide-open.

The way she'd felt kissing Dave.

It all poured back through her, flashes and then long, rolling waves. Heat, sensation, desiring and being desired, satisfaction that somehow brought even deeper longing. There was no use denying it, she still wanted Dave Currick. As badly as ever. And he'd demonstrated that maybe he wanted her, too.

But that wasn't the question. The question was whether she could risk letting herself slide back into believing in this, in *them*. Because if she did, and it didn't work out, she didn't know if she could survive it a second time. To lose it all again—the sense of family, the sense of belonging, the sense of being loved.

To lose Dave again.

But how could she even hope for anything else to happen when whatever was happening between them had started with a masquerade? Last time had at least started off honestly, and look how that ended. So what chance was there when they started off with a lie?

Besides, she should know by now that wanting wasn't enough. He'd wanted her before—that hadn't seemed to change right up until the moment he said they should see other people—so that certainly wasn't anything to base hopes on this time.

No, she had to be levelheaded, and remember what was most important—the future of the Flying W.

And while she did that, she could spend her nights appealing fervently to the ceiling for some mathematical equation that would halt memories and desire.

What the hell had he been thinking bringing up Ruskoff?

Not thinking, not thinking at all.

But dammit, it should have been him beside her at Henry's funeral, not Ruskoff. That image kept eating at his gut. Ruskoff standing beside her at the grave. Ruskoff with his arm protectively at her waist. Ruskoff handing her into the car.

It should have been him.

But he'd never meant to let her know. Jealousy had goaded him into that. Yeah, he was jealous, and he didn't like it.

It had started with one of her flying visits right after Henry hired Ruskoff.

Riding out alone on Brandeis, Dave had topped a rise near the fence that divided the two ranches, and he's spotted them. He hadn't even known Matty was home, so there'd been shock, but it had been more, too. There she was, smiling up at the new hand, and handing him a water jug. It wasn't something he hadn't seen her do a thousand times with a hundred or more men in the years they were growing up. But this was different. Maybe because he didn't know Ruskoff. Maybe because he no longer had a claim to Matty. Maybe because it had started the drumbeat of a single thought in his brain.

It should have been him.

Standing beside her. Consoling her. Protecting her. Loving her. Always.

He shook his head at his own foolishness.

Always looked damned shaky, he thought dryly. But he did have *now*. So instead of letting stuff he couldn't change eat at him, he should do his damnedest to protect her. And right now where she needed protection was with the Flying W.

She'd been so excited about getting the grant.

But would it be enough? And what would happen if the commission ever found out she'd only married him to get an address that qualified?

She'd put everything into the ranch, that was clear from what Joyce had said.

There were so many things that could go wrong with a ranch, and without a financial cushion each could be a death knell. But Matty was letting her love for the Flying W push her. She was being impulsive, as always. And this time her leap could land her down in the depths of a chasm.

Unable to sleep, Dave got up and headed for the kitchen counter where he'd left his briefcase. Might as well get some work done.

But on his way through the family room, he saw the official envelope atop the stack of Flying W papers Matty was still working her way through. He stopped and stared at it for a moment, before continuing on. Then he stopped again, walked back and picked up the envelope. The light wasn't good enough to read it, so he took it with him to the kitchen.

He read the acceptance letter quickly. The multiple sheets of instructions, warnings, musts and shall nots, he read through more slowly. After two readings, he put the papers down safely out of harm's way and got himself a drink of orange juice. He sipped it slowly as he stared out the window over the sink. If his eyes had been focused on the moment, he'd only have seen himself reflected back in the glass. But he was looking at something else entirely. Something without form or substance—possibilities, specifically possibilities for trouble.

Trouble for Matty.

He drained the last quarter of the glass, put it in the sink and took his laptop out of his briefcase. Standing at the counter, wearing only boxer shorts—and those in deference to Matty being in the house—he had a letter drafted in ten minutes.

Two minutes more, he had the laptop and briefcase closed, and the envelope and its enclosures back where he'd found it. He'd polish the letter at the office and have it off in the morning mail. The rest of what he needed to do would take a trip to a bank in Jefferson, but he could do that tomorrow.

And Matty need never know that he was protecting her, the way he always had.

Chapter Eight

Matty was stretched out on the family room couch watching a Fred Astaire and Ginger Rogers movie from Donna Currick's extensive collection when she heard the outside kitchen door open.

It was the third night in the past week he'd gotten home after ten.

She frowned as the thought surfaced. She wasn't keeping track of him.

"These leftovers for me?" He came into the family room carrying the plate she'd left for him, and since a forkful of cold roast beef was already headed for his mouth, she figured he knew the answer.

"You could have heated it up."

He mumbled something as he chewed before finally saying, "It's good like this. And faster."

He gestured with the fork for her to bend her knees to make room for him on the couch. When she did, he sank into the cushion with a faint grunt. She sat up, with her legs

stretched between them. It made it easy to watch him while
he ate, his absent gaze fastened on the TV screen.

His shirt was rumpled, with one more button undone than
his usual conservative two. His thick hair showed evidence
of a pair of big hands pushing through it. His five-o'clock
shadow bristled with an additional five hours of growth.
Lines at his mouth seemed to have dug deeper. She knew for
a fact that the shadows under his eyes were new.

"You better look this tired because you're working too
hard and not because you're out carousing, or I'm going to
demand Brandeis as immediate compensation."

His lips twitched in an abbreviation of his usual grin.
"You're not getting your hands on Brandeis over this, kiddo.
It's about the farthest I could get from carousing."

"Owen Marshall?"

He glanced at her, then away. "Yeah."

That's all he would say, she knew, because Owen was his
client. But she'd heard bits and pieces over the past week,
from folks in town, from what Cal had picked up from a
hand who was helping them, from Dave's foreman Jack. The
Marshalls owned a big, thriving spread at the other end of
Clark County. Owen was the strong-minded head of the family. At sixty-something he'd expected there to be plenty of
time to arrange for the next generation to take over the ranch
smoothly. Then he'd collapsed, and they'd discovered wide-
spread cancer. Now they were in a race to arrange matters
so the ranch didn't get eaten up by taxes, disputes or family
squabbles.

It wasn't that much different a situation from what Great-
Uncle Henry had faced. Except he never had acknowledged
he might die, Matty had been the only one to inherit—and
they hadn't had Dave Currick working to prevent the mess
she'd found herself in. The mess he'd been so instrumental
in giving her a chance to dig out of thanks to his willingness
to marry her. There wasn't another soul on earth she would
have asked.

She swallowed. And changed the subject of her own thoughts.

"I called all the people on your list for that legal get-together. They're all coming," she announced.

"So I hear. Thanks." He put his empty plate on the chest. "I also hear you've done more than invite them. Ruth was saying how impressed the various office managers are at your efforts to find out their bosses' special likes and dislikes."

Now it was her turn to watch the screen while he studied her. "If you're going to have someone as a guest you should make them as comfortable as possible."

Especially if you wanted something from them. But she wasn't going to share that piece of the fund-raiser's creed with him...not yet.

"Besides," she added, "it helps me to know what to buy."

"Chips and beer," he suggested.

"I think you've taken care of the beer." She shifted the subject. "I, uh, thought I'd let you know, I've got somebody coming by tomorrow, around ten."

"I'll be gone by then, so I won't be in your way."

"I didn't mean it that way. I just meant— Besides, it's your house."

"Most people would say it's our house, considering we're married."

She opened her mouth, then closed it. Maybe he was trying to goad her, maybe not. Either way, he was clearly exhausted, and she wasn't going to get into that wrangle now.

"Anyway, I wanted to let you know. I also left a folder on your desk with some stuff to look at. You must be swamped now, but when you have a chance."

"What kind of stuff?"

"It's material I've accumulated. I'd thought about it for the Flying W, but without the capital... But you could make it work on the Slash-C, especially where the creek drops down from The Narrows—"

"Whoa, Matty. Pretend you're talking to someone with a brain of mush and keep it simple, okay?"

She smiled at him. "If you piped that creek and had a turbine at the bottom, you could generate electricity. It would probably be only marginally profitable, so it would take a while to earn back your investment, but with the improvements in turbines it's a better deal. And it would protect you some against rising energy prices. You know you wouldn't be able to use the power directly?"

"Yeah, I know that. The electric company pays you for the power."

"Right, they have to even out the flow, clean it up, to prevent spikes. But if the price they're charging for electricity goes up, so does the price they pay you, so it is a cushion that way."

"How'd you get the idea?"

"Riding back and forth, seeing the creek where the trail cuts through The Narrows and then drops sharply," she explained. "That would be ideal."

"How'd you know about it in the first place?"

"Oh, I read about it a while back—must be three or four years ago. I updated the numbers recently, thinking if the price of turbines comes down enough..." She sighed. "I'd love to do it for the Flying W, but we don't have the capital. At least not yet. But the grant money is going to start us toward where we could think about projects like that. This is exactly the sort of difference I thought the grant could make. It's too bad the committee can't see the good that came from getting around stupid rules."

She expected a response to that—at least some crack about how she'd gone about getting around the rule. But he said nothing.

He seemed to have gone still, and he'd turned away from her to stare hard at the screen.

Only then did she become aware that her left foot had been rubbing slightly against him, the sole of her bare foot sliding a few inches up, then dropping back down against the side of his hip. She jerked both her feet back, wrapping her arms around her knees.

"Anyway, I thought it might be something you'd be interested in for the Slash-C."

Dave muttered something under his breath.

"What?"

"Jeez, you can see right through her dress."

She followed his gaze toward the TV screen. Fred and Ginger were dancing their climactic, dramatic dance. Her dress clung to her body, but covered her from throat to toes—until the light behind her shone through it, revealing her legs all the way to the top. "Not most of it."

"Enough."

"It's no worse than a bathing suit."

"All right, all right. I just don't remember this being so…"

She relaxed. He obviously hadn't even noticed her foot's reprehensible behavior. She released her grip on her knees and let her legs straighten—though she was careful not to let her feet touch him.

"I should hope not. You were a kid when we watched these."

"That doesn't mean I didn't notice things like the female form at a pretty young age." He gave a low whistle. "Things like those legs."

He cast a long look at her legs, stretched out on the couch between them. A sparkle of heat lit in her chest, until she sternly dampened it with logic. There was no backlighting here, and the knit of her sweats was far from see-through. If he thought about her legs at all, it was how they failed to measure up to the dancer floating across the screen.

"Are you telling me that you lusted after Ginger Rogers when we were still practically in the *sandbox?*"

"I don't recall a sandbox, but putting that aside I'd have to be pretty stupid to lust after someone who's probably old enough now to be my grandmother. Especially since I'd be lusting after what was only an image on the screen in the first place. Long gone, and only an illusion to start with. You really think I'm that stupid?''

An edge to his words let her know he wasn't talking about Ginger Rogers anymore. She suspected the *long gone* was *them,* and the illusion was the belief they had once held that they were meant for each other.

She pushed a twinge aside. ''So if it wasn't lust, why did you watch all those old musicals?''

''With my mother? What choice did I have?''

''Your mother never made you watch those movies—you wanted to.''

''Maybe I didn't want to be left out.''

She considered that, remembering the coziness of those occasions. She certainly hadn't wanted to be left out. But she'd been a lonely child being raised by loving but elderly grandparents. ''You mean because everybody else was watching?''

''Mostly.''

''Mostly? Come on, why else?''

''Well, something Dad said once stuck in my head.'' The left side of his mouth curved up. ''I asked why he watched those movies, when I knew he liked car chases and Westerns, and he said that he figured as long as Mom got a chance to dance with Fred Astaire now and then in the movies, she wouldn't miss being Ginger Rogers so much that she'd go looking for a real partner.''

''Your father's very wise.''

''I suppose so, but let me tell you it was a confusing thing to tell a six-year-old. I kept watching those movies waiting for Ginger Rogers to be replaced by my mother. Yeah—go ahead and laugh,'' he invited in mock indignation, ''but if it hadn't been for the other reason Dad told me for watching those movies, I could have had real emotional scars.''

''What was the other reason, then?''

"Because if we watched Mom's movies without squawking, she couldn't complain when we watched *The Three Stooges*."

"Now that sounds like the Dave Currick I remember!"

Dave rolled over and answered the phone with a growl.

He'd been up all night the night before with a colicky horse. In the morning he'd had a court appearance that went longer than he'd expected, followed by lunch with a client. Then back to the courthouse to file papers for the Marshalls, before he'd holed up in his office trying to find a solution for the lunch client's title problems. By the time he'd gotten home well after midnight, all he'd wanted to do was crash.

Updates he'd received all day on the colt had been good, but he wanted to see for himself. Intending to go check on the horse before he gave in to his body's complaints, he'd shucked off his slacks, white shirt and sports jacket, dragged on a T-shirt and jeans. Then he'd sat on the edge of the bed to pull on the thick socks he wore with his work boots.

Next thing he knew, the phone was ringing.

"Oh, Dave, did I wake you? I was sure I'd figured the time difference right…"

"Mother? Where are you?" He'd gotten in the habit of making that his first question since she and his father had started frequent trips after his father retired. Sometimes the answer was as domestic as Des Moines, sometimes as exotic as—

"Bangkok, dear. But we'll probably leave tomorrow for Hong Kong. That's why I'm calling. I meant to call you in the afternoon, so I wouldn't disturb you and Matty, in case…"

He grinned with a tinge of grimness as he sat up. "In case what, Mother?"

He pushed down the spread that covered him. Had he pulled it up before he fell asleep?

"I have no intention of beating around the bush about this,

Dave. I want grandchildren. They're a parent's reward for surviving their own children. And since Lisa shows no intention of obliging, I'm putting all my eggs in one basket—you.''

"Follow the Fleet."

His jacket, slacks and shirt were no longer on the chair where he'd tossed them. His boots were out of sight.

"What?"

"Follow the Fleet," he repeated, looking around the room more closely. The drapes had been closed over the window that would have let a stream of earliest-morning light splash right across where he'd been sleeping. He usually left them open for that very reason. "That's the movie that song's from—the one about putting all your eggs in one basket."

His mother's laugh came over the line. "You're right! Imagine you remembering that from all those years ago."

"It wasn't all those years ago. About a week ago. Matty's been digging out your Fred Astaire-Ginger Rogers videos, and we've been watching them."

About a week since he'd discovered how erotic a foot could be. Now he couldn't even look at Matty's cowboy boots without lusting for her.

"Isn't that sweet. And doing some dancing, too, I hope," his mother said archly. "Maybe cheek to cheek."

Better yet, mouth to mouth, the way they'd been last night—in his dreams.

"Mother, don't push."

"That's what mothers are for, Dave. Now, if I were a grandmother..."

"Isn't it time for me to say hello to Dad?"

"He went out for a walk."

Through the open door to the bathroom, Dave could see that the edges of the mirror bore a frosting of steam. Like someone had taken a shower in there some time before. While he'd slept. He felt his mood lighten. So, Matty had broken her own rule about his having to be out of the bedroom before she'd use the bathroom. Once broken, a rule became easier and easier to bend.

Considering all the efforts to let him sleep, it figured she wasn't in the house or she'd have answered the phone.

"Ah, so you figured it was a good time to meddle in your son's life."

"Of course, dear."

He chuckled. He and his mother had always been able to talk and tease...except over his relationship with Matty six years ago.

"Mom, after you married Dad did you ever regret what you gave up?"

"Regret? No. I would never exchange the life I've had with your father and with you kids on the Slash-C. Not for anything in this world. From the moment I saw him in that hotel lobby in Denver..."

Dave must have heard that story a thousand times. How Donna Roberts had arrived in Denver as part of the chorus and the star's understudy in a road company of "Sweet Charity"—her first big break. How Edward Currick, in the city for a stockman's regional meeting, had taken one look at her amid the gaggle of attractive young women trying to sort out luggage and room keys, and had fallen immediately.

Ed had stayed on after his meeting, attending all the show's performances. They'd spent every available minute together in the two weeks of the company's stop in Denver. But they'd told each other and themselves that it was just one of those things. A variation on the classically intense, vacation romance.

So when the show's run in Denver ended, Ed went back to Wyoming and Donna went on with the company to San Francisco.

Ten days later, he'd shown up at the stage door, having driven two days. He stood in the rain, not saying a word, and she'd gone straight into his arms.

The next day they were headed back to Wyoming, and Donna's mother in Indianapolis was deep into wedding plans.

"Would I have liked to have danced and sung on Broadway, too? Absolutely. But I knew the choice I was making, and I made it gladly."

He didn't realize how long he'd been silent until he heard his mother's sigh.

"Have you asked Matty why she came back?"

He saw two roads ahead. If he told the truth and said no because he was afraid the answer was she'd just come back to get the ranch in shape to sell it, then his mother's natural questions would lead to more truth—truth about this marriage being a sham.

"It's pretty obvious, isn't it? She inherited the Flying W, and wanted to get it back on its feet."

"Yes, but why did she want to get it back on its feet?"

And the road circled right back to where it was before.

"Maybe she was tired of all that convenient city living. Had a real yen for eighteen-hour days in the saddle and no money."

He'd expected a rebuke for his sarcasm. Instead he got a soft, "Oh, dear."

"Mom, you better hang up. You're going to have to cash in your return tickets to pay for this, and you'd have to live out your days in Thailand. Probably have to take a job as a geisha."

"That's Japan," she corrected. But he hadn't distracted her enough. "I've got something more to say to you first. You and Matty have a lot of things going for you—friendship, shared experiences, chemistry. But you came back together so fast that you're bound to have a period of adjustment while you learn to see each other realistically. Dave, are you listening to me?"

"Uh-huh. A period of adjustment. I'm surprised at you using a cliché like that."

"David Edward—" when she added the middle name he

knew his mother meant business "—you can tease, but this
is serious. The period of adjustment is especially important
for two people like you and Matty. You're opposites in so
many ways, and that's good because it balances out a couple
in the long run. But in the short run it can make for a lot of
friction—until you get that balance right. You know what I
mean."

A remembered phrase floated to the surface of his mind.
"Balanced polarities."

"Exactly. But where did *you* come across that term?"

He chuckled. "A woman in a flower shop in Jefferson said
it about Indian Paintbrush when I said it reminds me of
Matty. I meant the bold color and how tough it is and how
it brightens things up. Mom? You there?"

"Yes, I'm here, dear. I was thinking about Indian Paintbrush and Matty."

"What about them?" he asked warily.

"Did you know Indian Paintbrush is Wyoming's state
flower?"

"I suppose I learned it sometime, but I can't say I've
thought about it much. Does this have a point, Mom?"

"Oh, yes, it has a point."

When a silence followed that statement, he laughed out
loud. "But you're not going to tell me, are you?"

"No, dear. I think it would be much better if you figure it
out yourself."

He wondered how different things might have been if his
parents had felt that way six years ago.

It was the end of spring break and, while his mother
cooked Saturday breakfast, he was talking about his plans to
work in Denver that summer in a law office. Then he made
a casual comment about what he'd thought had always been
understood—that somewhere down the line after he had a
practice going, he and Matty would be getting married.
Maybe it was on his mind because they were about to part

again—heading off to the separate schools that had been his parents' and Grams Brennan's idea.

He'd been totally unprepared for his parents' reaction.

His father had surveyed him with a frown, then turned and said, "Donna?"

She put down the spatula she'd been using to keep the scrambled eggs from sticking, exchanged a look with her husband, then faced her son. "We're not sure that's a good idea, Dave."

"Not a good idea?" he'd echoed in shock. "Why? What have you got against Matty?"

His mother put her hands on her hips. "Not a thing, and you know it. I love that girl like she was my own."

"Then why the hell wouldn't it be a good idea?"

"You're too young."

"I know Matty's young, but we're not talking about getting married tomorrow. I want to get started in a practice. In fact, I haven't brought it up to Matty at all. But down the road when I think it's time—"

"Dave," his mother had interrupted, "I love you more than you'll ever know until you hold a babe of your own in your arms. And no mother could be prouder—you've got character and brains and compassion. But you could use a couple of slaps from the wide world to bring you a dose of reality. Both of you, I suppose, but you more than Matty. She's had her share of blows, with losing her parents young like that. But you... You're so *sure* all the time."

He'd been torn between irritation and amusement at this show of illogic from his parents. "You're the ones who always taught me to be confident. That carrying my tail between my legs was a sure way to get picked on."

"This isn't about getting picked on and it isn't about confidence. It's...it's..." Ed Currick had shrugged and looked once more to his wife.

"You get something set in your mind, Dave, and you won't see it any other way," she picked up immediately. "If you weren't so easygoing in most ways, you'd be a real jerk.''

He gaped at her. His *mother,* for heaven's sakes!

"Donna, don't you think maybe that's a bit hard on the boy?" His father's comment would have been more welcomed if it hadn't carried that phrase *the boy.* He was twenty-three, a college graduate and doing well in law school—*not* a kid.

"Not if it keeps him from tying up Matty in a marriage when they're not ready for what it really means being a husband and wife."

"That's up to me and Matty. That's our decision."

"Is it? Is it up to you *and* Matty? Or do you really think that it's just up to you? You decide what's best—for you, for Matty—then Matty will go along with it."

"You make it sound like Matty's a puppy following at my heels, doing everything I say. If Matty didn't want to get married, she'd be hollering it from the rooftops. If Matty didn't love me…"

He hadn't been able to finish that thought.

"She does love you, Dave. Has all her life, one way or another—from the time she truly did follow you around like a little lost puppy those first years after her parents died. And that's just it. What chance has Matty had to know if she wants to marry you or not?''

What chance has Matty had…

He hadn't liked the taste of that question rumbling in his gut. Hadn't liked it at all, when he'd plunged out of the kitchen and caught a mount in hopes of a head-clearing ride. But his head hadn't been any clearer when he headed for the Flying W.

Matty hadn't been there. He'd felt oddly relieved, but decided it was only because he needed to completely digest his parents' strange reaction before he told Matty about it.

Instead he'd ended up pouring out the whole conversation to Grams Brennan.

She'd listened silently to his complaint about his parents, especially his mother, then she'd looked at him square.

"Some might be taken in by the way her talking jumps around, but nobody with a lick of sense has ever said Donna Currick was a fool when it came to knowing people."

He'd been too stunned, felt too betrayed to say any more.

"I've lived a long time, boy, and there's three things I've seen in this world that seem to make a body happy or miserable. It's not money or health or any of those other things most people talk about. It's knowing where you fit in this world, being able to go after your dreams, and love. You and Matty say you're in love. Well, I'm not here to doubt you on that. But what about the other two?

"You've got your dreams, Dave. Some people are near born with 'em—and that's you. Born with your dreams and born with knowing where you fit in this world. Some would say you're pure lucky. I'm not so sure about that. Sometimes what you work for's better for you than what you're given. But what is, is.

"Now, Matty's another matter. She's latched onto this place like a lifeline since that accident took her parents. She's held on so tight I'm not sure she could see anything beyond it. And as for dreams... Well, why would she ever need to find her own when she has yours?"

"But Matty's always wanted to ranch, just like me."

"Just like you," she'd repeated, and the words had felt like a chain going around his neck. "Could be that's the road her life's meant to take. But if it's not, your dreams better be mighty strong, Dave, because they're going to have to carry two folks—along with any others you bring into this world—for a lifetime."

He'd spent a lot of the afternoon sitting on a ridge, staring at nothing and thinking about too much. They'd gone to a movie that night, but he hadn't heard a word of it. Matty had asked what was wrong. He said he thought he might be coming down with the flu.

By the next day, he'd made his decision, and he and Matty had gone on their last ride.

His father had called him at school the next week to tell him Matty was transferring immediately to Tulane in New Orleans. He supposed she could have gone farther geographically, but she sure couldn't have picked a place more different from Wyoming.

"It's for the best," his father had said. "You'll see, it'll work out for the best."

And he couldn't argue. How could he argue with any of those sane, adult voices who had said Matty was just going along with him, letting him be responsible for her future, making his dreams carry the both of them when she'd taken off like a coiled spring waiting to escape?

He'd been angry about that for most of the first year. The anger had faded. Even the hurt had faded some. And what was left after they were gone was the fact that he still loved Matty.

Chapter Nine

It was the Thursday night before the all-day session scheduled with his legal cohorts on Saturday.

Matty had gotten in enough supplies for a couple of livestock conventions. Dave not only had the evidence of his own eyes, but Tim Balder from the Knighton Food Stop had stopped him in the street to announce with excitement that he'd gotten in the special ham Matty had ordered.

She'd scheduled Pamela Dobson for an extra session tomorrow, after having her spend time earlier in the week doing things like wiping baseboards, cleaning switch plates and polishing light fixtures.

"You never asked for such things. 'Course, you're just a man," Pamela had grumbled, managing to complain both that Matty had asked her to do that work and that he hadn't.

From Ruth Moski he'd learned that Matty had made another round of phone calls to the various office managers of those who would be coming—gathering a fan club along the way, apparently.

Matty had told him nothing.

What neither she nor anyone else needed to tell him was that she was doing all of this in addition to working rancher's hours—sunup to sundown—and rancher's work.

She'd fallen asleep at the dinner table last night, her head drooping lower and lower until her chin rested on her chest. He'd considered picking her up and carrying her to bed, then locking her in for a couple days of enforced rest. At least it would be rest if he made sure he was on the other side of the locked door.

Matty had jerked awake before he could act on that thought.

He'd vowed she would have a restful evening tonight, though locked bedroom doors would not figure into it. He'd gotten home at a decent time and had things all set up before he heard her coming in the back.

She looked like a walking soil sample. From the fine dust that added a reddish tinge to her hair, face and shoulders down to the muck of a well-fertilized bog up to nearly her knees, and with a long swipe of dried clay along her right side.

"What the hell—" He started toward her.

She held out a peremptory stop-sign hand.

"If you laugh, Currick, I'll be a widow before midnight," she started in a dangerous tone. And that reassured him no end. She wasn't hurt. She was spitting mad. "Juno picked up a stone and I tried that gray colt Henry supposedly trained. The wretched animal was a perfect gentleman until we got too far out to replace him. Then he did his best to run me into the ground."

"Why didn't Ruskoff—"

"Don't even say it. I heard enough of that from him. As if I couldn't handle a rotten-tempered, untrained, sneaky piece of male horseflesh."

Was it his imagination or had she emphasized the adjective "male"?

"Tell you what," he offered, "have some appetizers to get your energy up, take a shower while I cook dinner, and then we'll watch a video. How does that sound?"

She looked around the kitchen that clearly hadn't been disturbed since this morning's cleanup. "Appetizers?"

He opened the refrigerator and pulled out the jar he'd stored there. "Voilà! Chilled as you prefer, madam."

"Cashews? Right before dinner?"

"If you'd rather have carrot sticks—?"

He'd barely started the motion of putting the jar back when she grabbed it.

"You think you're going to get away with waving cashews in front of me and then try to fob me off with carrots?"

He shrugged. "Up to you, Matty. Now go get cleaned up, and let a master work his magic."

Twenty minutes later she came into the kitchen with her wet hair slicked straight down her neck and wearing one of the casual outfits that often seemed to double as pajamas for her—long pants and a short-sleeve T-shirt, this time topped by a big cardigan sweater. She seemed to think it was the epitome of asexual propriety. When she was standing still she was almost half right. But when she moved...ah, that changed everything.

Half a dozen times he'd been tempted to tell her how the material flowed against her body whenever she moved, caressing the line of her thighs, the curve of her breasts, the indentation of her waist.

That temptation never lasted long. What, was he nuts? This sweater was bad enough. If he said a word, she'd cover up faster than a blizzard covered the grass.

Although, at this point she could wear her winter coat at all times and it wouldn't make any difference for him. The other night watching the movie on the couch, with the sensation of her foot absently stroking his hip still vibrating through his bloodstream, he'd had all he could do not to stroke his palm over the curves of her legs, and a lot of other curves. And she clearly hadn't had a clue.

Now, as she passed near where he was propped against the counter, waiting for the timer to ding, she drew in a deep breath.

"It smells heavenly," she said on the exhale.

His own breathing had developed a hitch after taking in the scent of her, clean and wet and with that Matty-smell that tormented him each time he followed her into the bathroom. "Heavenly" was the word all right.

"I hope you didn't ruin your appetite for dinner."

She chuckled. "I think I could eat half a side of beef right now and not ruin my appetite."

The oven dinged, and the next few minutes were a flurry of carrying dishes and glasses out to the family room, setting up the VCR and digging in.

Matty bit into the pointed end of a pizza slice with relish. "Mmm. Nobody heats up a frozen pizza like you, Currick."

"It's a gift," he agreed.

They ate in companionable silence, sitting almost hip to hip so they could reach the pizza, while Fred and Ginger danced. That lasted until a familiar song started.

"I'd forgotten this is the movie with 'A Fine Romance' in it," Matty said.

"How 'bout that." So had he, until he'd dug through his mother's collection looking for the song he'd teasingly told her at the reception was "theirs."

As the stars sang the ironic lyrics to each other in a fake snowstorm, the atmosphere in the family room seemed to have become tropical. He sure hoped he wasn't alone in having the phrases about no kisses and no embraces reminding him that there *had* been kisses and embraces between them since he'd sung the words to her.

The rest of the movie was nowhere near enough to divert his mind from that train of thought. Not when each breath brought her scent to him, not when each twitch pressed his hip against hers. And not when the movie shifted to a song called "Just the Way You Look Tonight."

She looked like the woman he'd never stopped wanting to make love to. Tonight, and every night.

He shifted slightly to see more of her, and felt a clutch of fierce response when he saw the points of her breasts straining against the fabric of her top.

As if he knew the line were coming, he tuned into the movie in time to hear Fred sing a reminder to Ginger of how he'd held her when they danced, but this time they weren't going to dance, and Dave's mind was swamped by images of how he could hold Matty as if they were going to dance, and what they might be doing that wasn't dancing. Neither of them moved except to breathe, deep and fast.

Thirty seconds later, the movie ended and the screen went blank.

She jolted to her feet.

"It's late, I better get to—uh, get some sleep. Going to be another full day tomorrow. I'll just..."

She bent, reaching for the dishes on the chest. The motion dropped the V-neck of her top at the same time the fabric snugged across the points of her breasts. Another few inches and—

"Don't."

She froze at his guttural order, her eyes wide on his face. He saw recognition hit her because it was followed by a wave of color appearing at the point of the V, then sweeping up her throat and into her cheeks.

"Don't bother," he managed to say in a more natural voice. "Dinner was my treat, so I'll clean up, too."

She straightened and turned away in a jerky motion. "Thanks. In that case, I'll say good night."

He watched her go. She paused at the doorway to the west room, reaching into the dimness to flip on the light. It backlit her, shining faintly through the fabric of her outfit, outlining her body.

For her sake, he thought, he hoped she'd have a more restful night than it was going to be for him.

Dave came out of the master bathroom at noon Saturday to find Matty pulling a pillow out of the narrow linen closet tucked into the corner of the bedroom.

"What's that for?"

"Randy's back. I want to make sure he's comfortable."

From the minute his fellow lawyers had started arriving, she'd been pouring coffee, tea and juices and handing out doughnuts, pastries and fruit like the Salvation Army after a flood. Anytime one of the group out there looked as if he might consider vaguely wanting something, she jumped up and got it. When he'd tried to tell her to let them get it themselves like usual, she'd shushed him and kept on.

What she'd kept on with was the two-pronged presentation she and Taylor had made this morning about the grant regulations. And if he hadn't been irked at her fussing over the legal wolves scattered around the family room, he would have had only admiration for how they handled the group, stirring their interest, challenging them and winning them over one by one. Before this lunch break—while they scarfed down gourmet ham and roast beef sandwiches, potato salad and vegetable salad—they'd agreed by a vote of 10 to 1 to use the grant regulations as this year's project. The dissenter was Bob Brathenwaite.

"The only way Randy could be more comfortable is if you stood over him and fanned him like a slave girl for the pasha," Dave growled.

But she'd already disappeared into the bathroom.

"What? I couldn't hear you, Dave."

"I said—" He started loudly, then she came back into the room with a box of tissues—no doubt for Phil's cold. "Never mind."

"I'm forgetting something..." She snapped her fingers

and started back into the bathroom. "Oh, Dave, don't you…"

Her words faded off in the creaking sound of the medicine cabinet being opened. "I can't hear you, Matty."

"I said—" she poked her head out of the doorway "—don't you think it's going well?"

"Going well? If you mean for…" But it was no use, she'd disappeared back into the bathroom. He strode in after her, surveyed to find the most central spot, and leaned back against the counter beside the sink. She hardly seemed to notice as she moved around him to get to the medicine cabinet, where she hunted for something elusive.

"Now where on earth can the aspirin be?"

"Who's it for?"

"Kyle has a headache."

"You mean a hangover. He's been on a bender ever since his wife left him. She had good cause from what I hear," he added darkly.

She withdrew enough from the cabinet to meet his eyes around the edge of its door. "Really? Why didn't he say so. A hangover calls for something else entirely."

And then she disappeared into the cabinet again, apparently without absorbing a single word of his veiled warning about Kyle and his womanizing. Hadn't she noticed how Kyle had been flirting with her?

While she put the bottle on the counter, she nudged at the cabinet door with her elbow. It stopped short of closing completely, but she was washing her hands, paying no attention. He turned, and watched the motion of soapy water over her long, straight fingers and the way the gold ring glinted.

The ring looked good on her hand. As if it belonged. He hoped Kyle and any of the other wolves in the pack out there in his family room had noticed how natural the ring looked, too. But just in case, he might do some reminding after this little break.

"I really do think it's going well. They're digging into the issue, aren't they? I don't know all the legalese, but I can tell you guys think you have a good chance of getting this revised regulation passed.''

''Don't get your hopes up too high, Matty. It would have to go through committees and then be voted on, and you can never tell with stuff like that.''

''I know.'' She sounded a little impatient with his reminder as she turned her back to dry her hands on a towel hanging from the rack on the back of the half-closed door. ''I don't have my hopes up. But I still say thank you. To all of you, but especially you.''

''Why me, especially?''

As she turned, her gaze snagged on something beyond him and she gave a faint cluck of her tongue. Following her look, he realized her focus was on the partially opened medicine cabinet door.

''Because you could have given it all away—I mean why I set this up. Taylor might have some suspicions, but you're the only one who knows for sure. You could have ruined it all with a few words. Thank you, Dave. I mean it, I'm really grateful.''

She stretched up on her toes to reach around him and push the medicine cabinet door closed.

''No problem, Matty.''

He turned his head back from following her motion and there they were, nose to nose, eye to eye and, most importantly, mouth to mouth.

Still on her toes, as if she wasn't thinking about it at all, she brushed her lips against his.

He was fully, achingly aware that it was the first time she'd kissed him. Not accepted his kiss, not kissed him back. This time she'd initiated the kiss.

The first time in six long, long years.

And this was hardly even a kiss, just a brief brushing of lips against lips. But it was between him and Matty, so it could never be that simple.

The natural retreat of her action halted abruptly, with Matty's face six inches from his. He held absolutely still, not even sure he was breathing, but fully aware his heart was beating pure heat through him.

Her gaze was on his mouth, as if she might have felt that same sizzle at the brief touch and was trying to figure out how it had happened. Her lashes raised then, and he stared into the heartbreakingly familiar depths of her blue eyes.

His muscles twitched with the urge to haul her to him. His jaw ached with biting back his desires.

And then, she was moving.

Toward him. Closer. But slowly. So damned, excruciatingly slowly.

She reached up to slide her hands around the back of his neck, drawing his face toward hers. And when her mouth touched his this time, there was nothing fleeting or brushing about it.

Matty kissed him the way she always used to kiss him—as if her soul and his depended on this kiss.

When her lips parted and her tongue touched his lower lip, his restraint gave way with a growl. He opened his mouth to her at the same time he gathered her to his chest with one arm across her back and the other under her bottom. He opened his legs to bring her in as close as he could.

It was like she'd been holding him off with a stiff-arm ever since she'd come back to Wyoming. Once or twice her locked elbow had weakened a bit and he'd gotten closer, but each time she'd stiffened that arm right away. He wasn't going to give her the chance this time.

He wanted nothing between them. No questions. No doubts. No six years. No space.

And a certain part of him was doing its best to close the little space between them by expanding in hard, hot surges.

He shifted so he could slide his palm from the turn of her jaw, down her throat. It took a firm tug to open the top half of her shirt.

Bless the snaps on Western-style shirts.

Instead of fumbling with buttons, his palm absorbed the cool, soft sweep from her collarbone down to the rise of her breast.

And he blessed Western-style shirts again when he felt her fingers tug open his shirt, and perform some miracle that turned her hands, so competent with rope and reins, into instruments capable of the softest, smoothest, most enticing touch known to man.

Another time simply being touched by Matty would have been more than enough. Not now. Something primitive drove him to possess her.

There was still space between them and that had to go.

One stroke of his hand caught the fabric of her shirt and the strap of her bra, pulling them off her shoulder, baring her to him. He touched her rosy nipple with two gentle fingertips, circling it lightly, awed at the way it pebbled.

A breathy sound came from Matty that hit him like lightning. He couldn't wait another second. He bent his head, and she arched her back, pushing against the apex of his legs at the same time she offered him what he most wanted.

He flicked his tongue over the nub, felt the answering tightening as a surge in his own bloodstream, then took her into his mouth, drawing on her.

Matty moaned, and her hips rocked against his while her hands roamed over his shoulders and back to the rhythm he'd set.

His torment was getting what he most wanted made him crave that touch more at the same time it awoke a craving for another, deeper touch.

He'd found the opening where the back of her shirt had pulled from the waistband of her jeans. He fumbled at the hooks on her bra, needing more, needing everything.

The last hook gave and he began a trail of kisses toward her other breast.

"Oh!"

The sound could have come from Matty, but he didn't think so. It didn't resonate through his nerves the way the sounds she'd been making had done.

He wanted to ignore it. He wanted to forget control, forget responsibility.

The hell of it was that he might have if it hadn't been Matty he held in his arms. But if it hadn't been Matty, he wouldn't have been driven to a pitch where he was tempted to forget those things.

Because it was Matty, he had no choice but to take care of this.

With more reluctance than he could ever remember, Dave lifted his head and looked over Matty's bare shoulder. Taylor Larsen stood in the doorway, one hand still splayed on the door, her mouth rounded from that "Oh!" and color surging up her neck. She was as frozen as a deer in headlights.

"I'm sorry! I didn't mean… I didn't know anyone was here."

Matty started to pull back, but he wrapped both arms across her back and drew her hard against his chest. He thought he heard an indignant sound from her, but he had enough to worry about with trying to slow down the way his body was reacting to her.

"Hey, Taylor," he managed to say.

"There was a line for the other bathroom, and the door was open—both doors. I never meant—I'm so sorry."

"Honest mistake. No harm done." Other than he might die of frustration in the next twenty seconds.

"I'll just, uh, go." She fled.

He loosened his hold on Matty, and she eased slightly away from him, but not completely. She left her head down and her forehead dropped against his shoulder, so he felt her slight puffs of breath as rhythmic tingles against his bare, heated skin.

"Oh Lord."

When Matty repeated that twice more, he thought he'd better try saying something.

"I'm glad it was Taylor," he offered.

Her head came up, her eyes questioning. "Are you? Why?"

"If it had been one of the guys I would have had to shoot them, and that would get messy. Not to mention, I sure as hell would get sued."

She stared at him uncomprehendingly.

"Because they're all lawyers, Matty," he explained with a teasing patience that cost him.

"I know *that,* it was that crazy talk about shooting—"

He sighed deeply. "I did my best, but with the mirrors, if you'd backed up another inch... You're not exactly decent, Matty."

She pulled back from him and looked past his shoulder, her eyes apparently catching a good look at her state of disarray in the mirror. "Oh Lord." A tide of color an even darker shade than the one that had suffused Taylor's face started rising as she fumbled ineffectively with snaps and hooks and eyes.

His fingers itched to pitch in, but he had a feeling they were more bent on undoing than doing. And at this point, restraint was definitely the wiser course. As it was, movement of any sort threatened to leave him with cause to be red-faced himself.

With her head bent over her task, Matty muttered something.

"What?"

"That was...uh..."

Hell and damnation. Blast it to hell and back.... His string of mental curses went on, running out of vocabulary long before it eased the feeling behind the words. She was going to say it was a *mistake.* Or it was *gratitude.* Or it was the *past.* Or some other damned stupid phrase—some *lie*—and it was none of those things. It was the fire that had always existed between the two of them from the first days they'd had the hormones to fuel that kind of fire.

He crossed his arms over his chest, waiting.

She glanced up at his motion, then down as she snapped the last snap.

"That was...well, I don't know what that was."

She followed that stunning statement with a nervous little chuckle that almost made him reach out and draw her into his arms. But before he could, she drew a deep breath, straightened her shoulders and met his eyes.

"I'm sorry, Dave. I apologize."

"It's okay, Matty."

"No, really, I'm the one who set the rules, and then to—"

"I said it before—it's okay."

"Right, before." Color surged up her face. Damn. He hadn't meant to remind her of their kisses after she got the grant approval. "This is the second time I've had to apologize for my behavior, and I promise there won't be a third time—"

"Shut up, Matty. I said it's okay."

He saw her open her mouth, then close it. She swallowed twice.

"Okay. Then I guess I better get back out there." She gave a vague wave.

"Guess you better."

At the door, she turned back, not quite meeting his eyes. "If you're sure it's okay—I mean, if you understand that what happened doesn't mean I'm going back on what we agreed to."

"I understand that, Matty."

He must have sounded grim, because her gaze met his and she frowned slightly. "Are you sure you're okay with this? Because you sound a little—"

"I sound like a man who needs a few minutes before he can move around real comfortable, that's all."

Her gaze instantly dropped to his groin, and damned if Matty Brennan Currick didn't blush at the sight.

"Oh, I didn't know you felt...I mean, I had to know, because I couldn't help but feel...I mean, not *my* feelings, because we're not talking about *my* feelings— Oh, hell!"

With that she turned and hurried out of the bathroom, then slammed the bedroom door behind her.

And Dave knew that after her final, hot look and those very interesting fragments of the thoughts apparently tumbling through Matty's mind that it would be a few additional minutes before he could comfortably—or decently—join their guests.

Chapter Ten

Dave paused at the doorway to the family room. Matty was distributing the items she grabbed earlier.

Her eyes came to him then skittered away.

He strode into the room.

"Thorne" was all he said by way of warning before tossing the bottle of pain reliever he'd spotted on the bathroom counter. He aimed it in the general direction of Kyle Thorne's head. Kyle had been a top college baseball prospect—a catcher—and his instincts brought his hands up in plenty of time to catch the bottle, as Dave had expected. The abrupt movement also made him wince against what was no doubt a throbbing head, also as Dave had expected.

"Hey, what's the idea?" Kyle complained in an unappealing whine.

"I understand from my wife that you need some morning-after cure, Kyle. Or more accurately, some afternoon-after cure."

A couple of the guys had gone outside to smoke and Taylor was nowhere in sight, but he sensed heightened awareness from most of the rest of the room. Except Randy Duff, who was rearranging the extra pillow Matty had brought him.

Matty's lips parted as if to protest, but after her gaze met his for another of those fraction-of-a-second exchanges, her mouth closed into a firm line. After all, what could she protest? That he'd called her his wife?

She grabbed a handful of empty glasses and headed toward the kitchen.

Randy let out a gusty sigh as he pressed his aching back against the pillow. "She's great, Currick. Makes everybody comfortable. Works the room like a pro. Boy, she'd make a terrific political wife."

"Hands off, Randy."

Even Randy recognized the tone of that order. He raised his hands in a sign of surrender, but he also chuckled. "Ease up on your trigger finger, Dave. I've already got a terrific wife, and absolutely no political ambitions. I was thinking of you."

A new tension seeped into the room, and Dave knew it came from Bob Brathenwaite. Randy had just inadvertently stirred Bob's unreasoning fears—or maybe not so inadvertently. The usually easygoing Randy truly disliked Brathenwaite.

"No, thanks," Dave said curtly, hoping to end the discussion now that he'd made his point to these men.

"No thanks, to the politics? Or—" Kyle looked in the direction Matty had taken "—the wife? Because if your act-in-haste wedding means you're repenting at leisure and the lady's going to be free…"

Dave moved directly in front of Kyle. He never let his voice lose its calm, but he didn't bother to mask his expression. "The lady is not free. She's not going to be free as long as I'm alive. And if I die and you put one hand on her, I'll come back from the dead and rip your heart out."

Into the silence that followed, Phil blew his nose like a bugle.

Randy, settled comfortably against his cushion, declared, "Guess that about covers it."

Matty got around the corner out of sight, then turned back to the family room to listen. She pressed the glasses against her midriff to keep them from clinking against each other.

Her hands were still shaking from what had happened between her and Dave in the bathroom—what she had initiated. Despite all her promises to herself and him that she wouldn't.

She wanted him.

But if she'd given up her pride by asking him for help to save the Flying W, she wouldn't give up her honor by breaking her pledge that this would be a platonic marriage. It was wrong. Dishonest.

He didn't seem to feel that way, pointed out a voice in her head.

You weren't exactly an impartial observer, another voice shot back.

"Matty?"

She jumped at the soft voice that came from behind her instead of inside her, and spun around to face Taylor, who must have been in the kitchen all along.

"Sorry. I didn't mean to startle you. I thought you saw me. I just wanted to say how sorry I am about walking in on you two that way. I feel like such an idiot."

"No, Taylor, I'm the one who apologizes. We shouldn't have been—"

"Actually it was sweet seeing a married couple like that, especially when at first…"

Taylor didn't need to finish the thought. Matty knew the lawyer was thinking that she and Dave hadn't seemed very loverlike at first.

At first? What was she thinking? They shouldn't seem loverlike at all. Except of course for appearances' sake. Although what Taylor had just walked in on most definitely had looked loverlike. It felt loverlike, too.

"Dave and I have—had—a lot of issues from the past that needed working out even after we, uh, decided to get married."

"Well, I'm glad to see you've worked them out so well," Taylor said with a warm smile. "I'll admit I was a little concerned with the marriage coming right on the heels of the grant commission's refusal to give you an exception. But if that was the only reason for the marriage you wouldn't be having all of us work on getting the regulations changed legally, would you? Besides, I can see what there is between you." She gave a rueful laugh. "Even not counting what I walked in on earlier."

Matty's stomach felt unsettled. Probably because Taylor had been nothing but a good friend and hardworking attorney for her, and she didn't deserve to be lied to.

"Anyway," Taylor added, "it gives hope to those of us who've found that when they talk about wide-open spaces out here in Wyoming, they're talking about the lack of eligible men. I haven't had a real date since I moved here two years ago, not to mention other, um, activities."

"I know *exactly* what you mean." As soon as she'd finished her wholehearted agreement, Matty caught sight of Taylor's face and hurriedly added, "I mean when I came back for visits. Before getting together with Dave."

But the surprise didn't fade from Taylor's expression. "I thought you and Cal Ruskoff— Oh! I'm sorry. That's so rude of me. It's none of my business."

"Well, if it's rude, so's the rest of humanity, because I suspect that's what most people thought. Truth be told, I would probably think the same thing if I were outside looking in. But no, Cal and I weren't ever, uh, an item."

"That's…" Apparently at a loss for words Taylor gave a slight shrug.

''That's a damned shame, is the phrase you're searching for, I think.''

Taylor chuckled. ''A damned waste was actually what I was thinking.''

''That, too. Cal's a fine-looking man.''

Taylor held up her soda glass in a toast. ''To fine-looking men.''

''Fine-looking men,'' she agreed. She put down the dirty glasses and picked up a bottle of soda. ''Especially the ones who are as good at heart as they look.''

''And to the women who have them,'' Taylor finished, clinking her glass to the bottle.

Taylor Larsen had a lot more humor in her than Matty had given her credit for. She might be the woman to bring Cal out of that shell he wrapped around himself. When things settled down between her and Dave maybe she'd try her hand at a bit of matchmaking— No, what was she thinking? When things settled down between her and Dave, they'd go their separate ways, and if Taylor was half as smart as Matty thought she was, the woman would zero in on Dave. Cal was a terrific man, and there was no denying he had a nice body, but he also had that shell and besides, he wasn't... Well, he wasn't Dave.

Matty solemnly clinked the neck of her bottle against Taylor's glass. ''Amen.''

Dave came around the corner to the kitchen at that moment.

''Speak of the devil,'' Matty murmured.

He'd closed his shirt and tucked it neatly into his jeans long before he'd come out to the family room, yet it seemed she could still feel the sensation of his chest—smooth skin, muscles, prickly hair—against her palms. And that was the least of it, because it also seemed she could feel his hands and mouth on her flesh.

''What's this I hear about *amen* and the *devil?* You two having a revival meeting in here?'' he demanded.

"Guess you could say that," Taylor said with a grin.

It was a good thing Taylor had answered, because Matty's own words had stunned her into stupidity.

A fine-looking man who was as good at heart as he looked... Speak of the devil.

Dave fit the bill from head to toe. She'd known that from the time she was a kid. And now she was married to him. But he wasn't hers. Not really. Not for good.

The taillights of the last car disappeared and still they stood side by side at the door where they'd waved off all the lawyers.

Matty broke the silence with spurious cheer. "Well, I'd better get this place cleaned up or Pamela will have a fit."

"We could leave it tonight and do it tomorrow."

The wicked voice in the back of her head immediately began thinking maybe he had other ideas for tonight. This was getting out of hand.

"No, I'm going to meet Cal early. I took today off, but we want to finish setting up that irrigation system. So, I'm going to clean up, then get to bed as soon as I can so I can get some sleep." She might have sounded harsh, but that wicked voice needed to be kept in line.

"I'll help clean up, then."

"No, no, I asked you to leave it all in my hands and you agreed, and that includes cleanup."

"Tell you what, I'll organize the papers and put away the books in the family room, and then we'll see."

She couldn't argue with that, since he'd know which papers to throw away and which to keep to support the draft of new regulations they'd written.

A few minutes later he came into the kitchen with more dirty dishes. "You handled this very well."

She turned from closing the refrigerator after putting away the last of the leftovers. "You should take some of the credit."

"All I did was buy beer."

"I meant for my learning how to handle things like this. If I hadn't left here six years ago, I doubt I would have learned those skills. And if you hadn't, uh, done the honorable, responsible thing, I wouldn't have left. As much as I hate to admit it, it ends up that you were right six years ago."

"Glad I could contribute to your happy life," he said dryly. "Even by accident."

"Yeah, there you go, being perfect again—even by accident." She picked up a cloth to dry the few dishes she'd washed by hand. "So, were you surprised I was good at pulling off a gathering like this?"

"Impressed. And I wasn't the only one. Randy Duff said you'd make a good political wife."

"Are you sure that's a compliment?"

He chuckled before tying up the filled trash bag and putting in a new one while she finished filling the dishwasher.

She broke the oddly companionable silence. "Have you ever thought of going into politics, Dave?"

"Me? No. Why?"

"You'd be very good."

"Are you sure that's a compliment?" he echoed with a wry smile.

She laughed as she closed up the dishwasher, but came back to the question. "You've never considered politics, or wanted to run for office?"

"Never wanted to. What's this all about?"

"I just thought…" She wiped one counter clean and turned the corner to the next one. She could let this go, but if she was right, she wanted Dave to have his guard up. "If you'd considered politics it would explain the odd tension I got from Bob Brathenwaite toward you."

"Brathenwaite? I thought he was on his best behavior today. Hardly said a word. You sure you don't mean Kyle?"

"Why would Kyle be tense around you?"

"Oh, just a little discussion we had."

His shrug was a clear indication he wasn't going to explain more fully. It was all beside the point, anyhow. "Well, I didn't get that sense from Kyle. But with Brathenwaite, I'd say watch your back."

He stared at the final wad of used paper napkins he'd been about to throw in the new trash bag, and muttered a soft curse.

"You *do* know why he feels that way. What is it, Dave?"

"I can't believe he'd still…" He threw the napkins in the bag, then leaned back against the counter, facing her. "About three years back some of the state movers and shakers in Brathenwaite's party came to me and asked if I'd run against him in the primary. They said he wasn't effective. From what I can tell it was more like they couldn't control him tight enough to suit them."

"And what did you say?"

"I said no, thanks. They kept after me for a while, but I kept on saying no until they got the meaning clear in their heads."

"But then, why would Brathenwaite…"

"Because *somebody* leaked it to the *Jefferson Observer*."

"Who?"

"No proof, but I suspect it was one of those movers and shakers."

"To start a groundswell of support for you or…" She looked up at him. "How did Brathenwaite react?"

"Bingo. He fell right into line."

"So you're the threat they hold over his head. No wonder he doesn't like you."

"Hey, it's not my fault!"

"Maybe not, but it must be hard for him, knowing you could have his job with the snap of your fingers." He grimaced, dismissing that assessment. But Matty was quite sure that if he'd wanted it, Dave Currick would now be state representative. "No doubts?"

"Nope. I know what I want. Always have." He looked at

her across the kitchen. His voice dropped, and she felt it like a vibration all the way to the deepest part of her. "And I've got most of it."

Six days later, Matty rapped on Dave's office door and headed in.

"Hi."

He was standing by the bookshelves, holding an open law book. When he heard her, he looked up quickly, and a smile creased his face. Matty felt as if a huge, warm hand wrapped around her heart and squeezed gently.

This was exactly why she'd decided to come into town this evening, the rational corner of her mind reminded her.

"Hi, yourself. This is a nice surprise."

"I, uh, I had some things to do in town. Jack gave me a ride in, and I thought I'd catch a ride back with you. If you don't mind."

"Don't mind at all. I'm finishing up right now. Just let me get this citation down and we can head home."

"Good, but I thought we could go home...later."

"Later?"

"Yeah. It's Friday night, you know." Some gremlin of nervousness had hijacked her usual voice. "I thought I could take you to dinner and a movie afterward. Your choice—where to eat and what to see."

He studied her a moment. "Dinner's easy. Chinese. That way we'll be hungry enough to eat popcorn at the movie. As to what to see...well, I suppose some of that might depend on what's prompted this unexpected invitation."

"We've spent so many nights watching old movies, and I thought it would be a nice change to get out of the house for an evening."

"Sounds good." He nodded judiciously, and Matty didn't like the way he'd said that—not as if he agreed, but as if her explanation had sounded like a plausible lie that he'd seen through. "Probably a smart idea to let people in town see us together a little more often."

Smart idea was what she'd been going for with this invitation, and being out in public had been her goal. But it hadn't been with any idea of making an appearance to shore up their image; it had been to avoid another cozy, intimate evening at home.

After the episode in the bathroom on Saturday, she'd spent all week keeping their evenings to a minimum. She'd stayed out as late as she could each night, but that still left time before bed. The effort of making sure they didn't accidentally brush, didn't sit near each other, but also didn't sit across from each other had worn her out. She'd pleaded a headache Wednesday night, and gone to bed. Then became even more intimately acquainted with the ceiling of the west room as she strained to hear each move he made. So she'd fibbed and told him she had a meeting early this morning at the Flying W, and she'd spent last night at her ranch. She hadn't slept a wink.

That's when she'd decided she'd try this—staying out in public late enough that it would be time to go to bed when they got home.

Forgetting all that planning for the moment, she let herself sound miffed at his intimation that she was so calculating. "I didn't mean it like that."

"Didn't you?" he asked in that low, rumble of a voice.

"No." She said it too loudly, too firmly. When it was clear he wasn't going to argue, she continued. "Besides, I have reason to celebrate. I got good news today."

He looked up from where he was jotting something. "Always glad to hear good news."

"The man who came out to the ranch a while back, remember I told you he was coming by? Well, he's someone a friend from the university in Chicago told me about, and I started talking to him last fall. He's doing research on alfalfa seed that's resistant to weevils, and he's going to use the

Flying W for some of his test fields next season. And he's paying us. A lot—at least by my standards." She grinned. "Enough that even if I don't get another grant, the ranch should be okay."

He seemed to go still for a moment, then he grinned back at her, closing the book and coming around the desk. "That's great news. I had no idea you knew about programs like that."

"I didn't until I worked for the university. I read about his research, then got a mutual friend to introduce us. He was interested in the Flying W, but had to see this spring's regular crop to be sure. And now I've got the contract, signed and sealed."

He reached toward her and she tensed, but all he did was take her jacket from her hands and hold it out for her to slip into.

"See, Currick," she said, slipping one arm in, "you don't know me as well as you like to think."

"You're right. I don't know what's behind this sudden togetherness." He pulled the jacket collar up under her hair, and shifted it to line up the other sleeve with her outstretched arm, slowly completing a circle around her.

"I thought we could go see a movie. Like we used—"

The back of his hand, the one straightening the twisted lapel of her jacket brushed her breast. Her lungs seemed to stammer, starting and stopping without making much progress in getting her the oxygen she suddenly lacked.

They both went still. Yet she could feel her breast tightening with pleasure. He moved his hand then, the ridges of his knuckles stroking slowly, lightly across the fabric that covered her sensitized breast.

"Like we used to?" he suggested, conjuring up times they'd spent together doing exactly this, and more.

The door swung open and Ruth Moski's brisk, efficient stride had her well across the threshold before their reflexes kicked in and they jumped apart.

"No need to look so guilty, you two. You are married. It's to be expected with folks still practically honeymooning. You'll get over it eventually," she said as she crossed the room, deposited files on Dave's desk and headed back. "Besides, it's not like it's anything I haven't seen before. We've got a satellite dish you know. And Hugh can't watch sports twenty-four hours a day."

As the door closed behind the older woman, Matty could have sworn she heard an evil chuckle. But she was more concerned with what Dave was saying.

"It's getting to be a habit, the two of us caught in a compromising position."

"The solution is for us never to be in another compromising position."

"That's one answer," he agreed. One more thing she'd forgotten about Dave Currick—how incredibly irritating he could be when he was being agreeable. "Of course, it *is* good for our masquerade."

Matty took one look around the still-lit theater and had her fear confirmed—it was a Friday night make-out special.

By the time they'd finished dinner, interrupted by more than a half-dozen people who had stopped by their table to marvel at their sudden marriage and offer congratulations, the only movie they hadn't missed was the ten-thirty show at the Bijou, the gaudy old vaudeville theater built during Jefferson's railroad boom.

Fenton Trimble had run it as a movie house since it probably showed first-runs of Fred Astaire and Ginger Rogers. Long ago he'd come up with a weekend schedule that brought in the most business. Early evening on Fridays, he had family fare for young parents to bring their kids. Then he showed a current movie, pulling in adults and older families. Last, he showed a movie that had already made the rounds of cable and network TV that would finish up in time for high school dating couples to get home by midnight or twelve-thirty curfews. It didn't much matter what the movie was, because not much of it was going to be watched.

She and Dave had spent their share of time sitting in this theater not watching movies. Maybe that's why she'd automatically bought the tickets and the snacks—individual popcorns so he could have his extra butter and a soft drink to share—without checking what the movie was. But unlike when they were kids, tonight the movie did matter to her.

Only she didn't realize that until they had started down the right-center aisle and she saw the announcement of tonight's movie on the screen.

Oh, no. This was *not* her idea of a back-on-an-even-keel, friendly-but-distant movie.

"Dave, you know, it's getting late. Maybe we better just forget this."

"No way. We've got the tickets. We've got the popcorn. And—" he flashed her a triumphant grin as his free hand at the small of her back guided her to some empty seats in the quickly filling theater "—now we have the perfect seats. Besides, I'm looking forward to seeing *Body Heat* on the big screen again."

She cut him a look as she settled into a seat. She dug her hand into the popcorn.

"Love all those plot twists," he added innocently as he took a popcorn from the tray. "Hey, you're eating my popcorn."

She realized he was right as she licked an extra drizzle of butter off her thumbnail.

"Sorry. I didn't mean—"

The words clogged in her throat as she looked up and saw Dave's eyes on her mouth.

Simultaneously the lights dimmed and a couple appeared at the end of their row, asking if the seats beyond Matty were open. Making room for them to pass, then getting resettled consumed most of the preview time.

Within a couple of minutes of the movie starting, the couple to Matty's left was fully engrossed in each other. That should have meant that she would be perfectly safe with her arm on the left armrest. Instead she kept getting poked in the arm and twice was kicked in the leg.

Her only protection was to cling to the right side of her seat—the side by Dave. Where she was fully aware of *his* body heat. The sort of heat she'd felt when his hand had brushed her breast earlier. A heat that pulsed through her, pooling deep inside. A heat that never seemed to entirely leave her recently...

Plot twists.

That's what Dave had said, the sadist. Fine. Just fine. She was going to concentrate on the plot twists and ignore everything else, if it killed her.

Chapter Eleven

Plot twists? What had he been thinking?

Had he ever been as randy as this boy seated in front of him?

Oh, hell yes.

Dave yanked his mind away from the long-forgotten nuances of making out.

The movie. Watch the movie.

The boy in front of him yawned loudly and stretched, then dropped his arm around his date's shoulders.

This kid was hopeless. He was trying so hard to touch his girlfriend's breast without anyone knowing—including her—that everybody in the theater had to know what was going on.

Relax, kid. You've got time. Dating's all about giving you chances to bump and brush and touch and, occasionally, talk. And when it happened without plotting, without manipulating, it was magic.

Like this evening in his office.

That first touch had been purely accidental. It was bound to happen now and then, especially with the two of them living in the same house, seeing each other so much. If Matty had eased away, that would have been all there was to it. But she hadn't. She'd stilled, and even more than that, he'd seen the wonder in her face at the sensation of his hand on her breast.

Plot twists. Dammit, concentrate on the plot twists, Currick.

William Hurt was getting drawn in deeper and deeper into Kathleen Turner's web...and her character's name was Maddy. Amazing. Of course his Matty had never flaunted her charms that way. She didn't have to. An accidental touch, and he was gone.

Even with the double barrier of her shirt and bra, he'd felt as if he were experiencing the silken texture of Matty's skin under his hand. He had felt the budding of her nipple, pebbling under his palm, just the way he had Saturday. If he could have touched his tongue to it... He shifted in his seat, trying to ease the restriction in his crotch.

Matty touched his arm. He jolted involuntarily, and she started to snatch her hand away. Just as fast, he clamped his free hand over hers, against his arm.

"Sorry, I jumped, Matty," he whispered, but without turning his head. If he turned and found her lips a breath away, these kids would see something that would give Kathleen Turner and William Hurt a run for their money.

"I didn't mean to startle you. I thought..."

"What?"

"We don't have to stay. It's getting late. And if you're tired..."

"No. I'm fine. I want to see the end."

Needed to see the end. When it was clear, even to the guy who was in prison—a prison of his own making for having done murder—that the woman he'd built her up to be in his head had never existed. And neither had her feelings for him.

* * *

The silence in the truck gained mass with every mile that brought them closer to the Slash-C.

She couldn't take it anymore.

"Were we ever that young?" She tried a chuckle.

"Must have been," he said neutrally and irrefutably.

"Boy, and we thought we knew everything, didn't we?"

"Uh-huh."

"But we know different now. When I think how naïve I was back then, all starry-eyed and optimistic. Guess life teaches us all lessons, doesn't it?"

"I suppose so."

"I know it's taught me a lot. Why I can hardly even remember what it was like to be the person I was six years ago—a child really. It seems like it happened to another person."

"And with your ranch starting to shape up, you'll be able to get back to that new life where you were a new person soon, right?"

She glared at him, but the reflection from the instrument panel did little to illuminate his profile.

"I'm tired of you jabbing at me about leaving, Dave. I couldn't believe it when you suggested I sell out and walk away from the Flying W."

"I didn't—"

"You did! The morning after we got married, sitting on the bench by the shed, you said it."

"I wasn't suggesting it. I wanted to get it out in the open. So we knew where we stood. That you'd get the Flying W back on its feet so when you sold out you'd collect some money and could go back to your PR job in Chicago."

"You can't believe that. That I'd sell the Flying W?" She blinked against a sharp sting in her eyes. "How could you think I'd walk away from the Flying W? You've always known I wanted to ranch, that the Flying W is *my* ranch. I'll spell it out Dave—I'm not selling the Flying W. Not any of it—if I'd been willing to sell some of it I could have adjusted the percentage of my acres to qualify for the grant, or I could have used the money to buy irrigation equipment myself and we wouldn't have been in this—'' her hand fluttered in a futile attempt to grab the right word for what had happened between them ''—this *thing*.''

Dave's right hand clamped over her wrist, holding it still, while he steered the slowing truck on the empty highway with his left hand.

''Are you telling me that ranching's your dream? That it's what you want to do?''

''Of course it is. Why do you think I've spent years reading up on ranching improvements. How do you think I knew about new irrigation methods and test crops and getting your own power from turbines?''

He squeezed his eyes closed. ''I've been a fool. I should have listened to my mother.''

''What are you talking about?''

He was grinning as he released her hand and hit the accelerator.

''About periods of adjustment and unanswered questions and balanced polarities.''

''Okay, now you've really lost me.''

''What? You've never heard about how Indian Paintbrush represents balanced polarities?''

He went on, talking about essences, and yin and yang and other things she never would have expected to hear from Dave Currick, until he stopped the truck by the house, and turned off the engine. After a moment of staring straight ahead, he turned his head toward her. With the lights off and the crescent moon obscured by clouds the light was uncertain at best. So how could she be sure—sure right down to her bones—of what she saw in his eyes? Because she wanted to see it?

''It's, uh, getting late.''

She reached behind her for the door handle, not able to

break his look, but seeking an escape. The door swung open and she went with it, just missing tumbling ignobly in the dust. Without checking his reaction or waiting for him she hurried inside through the kitchen door, using her key.

But when she reached the corner where the kitchen, the entry hall and the family room met, she stopped. The automatic lights had come on, leaving the area lit as it had been the first night they'd come back together to the Slash-C, their wedding night.

Dave came up behind her, but didn't touch her.

"It was a nice evening, Matty. Thank you."

He sounded oddly formal, as if he was bringing her home from a date. With the twist that he was thanking her, and of course that he would not get in his truck and drive away. He'd walk down the hall and go to sleep in his big bed, not twenty-five feet from where she would go to bed.

She turned toward him, but also backed up a step, finding herself propped against the back of the couch, as she had been that first night. Although this time there was no anger between them. She swallowed.

"You're welcome, Dave. I enjoyed it, too."

He cut her safety margin to less than a foot. "It's customary to end an evening like this with a kiss."

"Yes," she breathed. Fearing he might misinterpret that— or might interpret it correctly—she added, "It is. Customary, I mean."

"Shouldn't break with custom. That's the sort of thing that leads to the downfall of civilizations."

Well, when he put it that way, it was a patriotic duty. "We can't have that."

"No, we can't. So what are you going to do about it?"

"Me?"

"You asked me out, remember?"

"I wouldn't say I asked you out, not like—"

He interrupted with a deep sigh. "Matty, with civilization

on the line, you're going to argue? Guess I'll have to take care of this myself.''

Her lips were lifting into a smile when he did.

The kiss caught fire as if the smile had been kindling. No, more like the entire evening had been kindling. Cords of kindling made of touches, looks, thoughts, all piled up waiting for the first spark to light the bonfire. And it did.

Because she couldn't do anything else if her life depended on it, she opened to his deep kiss, sinking back against the couch. But his arms gathered her up, holding her against him even as he delved into her mouth. He turned them once so he was against the couch.

After a time that could only be gauged by the weakness of her knees, he eased the kiss, lining her swollen lips with his tongue, darting inside, then back, tugging on her bottom lip with his teeth, then taking the kiss deep and involved again.

Lack of oxygen forced a slight let-up, though he held her just as tight, and she had her arms wrapped around his neck. Dave leaned his forehead against hers, and she felt his ragged breath across her skin.

''I want you, Matty.'' His voice was even more of a graveled rumble than usual. ''You should know that. And you should know how much I want you.''

More shaken than she wanted to admit, she tried his teasing sarcasm. ''If you give me some cliché now about how you want me more than you've ever wanted a woman before, Dave, I'll—''

''I won't. Because it's not true. I *have* wanted a woman this much before.''

''Oh.'' Her throat burned with some acid. ''I'm not surprised. It's like I said, six years can teach you a lot—''

''Matty.'' He started pushing her jacket off her shoulders. She hadn't intended to cooperate, but somehow she was shrugging out of the jacket. He tossed it onto the couch behind them.

"It's to be expected that we'd have other, uh, experiences and some—"

"Matty."

"—of them were bound to be pretty darned good. I mean, it would be sad, if they weren't, right?"

"Matty." He turned them again, and when she leaned back this time she discovered they'd reached the end of the couch. It didn't matter because he was still holding her flush against him. When had he taken his jacket off? But he must have, because now it was only the softness of his shirt that separated her hands from the firmness of his skin.

"After all, we were kids when we were together. What did we know about—"

He slid a hand up into her hair to cup the back of her skull and held her still while he kissed her with a ruthlessness she'd never have expected of Dave.

"You, Matty." He slid his tongue between her lips again, in a long, slow thrust that was not subtle nor open to misinterpretation, before repeating. "You."

She tilted her head to kiss under his jaw, then down his throat, touching her tongue lightly to his Adam's apple. He swallowed convulsively and dropped his head back as she continued her openmouthed exploration. Slipping first one button then another free and sliding the cotton back, she reached the hollow between his shoulder and collarbone. He'd always liked this spot. She licked it, then opened her mouth and sucked lightly. She liked it, too, because when he made that sound deep in his chest he was making now, more a rumble than a purr. She felt the vibrations echo inside her, spreading deeper and wider.

She was in danger. Deep danger. Right at the edge of losing thought and will and being left with only feeling. She scrambled back a fraction of an inch or so.

He slowly brought his head down and spread his hands across her buttocks and rocked against her, letting her feel his hardness.

"You're the woman I've wanted this much before, Matty. Every night you've slept under this roof."

Her back arched, brushing the tips of her breasts against his chest. Desire pulsed through her. She met his eyes and didn't try to hide it.

"Matty." His voice was rougher than usual, strumming over her nerves. "Make love with me."

He saw her answer in her eyes and wasn't going to give her time to reconsider. There had been too much time between them. Much, much too much time.

He twisted, bringing them down to the couch at the same time he maintained the contact all along their bodies. But something was sliding out from under them, maybe the universe.

They landed on the soft, old rug, partially caught in the canyon between the couch and the chest, with Matty on top of him, a giggle escaping her. She spread her hands on his chest, inside where his shirt was open, and seemed inclined to push off him. He wasn't going to allow that.

With one hand he shoved the chest, leaving them a wide wedge of space. With the other arm he captured her, pivoting and turning at the same time, so their legs tangled and he ended above her. If she'd had any doubts about his desire before, she couldn't now, because he was flush in the cradle of her legs, pulsing and pushing despite the layers of clothes between them.

He set to work remedying that. It wasn't elegant, because he wasn't willing to be separated from her long enough to make the tugging of fabric, the sliding of zippers, the yanking of material anything but urgently awkward. He didn't care.

He was greedy. Not content to wring every pleasure from each of her touches. He needed more. He needed her naked.

She had doubts. He knew that, could see it, though he didn't know precisely what the doubts were. It didn't matter.

He'd answer them, he'd take care of them. As he'd always taken care of Matty. As he always would.

The phrase *taking care of Matty* snagged in his mind.

He swore under his breath and raised up enough to jerk his jeans off the corner of the chest where they'd been dumped. Digging in the pocket was almost more than he could manage. At last he had the packet and was tearing it open. He levered away from her only the amount absolutely necessary.

"Dave, I can help—"

"No." It would be no help. He did it himself, only sparing a little oxygen for curses at how long it seemed to take.

He rolled back to her, bending on one knee to push slightly against the inside of her leg.

"Matty."

She answered the plea and opened to him. He was breathing fire, sucking it in in short, shallow gasps. He positioned himself, thinking he'd take it slow.

It was the last thought he had.

She wrapped her legs around him and took him inside her. Deep. Complete. Right.

They held like that for an instant that captured eternity.

He drew back to nearly the point of leaving her, then stroked in with one motion.

Matty made a sound, a sound he'd dreamt about too many nights to count, and there were no more measured movements, no more control.

Matty's hands were on him. Urging him to her, as if there was any chance in this life that he would do anything else. He heard her breathing change, felt the rhythm of it in puffs across his skin. And he felt the tremors start deep inside her, where she surrounded him, held him. Each tremor a pulsing stroke that left him no choices—if he'd ever had any. There was no slow.

Fast and wild. No time to breathe. Just climbing straight up, hotter and tighter and higher and—

She screamed his name, and the waves of its echo pushed him over the edge after her.

He didn't move for a long time.

At last, Dave rolled to his back, but with his side pressed against hers, one of his legs still trailed across hers. From the corner of his eye he was aware of clothes strewn around the otherwise familiar room.

Like those pieces of clothing, he was limp, bound to stay in whatever position he had landed in until something lifted him up.

Beside him, Matty drew in a deep, shaky breath. "My."

Dave rolled his head to look at her.

"That's all—" he had to stop to pull more oxygen into his depleted lungs "—you're going to say? *My?*"

"I…" She took two more quick breaths, then offered. *"Oh, my?"*

"That's better." His chuckle held relief. It had never been like this for him before, not even with her. He didn't want to be alone in that "never before." He crooked his arm above his head, and his fingers found strands of her hair spread out against the rug, stroking softly.

"I didn't expect…" Although her breathing was starting to return to normal, Matty didn't finish the thought.

"What?"

"That it would be like that."

"Like what?"

Matty heard something in his voice that made her both more aware of her own vulnerability, and wondering if he had similar feelings.

"I didn't think it could be like it used to be for us, but this was…even more." She turned to tip her head, touching her forehead against his.

"Yeah, it was." He brushed her hair back from her face, then stroked it. "Why didn't you think it could be like it used to be?"

"We were such kids. I thought…you know, rampaging

hormones and all that. You know what they say, about how you can't ever recapture the impact of those first experiences, because so much of it's the heady rush of discovery and exploration.''

''Is that what they say?''

''I'm sure I read it somewhere.''

''Uh-huh. Couldn't be that you're making this up, now could it?''

If she'd decided during the past six years that the reason it had been so good with Dave was that it had been their first experiences and they'd been awash in hormones, she wasn't ready to give up that cloak of self-protection. Especially not since that metaphorical cloak was all she was wearing.

''Well, it makes sense when you think of it. Those first times, you're not only discovering the other person, you're discovering the fear and wonder and excitement of making love. Of sex. That's pretty powerful stuff, you know.''

''I know.''

Two raw, low words. They sent a tremor through her that reminded her of all the parts of her body that reacted to that powerful urge. The obvious ones certainly made their reaction known, but a crazy heat also pulsed at the inside of her elbows, as well as an urge to arch her neck and curl her toes, along with the odd prickling at the tip of her fingers.

''But consider this,'' Dave was going on, and she could have thought that he was totally unaware of her response...except he chose that moment to take her arm from where it rested at her far side, draw it across both of them, then lift his head to lick and kiss the exact, heated spot on the inside of her elbow that craved his caress.

''Consider what?'' she gasped.

''Hmm? Oh. Consider that after those first few times, you're older and wiser. You have the value of experience. You can set aside nerves. You might even be said to have some...technique.''

She shook her head. "That doesn't match up to the exhilaration of fear and wonder and excitement."

"I've got another theory for you to consider, then. Maybe it's just us. You and me."

He bent his head over her arm once more, and she looked at the disorder of his thick brown hair while his tongue teased her skin.

"More likely it's a carryover from when we were kids," she said, oddly reluctant to let that theory go. "Plus, the fact of us being thrown together like we have been."

"So you're saying it's nostalgia and proximity and enforced abstinence, huh? Is that a multiple choice or all of 'em taken together?"

"I don't know," she said crossly. What was he doing, treating this like a scientist looking at a bug? Especially when what was building inside her once more did not mesh well with her idea of scientists or bugs. "Take your pick. Or maybe it was because we've never done it in a bed like normal people. It could be just the novelty of it."

"Guess there's only one way to tell." He came up on his elbow, and looked down at her. "But before we do. In case we find out it was nostalgia—" he kissed her "—or proximity—" And again, sliding his tongue past her lips before backing away enough to say, "Or curiosity or—novelty or—"

She kissed him. "Enforced abstinence."

"Right. I want something else before we take the risk of bursting the bubble."

"What?"

Not that it mattered. Was there anything she wouldn't give him at this moment?

He stroked one hand from her shoulder, across her breasts, then lower, following it with his mouth. His lips covered her nipple and the touch of his tongue brought her hips off the floor.

"That first time," he said, raising his head enough to look

into her eyes, "well, we were in kind of a hurry. And next time, we'll be testing that hypothesis of yours and it could be it'll be a grave letdown for both of us. So this time…" He stroked his hand up the inside of her thigh, pressing gently for entrance. She gave it. "I want to watch you, Matty. I want to see you shatter. Just for me."

"Matty."
"Hmm."
"It's time for bed."
She burrowed deeper into Dave's shoulder, then slid her bare foot up his calf. "This is fine."
"No. You were right before."
That got her eyes to open.
"We need to test this in a bed. To make sure it's not the novelty."
It wasn't.

"It wasn't the novelty," she said when she could breathe again.
"Nope. Guess we'll just have to face it, Matty. It's us." He rolled to his back, taking her with him.
She found that hollow above his collarbone again, tasted the salt on his skin and reveled in the hitch in his breathing. He stroked his hand down her back, over her hip, and then up under her hair to her neck, a long, lazy glide of his palm over her skin.
"I truly didn't bargain for this when I asked you to marry me for two years, Dave. It makes things even more complicated."
"Mmm." He was obviously drifting toward sleep. "No. Makes things simple. We stay together."

Chapter Twelve

She was gone.

He sensed it before he even came fully awake. He swept an arm across the empty sheets, still warm from her body.

He swore as he sat up. She'd run out on him. Just like when they were kids. Just like the night they got married. Well, dammit, this time he wasn't going to be easygoing, reasonable Dave. This time she was going to explain what the hell she meant by taking off. This time she was going to tell him exactly what she was thinking, if he had to damn well tie her to a chair while she did it.

He jerked on his clothes, muttering curses under his breath all the while, and headed out to saddle Brandeis.

Tears blurred Matty's vision, but she didn't need to see because Juno was picking her way along the familiar trail without a hitch.

What she needed to do was think.

She'd let herself drift to sleep without thinking about what he'd said, and she'd awakened nestled within Dave's protective hold, never wanting to move.

It wasn't any of the things she'd tried to use to explain what happened between the two of them. It *was* them. But there was still a canyon between that and Dave's certainty.

Makes things simple. We stay together.

It didn't feel simple to her. That's what she needed to sort out.

Because she'd jumped into this. Just like Dave said about her. She'd jumped into a new life when he'd broken up with her all those years ago. She'd jumped into coming back to the ranch when Great-Uncle Henry died, leaving her new life behind. She'd jumped into asking Dave to be her husband when she'd come up against a problem.

Her husband.

Only, not really her husband, no matter what he said.

The man she'd always loved.

Always? Still?

She had to think about this. Think it through before she took another step—a misstep. This was too big to do any more jumping.

Only she couldn't think lying next to Dave, with the sound of his breathing in her ear and the rise and fall of his chest under her hand. Especially not this sort of thinking.

Easing away from him was one of the hardest things she'd ever done. Not because she was trying to make no noise that would wake him, but because of the voice inside her screaming to lie down beside him again and feel his arms around her for as long as she possibly could.

The jangle of Juno's harness brought Matty's attention back to the present. They'd almost reached the end of the section of trail she and Dave had named The Narrows—a high and tight path between two outcroppings of rock that let only one horse at a time pass through. She heard hoofs coming fast behind her.

Dave. It had to be.

No one else would be taking this trail at dawn, especially not at that speed. No one else would have reason to follow her. No one else would have reason to call her to account.

Her leg muscles tensed in preparation for tapping her heels against Juno's sides, signaling the responsive mare to move faster. But she stopped herself. Better to face it now. Better to own up to jumping in headfirst—again—and go from there.

She let Juno keep going the few yards to where the path opened up beyond The Narrows, then turned her around, facing the way they'd come, and waited.

She'd barely brought Juno to a stop when she heard a horse's frightened cry, then what sounded like metal against rock, followed by a faint, dull thud. She hadn't even sorted out the sounds, much less consciously ascribed meanings to them before she tapped Juno's sides and urged her forward, toward the sounds.

Almost as soon as she started, she stopped. Responding to more sounds, she pulled back hard on Juno's reins, and wheeled the mare across the opening of The Narrows. In another second, Brandeis came charging out of the shadows toward them. Riderless.

Not letting herself think about that, Matty angled Juno so she partially blocked Brandeis' outlet, but not completely, so he wouldn't panic more. He took the opening she left him toward the fence along the trail here. Keeping Juno half a body ahead of him, she steered him along the fence, talking to him all the while. She slowed Juno, and to her relief, the powerful stallion also slowed.

Knowing an abrupt move now could send the stallion into a frenzy, she forced herself to reach slowly for the reins. Brandeis shook his head, but didn't pull away or rear. I seemed like an eternity before she had the two horses headed back into The Narrows, but it couldn't have been more than three or four minutes altogether since Brandeis had appeared.

"Dave?" she called. Not too loud, for fear of Brandeis.

bolting again, but loud enough for someone to hear. No answer.

"Dave?"

Nothing.

Her heart lurched painfully against her chest. Her eyes strained into the murky light as they followed a curve around a huge boulder that blocked the trail ahead from view.

She saw the patch of red first, and heard herself whispering, "Please, please."

It was all she could get out in the way of a prayer. But as she drew closer, it seemed to be answered as she realized the color was from Dave's shirt, not something else.

"Dave!"

Still no answer. She dismounted some distance away, near a scrub pine growing out of the rock where she could loop both horses' reins. It wouldn't hold either one if they pulled hard, but it was better than nothing. And the first rule in an emergency was to not be left afoot. Ed Currick had taught her and Dave that so many years ago.

"Please," she whispered again, as she hurried toward the figure awkwardly sprawled on the ground. There was more red. Blood. In his hair and down the side of his face. "Oh, Dave."

He groaned, and she had never heard anything so wonderful in her life. She dropped to her knees beside him as his eyes fluttered open. His mouth moved once with no sound. It took a second time before words came.

"Matty. You okay?"

"Am *I* okay? You're the one who's hurt! What happened? No— First, tell me where you hurt."

He blinked, and winced as if that motion hurt. "Brandeis…?"

"Is fine. Now, will you tell where you're hurt?"

"I'm all right."

He started to move, as if to sit up. She pressed his shoulder to the ground. With a moan, he subsided, closing his eyes, and she wasn't sure if it was her hold or pain that kept him still.

"Right. You're just fine," she said aloud. Inside she was uttering incoherent prayers of thanks that he was moving and talking.

Now she had to know how badly he was hurt.

Keeping her touch as gentle as she could, and thankful the light was growing stronger, she followed the path of blood back, parting his hair to find a gash in his scalp. Although it was still bleeding steadily, it didn't look too deep. With her own blood pounding in her ears, she placed her fingertips on his wrist and felt the strong, solid pulse there.

The bump on his head was bad enough for a concussion, but the light wasn't good enough to compare the size of his pupils. His talking and making sense were both good signs, though.

She allowed herself on exhalation of relief, then wiped her bloody fingers on the scrub grass before methodically running her hands over his body, testing for broken bones the way she would with a calf or a colt. It wasn't scientific, but she figured it was the same principal.

By the time she reached his boots, she was satisfied he had no major fractures, though she couldn't speak to smaller bones—or internal injuries. To check that out, she needed to get him to a doctor, and to do that, she would need help.

"Dave?"

His eyes were closed and for a heartbeat she thought he'd lost consciousness again, but then came a low, "Huh?"

"Don't go to sleep. You might have a concussion, and I don't think you're supposed to sleep."

"Uh-huh."

The vagueness of that answer made one decision for her. She wasn't going to leave him long enough to ride for help. She'd have to get help some other way.

"Dave. I'm going to the horses. I want you to stay awake. You understand?"

Another grunt.

"That's not good enough, Dave." She forced her voice to stay calm and even. "Answer me, so I know you understand."

"I understand."

"Good."

First, she checked Brandeis, making sure he was sound—in case she had to ride him after all. Next, she took everything she thought might be useful out of the pack she kept behind Juno's saddle. There wasn't much since she'd only been riding back and forth between the ranches. She'd hoped for a paper and pencil, but no such luck.

Instead she tied her red bandanna around the saddlehorn, freed Juno's reins, turned her toward the Flying W, slapped her on the rump and hoped like the dickens that Juno would do what Matty expected her to do, that Cal wouldn't have left the home ranch yet, and that he would understand the message.

It was a lot of hoping.

She wasn't prepared to leave it to hope. So if Cal didn't show up after an hour, she would light a signal fire up on top of the rock outcropping. Surely someone would see that.

She raided Brandeis' pack next and found a first-aid kit—count on Dave to be prepared—and brought her booty to where Dave was, she used the first-aid kit and a bandanna dipped in the creek along the fence line to wipe the blood from his face, and the worst of it out of his hair. More oozed sluggishly from the cut. She kept reminding herself that head wounds bleed worse than others. Drawing the split skin together, she used three butterfly bandages, but suspected he'd need stitches.

"Dave, you want some water?"

He'd said nothing while she'd worked and most of the time he'd kept his eyes closed, but she'd known he was conscious from the movement of his eyes beneath the lids.

"Yeah."

With the sky brightening quickly now, she put one arm under his head to raise it enough for him to drink, and he tried to keep going, so she used the other hand to press down on his chest.

"I can sit."

"No. Just lie still. I think you've got some injured ribs—broken or maybe cracked, but either way they've got to be hurting."

He started to protest again but she put the mouth of the water bottle to his lips, and his choice was to waste good water by letting it dribble down his chin or to drink. He drank—even banged up, Dave was too levelheaded to waste water.

She'd told him about setting Juno loose—hopefully to return to the Flying W barn. Now she informed him, "I'm going to gather makings for a signal fire in case we need it."

She worked fast, not wanting to leave him alone, so only a few minutes passed before she rounded the big boulder once more, and saw the stubborn fool struggling to sit up, trying to use his heel for purchase in the thin, rocky soil. She dropped the armload of fire-makings at one side of the trail and hurried forward.

"Stay still!"

Something more persuasive than her entered the picture—pain. He gave a sharp grunt that faded into a groan, and dropped back to one elbow.

"Is it your ankle?"

"Leg." His lips were thinned. "I think. Hard to tell."

She crouched beside him, and pulled the bottom of his jeans up as high as she could, then gently slid her hands inside them to skim over his flesh. The wiry hair there prickled her palms, but the bones beneath seemed solid and in place.

"Your leg seems fine," she said, drawing her palms slowly down his shin. She looked up at him. "Maybe it's—

what?'' His face had gone tense and he was breathing harder. ''Is there pain?''

''Not my leg now.''

''But you said—''

''Higher, Matty.''

''Higher? But—'' And then, crouched there on the ground, with her hands cupped around the tough muscles of his calf, she recognized the part of his anatomy his look was indicating, and she saw that part of him was indeed swollen.

And it made no difference that she needed to think things through. It made no difference how much had changed between them and what might never have been right. It made no difference that he'd been thrown and she didn't know how badly hurt he was. She felt the corresponding reaction surge hot and powerful into her.

''Matty, if you regret making love—''

''No.'' The word came out stark and louder than she'd expected. ''No, I don't regret making love with you, Dave.''

''Good, because I'm not dead yet, Matty,'' he said in the closest thing to his Dave drawl he'd managed since the fall.

''Oh, for heaven's sake.'' Angry at herself, terrified for him, she snatched her hands away, taking the hem of his jeans and jerking them back down over the top of his boot, and slapping them there—and nearly jumped out of her skin at his yowl of pain.

''Oh God, I'm sorry, Dave. I didn't mean to hurt your ankle.''

''Foot,'' he gasped.

But she was looking more closely at his boots, comparing the two of them. ''I don't think so, Dave. It looks like your ankle's starting to swell some even with your boot on. I can't be certain without taking the boot off, but if it is your ankle... No, I'm leaving the boot on until the doctor can see you.''

''Don't need a doctor.''

''Right.'' She might have had more to say on that subject as well as the general topic of stubborn males, but she heard hoofbeats, even before Brandeis nickered. "Dave, I think it's Cal. I'll be right back."

She went to Brandeis, holding his reins so he wouldn't decide the newcomer's arrival was an excuse to run.

Cal rode in on Reve, leading Juno, his rifle crooked in his arm. He looked decidedly grim in the instant before he spotted her.

"You okay?"

"I'm fine, Cal. But Dave got thrown."

"Is he—?"

"Bad bump on the head, and a cut. Ankle's swelling, could be broken. But his pulse is good. He's moving, talking. He's groggy, but making sense."

"When Juno came back to the barn with it barely light… What the hell happened?" He was already dismounting.

"Brandeis must have thrown him. You know how stallions can be."

"Looks calm now."

"Even the calmest horse can get rattled."

He slid her a look. "Even riding before daylight, I've never heard of Currick getting thrown by anything on four legs."

Neither had she. Not since they were kids.

Except the calmest man could get rattled, too. And maybe he'd been rattled, just the way she'd been.

"Not that you owe me any explanation, Matty." He looped the reins around the same scrub pine, and slid the rifle into a holder on the saddle.

"He was coming after me. We had a…fight." It was the fastest way to explain what had happened. Cal gave her a long look.

"Where is he?"

"This way."

The stubborn fool had himself half propped up against the rock wall of The Narrows. Drag marks in the dirt showed part of his struggle. The grayness under his tan showed more.

Matty glared at him, which did no good since his eyes were closed.

"You want to stay with him while I get a doctor out here?" Cal asked.

If Dave was seriously injured he shouldn't be moved—but of course he'd been moving himself so it was a little late for that. Even more, Matty was sure she'd have sensed if he was more seriously hurt than he appeared to be.

"No. We'll take him back to the Flying W. Then we can call—"

"Slash-C."

She and Cal turned in unison to Dave. He sounded almost completely like himself, except his voice was roughened by pain.

"We're on Flying W land," Matty started reasonably. "So it's shorter to—"

"Home."

"Flying W's closer," Cal backed her up.

"Home."

Cal stared at Dave another two beats, then turned to her with a lift of one brow.

The Flying W was closer. Dave would get medical attention quicker by taking him there. She looked into his face again. There was more to healing than medicine.

"Slash-C." She said it once to Dave, then turned to Cal and repeated, "Slash-C."

Cal dipped his head in acceptance. "Okay, how're we gonna get him there?"

"I can ride," Dave said.

"You are *not* riding—"

"I can ride," he repeated stubbornly.

"Maybe," Cal interrupted calmly. "But how're you going to get in the saddle with that ankle?"

That stopped Dave, though he did mutter "Foot" under his breath.

"He'll ride double behind me," she decided. "On Brandeis. He can carry double riders better than Juno."

Cal frowned. "If Currick passes out and starts to slip—"

"I can ride alone."

She ignored Dave. "You can ride along next to us, Cal. Besides, I'll need you to help get him up. I couldn't get him up behind you."

"Okay."

They brought the horses out of The Narrows first. Getting Dave upright was tricky in the confined area. Cal couldn't get in position to get his shoulder under Dave's arm, so the two of them could only tug on him and help him balance as he used his upper body to grab hold of the sharp rock face. Each grunt of pain was like a blow to her, and the perspiration on his forehead made her want to cry.

It was even worse getting him up on Brandeis, because all she could do was sit in the saddle, keep the horse steady and try to be something stable for him to grab on to as Cal boosted him up. He didn't make a sound through that whole maneuver, but she heard his hiss of pain as he finally settled against her back, with his arms around her waist.

"Lean on me, Dave," she ordered, when Cal left them to mount up himself.

"I'm okay." But she could tell from his voice how much getting on Brandeis had taken out of him, and that frightened her.

"You're stubborn as a jackass."

"Don't knock it. It's the only way I've been able to stay in love with you all these years, Matty."

Chapter Thirteen

It was a hellish trip back.

They had to take it slow, yet she knew that each minute was delaying the time Dave could get relief for his pain.

And what if she were wrong? What if he had more serious injuries than she'd thought. Maybe she should have insisted he stay up in The Narrows until they could get the doctor to him. Maybe she shouldn't have agreed to bring him the longer distance to the Slash-C.

Dave didn't speak until they'd dropped down from the higher ground of The Narrows to where the first true sunlight glinted on blooming wildflowers.

"Indian Paintbrush," he said quite clearly from behind her.

Its vivid red was among the blooms, but why would he bring it up? Could he be delirious? "What about it, Dave?"

"Reminds me of you."

She couldn't twist around enough to see him and had to be satisfied with looking to Cal, riding beside them. He gave a faint shrug, which he wouldn't have done if he thought Dave was raving.

Still, when she caught sight of the roof of the barn ahead she thought she'd never seen such a beautiful sight.

"Cal, ride ahead and see if Jack or any of the other hands are around to help."

"You sure you'll be okay?"

"I'm not going to fall off, dammit." The grumble was the first thing Dave had said since the comment about Indian Paintbrush. She'd known he was conscious, though, by his hold around her waist.

"Yes," she assured Cal. "Go on. And if you find someone to come back and help, go inside and call Doc Johnson in Knighton."

Cal spurred Reve into the placid canter that was his top speed these days.

It seemed interminable, but it couldn't have been more than ten minutes after Cal had gone out of sight before she saw two riders heading toward them. Amid a flurry of questions Jack and young Bryan came up on either side of Brandeis, and Matty felt immeasurably relieved to have flank riders for the last stretch.

They came to a slow stop near the porch steps that led into the office. Matty didn't dare risk turning around in the saddle to look at Dave for fear of upsetting his balance.

"Now what?" Bryan asked anxiously. "How'll we get him off Brandeis?"

"Gettin' him off is the problem," Jack agreed. "After that, we can carry him inside, but—"

"Try it and you're fired."

Dave's words had barely registered before she felt him release his hold on her.

"He's slipping!" With the other two in the process of dismounting, no one could help Dave. She twisted around trying to grab his shirt or anything she could hold on to, and then she realized he hadn't passed out as she feared, but was trying to dismount. "David Currick, you are the most stubborn—!"

He'd reached the ground, but his bad ankle gave way, and he started to stumble. She spotted Cal on the porch. "Cal!"

He'd already seen the situation, and moved in quickly, keeping Dave from going down by grabbing him around the chest. Dave gave a pained grunt and went even whiter.

"What on earth do you think you were doing, you stubborn idiot!" Matty scolded as she jumped down from the saddle and hurried over to him. "I just know you've got broken ribs."

"If I didn't before I do now, thanks to Ruskoff."

Cal's mouth twitched at the dry words, as he shifted to get a more secure and less painful hold on Dave. "You can't fire me. I don't work for you."

All the men chuckled, including Dave, as she glared impartially.

"He could have killed himself trying to get off Brandeis that way. Cal, did you call—?"

"Yup. Be here as soon as he can."

"Okay. You and Jack help Dave in. I'll get his bed ready."

When she reached Dave's bedroom well ahead of their slow progress, she stopped dead at the sight of the bed, with the pillows still imprinted by their heads and the covers still in disarray. The sound of the men behind her made her swallow all that she was feeling, and hurriedly smooth the sheets, plump the pillows and fold back the covers.

It wasn't until the others were gone and Dave was settled back against pillows that he let out a low-voiced curse.

"What is it, Dave?"

"You're right about the ribs. Cracked or broken. And, God, my head hurts."

"I know, but I don't want to give you anything until the doctor sees you."

"And my foot."

"It's your ankle, sweetheart."

"It's *my* ankle, and it's my foot that hurts."

"Okay, Dave."

"Did you call me sweetheart?"

"Yeah, I did." She waited warily.

He grunted, leaned back and closed his eyes.

"Afraid for a minute there that I'd hit my head harder than I'd thought."

Matty finally started to relax after Doc Johnson checked Dave, finding no sign of internal injuries, and declared he didn't need to go to the hospital.

Although, Doc added, a mild concussion, cracked ribs, a severely sprained ankle and numerous contusions were "nothing to sneeze at. Besides, sneezing'll make those ribs hurt like the dickens right now. What I want to know is what you were doing out at The Narrows in the middle of the night."

"A bet," Dave said before Matty could even start to think of an excuse to give.

Doc gave a snort that sounded distinctly disbelieving. "How'd you do this to your ankle?"

"Brandeis was rearing, would've gouged his flank on the rock, so I stuck my foot out to hold him off."

His stirrup striking rock must have been the metallic sound she'd heard.

"So you tried to stiff-arm a mountain with your leg. You know the human ankle is not designed for that sort of abuse, David."

"Neither's Brandeis."

"The horse isn't my patient. I'd probably get more co-operation if he was." Doc turned to Matty. "He'll need checking on, but nothing you shouldn't be able to handle."

"Matty's not going to be here to nurse me—"

She cut across Dave's protest. "Of course I am. Cal can handle the work without me until you're better."

"I've wrapped his ribs. That ankle will turn six shades of black and blue. Give him these pills so he can sleep at night. But all in all, a week in bed ought to fix him up."

"I'll be fine by tomorrow."

"A week," Doc answered so fast that he must have known he would need to repeat his order.

"Three days."

"A week."

"All right, all right, I'll stay in bed four days, but you can't expect—"

"A week. That's what I said, and that's what I mean. I'm giving orders here, not dickering."

"Now why didn't I think of that approach," Matty murmured from the other side of the bed.

Dave cut her a sharp look. She raised her hands in surrender.

"Well, I got some advantages in the dickering. I brought the stubborn cuss into this world," Doc said with self-satisfaction. He chuckled and winked at Matty as she came around the bed to escort him out. "'Course, Matty, you got some advantages I don't."

"Matty, quit tiptoeing around me, for God's sake."

Dave had definitely reached the cranky-patient stage of recovery.

"I'm not tiptoeing. I'm simply trying to walk quietly so you can rest."

"I've been sleeping for four days. I'm fine."

"You're not fine, and you haven't been sleeping. You've had more people come by than would show up for an Elvis sighting." Which might explain why they hadn't talked about what had happened—not about his accident, not about his following her, not about her predawn departure, not about making love.

Or maybe cowardice explained it.

At least if it was cowardice, she knew she wasn't alone,

because he'd steered as far away from the subject as she had. However, as an avoidance method it had left a lot to be desired, because all that time of not talking had left way, way too much time for thinking.

"You hardly touched lunch." She picked up the tray from the table next to his bed. "And when Doc Johnson comes this afternoon, I'm going to have him write down every single thing he says to do, so there's no confusion, and from now on you're going to do whatever he says if I have to tie you down—"

"Tying might be fun." He used a version of that old calm, mocking voice, although it didn't sound quite right. "But it might work better if I tie you, since you're the one who's prone to leaving suddenly."

Realization hit her so hard she had to put the tray down. It landed with a clunk, and surprise showed through Dave's assumed amusement.

Assumed was the key word.

She couldn't believe she hadn't seen it before.

Maybe because he was still hurting and hadn't done it as well as usual. Maybe because she had more experience with people. Maybe because she'd come to know him in these past weeks in a way she never had before. Maybe because she'd been so concerned with his physical condition that she'd stopped worrying about protecting her own feelings every second.

Maybe all those things together, and more, but it seemed so obvious now—Dave used that calm amusement to protect himself, to keep people from knowing what he was really feeling. He'd done it when they were kids, and he was doing it now. Had he been doing it all along in these weeks they'd been together?

Almost certainly. But she would examine the past against the light of that theory later, when she had time. Right now she had to deal with right now.

She sat on the side of his bed, crowding his sweats-covered

legs under an afghan. She could see that surprised him. She'd been so careful around him up till now. Careful to not crowd him, to not touch him if possible. Tiptoeing—sometimes literally, at all times metaphorically.

"We have to talk, Currick."

That surprised him, too. But he came back with that same tone. "Going to renegotiate our deal because you didn't bargain for nursing duty? You did promise in sickness and health—at least for two years."

"Cut it out, Dave. Stop hiding behind that damned mocking. That's what we've been doing—both of us—hiding behind things." Words were tumbling out too fast for her to even think about censoring them.

He pushed himself up against the pillows to sit straighter with barely a wince.

"Okay, Matty, we'll stop hiding. I love you. I've loved you as long as I can remember. I want to stay married to you—to have a real marriage, and what happened Friday night shows you want that, too. You can't deny what's between us."

"I don't deny that what happened Friday was…incredible." He took her hand between both of his, and she didn't resist. It was comforting to feel the rough warmth surrounding her flesh. "But it's not as simple as you make it sound. For a long time, I was so angry at you. So hurt and disappointed. I let it cloud my thinking about too many things. Even if the grant wasn't making such a huge difference for the Flying W, I'll always be glad we made this marriage bargain, because we've taken care of so many of those old questions and arguments and scars. Now we have the good things from the past. We didn't used to have that."

"That sounds like a line from *Casablanca*," he accused.

She summoned a ghostly smile. "It does, doesn't it? It's a little like that, too—we'd lost Paris, but now we have it back."

"I can't remember how many times you've told me there

should've been a way to end that movie with Bogart and Bergman getting together.''

"Maybe a sequel."

"We've already waited six years, Matty. I want us to make this marriage real. To have you in my bed every night, not down the hall or at the Flying W or in Chicago."

So much in her wanted to give in to the wanting, his and her own, to fall into his arms and feel his love. But the same doubt that had driven her out of his bed Friday night held her now. The worst of it was, it wasn't a doubt with definable edges that sat in her heart like an iron box; it was a fog that slipped through her fingers each time she tried to grasp it, burning off under the heat of their passion, but always sliding back in.

She bit the inside of her lip. "Dave, this is a big step. You agreed to marry me for a certain time and for a special reason. Before we consider changing that—"

"There's a special reason for that, too." Still holding her hand in one of his, he stroked the other palm along the curve of her thigh. "To have a family and a life. The one we dreamed about all our lives. Just the way I've loved you all my life."

"If you've always loved me, if that life together is what you've always wanted, why did you break up six years ago?"

"I was an idiot, that's why. I listened to the adults—Mom and Dad and Grams—and let them talk me into worrying that you didn't have dreams of your own, that you were just following along with mine. But that's not true. You said it yourself Friday night, ranching's your dream. We share it. I never imposed it on you."

"No, you didn't impose the dream on me." The heat from his touch on her leg was so much deeper than friction could ever explain. But the fog nudged at her. "It's so unlike you to listen to other people when—"

"Hey! Anybody home!"

Doc Johnson's voice came down the hall toward them.

Matty jumped up off the bed, though sitting beside Dave, holding hands and having his hand on her thigh were far from indecent, even if he hadn't been her husband in the eyes of the law and the community. But she couldn't look away from him.

Dave's gaze was direct and intent on her, promising that he would not let these issues die even if this particular discussion was over.

"Doc! Come on in," she called. "We're back here."

"Hope you don't mind me being early. I was through with a meeting in Sheridan, and I thought I'd swing by on my way to the clinic. So, how's the patient? Impatient, I bet." The doctor chuckled at his own joke as he set down a hard-sided case he used as a medical bag. "Matty, could you spare a thirsty man something to drink while I take a look at how this young man's healing?"

"Oh, of course. I'm sorry. I should have asked you—iced tea?"

"Sounds good. You, too, Dave?"

"Yeah. Please." His eyes were still on her.

Matty pivoted, finally breaking eye contact with Dave, and hurried to the kitchen. The automatic motions of preparing the iced tea didn't make a dent in the thoughts whirling through her mind.

If Doc hadn't come, might they have somehow discovered the source of her doubt? A doubt that had kept her fighting her feelings, even as she knew Dave was the one person on earth she could turn to when she needed help. Or would the warmth of his touch, and the heat of their desire have led her to ignore the doubt, and make love to him as she had wanted to do long before Friday night, and still wanted to do now?

She didn't regret making love with Dave.

She hadn't faced that truth until she'd told him so on the trail. Maybe at some level she'd been letting herself think he'd rushed her into making love. But that wasn't true. With all the talking she'd done that night she'd never said the words that would have stopped him.

Because she hadn't wanted to stop.

Because she'd wanted to make love with him more than she'd wanted her next breath.

Because she loved him.

That was a hell of a thing to realize about the man you were supposed to divorce in twenty months.

If Dave had his way there would be no divorce. But they'd started under false pretenses; how could they ever erase that? *Could* a marriage shift from a business proposition to something real?

She froze with her hands rapped around the frosty glasses she'd just put on a tray.

Oh, no.

What if at some subconscious level she'd been in love with Dave when she'd asked him to help her out by marrying her? That would mean she'd tricked him into marriage in the hope of tricking him into falling in love with her. How could she have done that to him? How could she have lied to herself and him that way? What kind of basis was that for a marriage?

"Matty?" Doc called. "You've got a couple of parched men here."

She picked up the tray.

Twenty months.

She didn't have to answer all these questions for twenty months.

At the very least, she could make the best of what she had now. Twenty months of loving Dave.

"Dave! What are you doing?"

All confusion dropped from Matty's eyes as she zeroed in on him. He was glad to see the confusion go, but he sure would have preferred if it hadn't been there at all when they talked about a future together. Just like the doubts he'd known she had before they made love Friday night.

"I'm getting up."

"Doc, you said he had to stay in bed a week!"

"It's a week—a work week." Standing beside the bed, Dave grinned. "A short work week."

"David Edward Currick—"

Doc patted her on the arm. "It's all right. He needs to be getting up a little more every day, as I'm sure he's been doing no matter what he's been told or how you tried to keep him tied down."

Tied down… If I have to tie you down… Tying might be fun.

He met Matty's eyes and saw his own reaction mirrored there, a jumble of desire and uncertainty.

But Doc was going on. "I counted on that when I told him a week. He's done better than I expected. Though you don't look as well rested as I'd hoped." He looked from one to the other. "Neither of you. Well, I suppose that's to be expected with a couple just married. You don't expect them to get much sleep at night anyhow, and—"

"Doc." Dave tried to stop the flow because the message now in Matty's eyes was that she wished the floor would open beneath her.

"—with something like this happening and you two having to be more inventive—"

"Doc!"

"What?" The older man looked at Dave half a minute, then turned to Matty before he started shaking his head. "Good Lord, you're telling me—no, don't tell me. I'm sorely disappointed. I never would have thought a little obstacle like a few sore ribs and a sprained ankle would get the better of you two."

"Dave had a bad blow to his head," Matty started, as if protecting his image.

He had to fight to keep from ordering Doc out of the room

right now. Because it had hit him, hard and hot, that the one time Matty hadn't had doubts was when the passion was flaring between them, when she was in his arms and they were making love. If that was the way to fight her doubts, he'd volunteer for duty every time. And soon she'd see there was no reason for doubt or confusion.

"Hogwash. He's got a head like a rock, as you should know better than most. I would have thought better of you two." Doc's stern expression abruptly dissolved into a chuckle. "That you'd be better at being a little wicked, anyway."

She came back from escorting Doc to the door and receiving a number of encouraging reassurances about Dave's recovery to find the bed empty and the bathroom door half open.

"Dave?"

"I'm in the shower. At least I will be if these pants will..." His voice trailed off into a grumble of curses.

"What on earth—?"

He was standing in the bathtub with the shower curtain pulled open. He'd discarded his shirt and socks. Now he seemed intent on taking off his sweatpants and boxers, which so far involved precarious hopping around on one foot on the slick tub surface.

"Be careful! You're going to fall! If you hit your head again or bang your ankle, even your ribs—"

"I won't do any of that if you'll come in here and help me. I want a shower, a hot, steamy shower."

Her lips parted. She fully intended to scold him again, except the heat inside her changed sources without even a blink.

"I'll help you get undressed if you'll promise you'll hold onto the faucet with one hand while you—Dave!"

Not only had the shower come on full-force, but his awkward hopping had been replaced by smoothly efficient motions that had him out of the rest of his clothes, starting on hers, and the shower curtain closed in no time.

"I told you I wanted a steamy shower." He was grinning that wicked Dave grin as he dragged her sodden shirt off her shoulders, tossed it over the curtain rod and started on her jeans.

She cooperated. Because she was still afraid he might fall. Because she wanted to.

"Remember the swimming hole?"

She stepped out of her jeans and panties. They, too, went over the rod, with the slap of wet fabric. But the wet fabric of her bra was frustrating him. He turned her around and finally released the hooks, sliding his hands over her in place of the cloth, while she tossed this final barrier over the rod.

"I don't want memories. I want now, Matty."

Now was going to be very short if he kept touching her that way. She bent to reach the soap and he groaned as her derriere pressed against him. He reached for her, but she stepped around him, feeling the beat of the water on her back now.

"You wanted to get clean, didn't you?"

"Not especially." But he didn't fight her as she soaped across his broad shoulders, down a back contoured by the muscles of ranching, over the rear end and tough legs of a rider. She gentled her touch to bare contact over the discoloration that remained at his ankle, then scooted around to in front of him, and began to work her way up.

At the top of his thighs, he growled a warning, and she skipped to the top of his shoulders. Then soaping over his chest, circling slowly around the male nubs that turned hard and beaded at her touch, then following the path of the dusting of hair as it narrowed, leading her down between his ribs, below his waist, before widening.

"Matty."

But she was done being warned. She cupped him, watching his response shrink the relative size of the soap bar as if it had been in a deluge. She felt the length and silkiness of him with her fingertips, shifting the soap to one hand in order to curl the other around him.

"My turn," he declared with another growl as he drew her hand away.

He took the soap and was gliding it over her back as his arms encircled her. He slid his tongue into her mouth, slow and deep, his arousal pressing insistently against her belly, her breasts sliding against his chest.

When she arched her back, his soap-slicked hands dropped lower, over the curve of her cheeks, down to the tops of her thighs. Then higher into the cleft, gently probing. She shuddered with the first touch.

The soap clattered to the tub, and he dropped to one knee in front of her. His hands holding her while his mouth found her. She was partly aware of the warm water streaming over her, of her hand gripping the towel bar for support, while the other tangled in his wet hair. But that awareness was a faint shadow to the gush of sensation centered on her core.

"Dave—"

Tremors racked her, and all that kept her knees from giving was the steadiness of his hold on her.

"Matty." He straightened to slide his tongue down her throat along her collarbone, then lower, until he flicked her nipple with a motion that nearly buckled her knees again. "I want to be inside you. Come to bed, Matty. Come to bed."

He wrapped her in a bath sheet, tucked another towel around his hips, then led her to the bed. But she saw his wince as he started to guide her down.

"Dave. Let me." She saw the question in his eyes, but he didn't resist as she gently pushed him back against the pillows. "Let me, so you won't hurt your ribs, your ankle. I don't want this to hurt you. Dave."

"You could never hurt me." In his gruff rumble of a whisper she recognized her own words from their first lovemaking so many years ago.

Her eyes were misty with memories and tenderness as she brushed the wet hair from his temple. But beneath the softness, a hard hunger pushed, and she saw it echoed in the sharpened planes of his face as she reached into the bedside table's drawer and brought out a packet.

She tried to be gentle, but the moisture lingering from their shower mingled with his sweat before she'd finished. His groan, though, told her it wasn't pain. At least not the kind he wanted to end.

She straddled his upper thighs, then bent to flick her tongue across his nipples while she cupped his weight in her hands. She felt the surge then, against her hands and under her as his hips rose in a response as old as man.

"Matty. Inside...I want to be inside you."

She gave in to that demand because it was what she wanted, too. She positioned herself, then guided him to her entrance. His hands bracketed her hips, flexing into her flesh, but he didn't try to hurry her. His hazel eyes seemed to burn with the heat arcing between them as he stared into her face as she lowered herself to take him inside, inch by glorious inch.

Sheathing him completely, she felt the tremors already starting. Or maybe they had never finished from earlier. Feeding them set the rhythm, built the pace until she was gasping to find oxygen in the overheated atmosphere.

His face was taut, his body glistened, and she felt the power of him beneath her, inside her. A part of her, as he always had been. Her love.

She called out as her body clenched with the power of a tremor. Dave's hips lifted, then again and again, driving her higher and higher, until the tremor metamorphosed to a glittering star shower that rained sensation through her blood and skin and bone, tingling and trembling there as she heard his harsh groan and felt the power of his release inside her.

And as she lay pillowed on Dave, still connected so intimately, that magical star shower slowly ebbed, gathering back in her heart, where it had originated from, though leaving a flutter of sensation here and a shiver of satisfaction there.

"All right, Currick, what's all this?" Matty came into the room the next morning carrying an armload of files with his briefcase hooked on one hand and trying to look stern.

"You're asking me?" he teased. "You're the one holding whatever it is."

"Mr. Innocent, huh?"

He'd been far from innocent the night before, and he liked it that way just fine. His campaign of not giving Matty too much time to let those doubts of hers take hold had been working very satisfactorily for the past twenty-four hours. *Very satisfactorily.*

"Like you have no idea that these are files Ruth dropped off because you threatened to fire her if she didn't bring them out here for you to work on."

"Well, if you let me drive into town—"

"Doc said no driving for two more days, and quit trying to change the subject from your having half your office delivered here."

"Hey, I'm getting behind. Besides, I've read three books and a half-dozen magazines, I can't take TV. Although..." He drew it out with a wicked grin. "I can think of a much better way to pass the time than working on legal files if you'd cooperate."

He reached for her, and she swiveled away with a chuckle. "Oh, no, you don't. I noticed you wincing, and you can't tell me your ribs aren't tender. You're not in any condition to be thinking of staying in bed all day that way today."

"Actually I'm in exactly the condition for staying in bed all day that way."

Her gaze dropped to his lap, and he saw the answering heat flushing her throat. But she was not to be swayed this time.

"I'll give you an hour—"

"That'll be a good start."

"—to work on the files," she clarified with her mouth so firmly turned down that he knew she was fighting a smile.

He took most of the files from her to free her arms, leaving her to set down his briefcase. He was flipping through files when her sudden stillness caught his attention. He looked up to see her holding a single file, with an envelope sticking out far enough to see the return address.

"You have a letter from the grant commission, Dave? There's not a problem is there? They're not after you or—"

He saw the precipice but couldn't let her worry like that. "No, no nothing like that, Matty."

"Then why are they writing you? Does this have something to do with the Flying W's grant, Dave?"

He wouldn't have chosen this way to tell her—hell, his first choice would be to never have her find out—but now that she was wondering, she'd never let it go. And with things so good between them, she'd understand.

"There is no Flying W grant."

Her eyes went wide. "I got the official notification."

"Yeah, you did. They gave the Flying W the grant, but I wrote to them and turned it down on your behalf."

She sank down on the edge of the bed near his feet. "You what?"

"I said that you'd reconsidered and you were withdrawing your request."

"But the grant money for the Flying W, the checks I've been getting…? Where's it from, Dave?"

He knew from her voice that she already knew. "It's from me. I repaid that first check you got, then sent the rest myself through an account I set up. I couldn't let you get in trouble."

"You couldn't let me get in trouble?" she repeated in an odd voice.

"No," he said cautiously, wondering what that tone meant. He didn't think he'd ever heard Matty use it before.

It wasn't angry, but it sure wasn't happy, either. "I wasn't sure they'd raise a big stink if anybody found out—as you said nobody was using that money—but I read all the conditions and checks and oversight they listed in that agreement and I decided it wasn't worth the risk."

"You decided." The words were as flat as the plains of Kansas.

"Yeah," he confirmed warily.

"You didn't believe I could turn the Flying W around without you pulling the strings."

"It wasn't a matter of faith," he said defensively, although she hadn't brought up the word. "I knew you'd sunk all your money in the ranch."

"How could you know that, Dave? I never told you."

The question was calm and cool. It scared the living daylights out of him. But he answered it with equal calm.

"I didn't go nosing around, Matty. Joyce Aberdick mentioned it the day she gave me those papers to bring on to you—the papers that confirmed all your retirement accounts had been converted to cash for the ranch."

"All my…?" Her eyebrows had dipped over her nose in puzzlement, but now one tilted up at an angle. "The IRAs."

"Yeah, that's what Joyce said. Your IRAs."

"Dave, those were the kind of IRAs that can be withdrawn without penalty. And that's not all my retirement money. I have a 401k in addition to some profit sharing. I am gambling on the ranch, but I wouldn't be destitute if it doesn't work."

"I didn't know."

"No, and you didn't ask me."

"If you're mad, I think I like it better when you yell, Matty."

"I'm not mad, Dave."

That didn't reassure him. "What are you then?"

"I'm…I'm touched that you cared about me that way and that you still look out for me, but…"

"But what?" He hadn't experienced dread before, not like

this, but he recognized it. And he knew it came from the misery he saw in Matty's eyes.

"It's what drives me away." A single tear slid through her bottom lashes and dropped to her cheek. "I know my leaving the morning after you married me and after we made love hurt you, and I'm so sorry for hurting you, Dave. But I've needed to go off by myself sometimes and think things through. To make a decision. My own decision. Because it's been so hard to make decisions around you. I think that's why I didn't tell you about the seed contract until it was a done deal. Maybe that's hard for you to get used to because I used to run *to* you and let you make my decisions."

"You make yourself sound like some weak-willed cream puff. You've never been like that."

"Then why do you try to treat me like one?"

"Are you still talking about my being the one to decide we should see other people six years ago?"

"We can start with that—you decided, and I had no voice in it. The night we came back here after the reception, you said you would decide the next morning how we would work out the details, clearly not wanting any input from me. After we made love, you said we'd stay together. Period. No discussion, no input from me. You'd decided, so that was it. But I can't live that way."

She dropped the grant commission envelope. It landed on his leg, balancing there for a moment before it slid off and fell to the floor.

"I thought all the problems between us were about the past," Matty continued. "But solving the past doesn't fix the future, Dave. It doesn't even fix the present. This isn't going to work."

"Matty—"

"I've been trying to fool myself into thinking you understood how I'd changed. I was wrong. You see me as I was when I was twenty, except for when you're seeing me as I was at twelve or five. Dave, I do jump into things. I am impulsive. And stubborn. But I don't need to be protected from that. It's who I am, and if that gets me into problems, then I get myself out of them. I have for a long time. At first it was scary, not having you around to rescue me. But, you know, after a while, I learned it wasn't all bad. And it's a hell of a lot better for my self-respect. I'm not the girl you knew. I'm not the girl who loved you so blindly, so unthinkingly.''

''Are you're saying you don't love me?'' She looked to her now empty hands. When her lips parted, he wouldn't let her say the words he couldn't bear to hear. ''That's bull. I know you love me, Matty. I know it by the way we make love. I know it by the way your eyes shine. I know it because you never, ever cut me slack unless I really need it. I know it in my *bones*. So don't try to tell me you don't love me.''

''I'm not trying to tell you that, Dave. I do love you.''

He'd waited so long to hear his Matty say that again; now it only made him think of heartbreak. But he wasn't going to give in. ''That's fine, because I always loved you, too.''

''No,'' she said with soft finality, ''it's not fine. Don't you see, Dave? You don't love *me*. You love the memory of me. I'm not that girl anymore. Maybe…maybe I never even was the girl you thought I was.''

''Matty, I know you have doubts, but—''

A memory of his own thoughts swept across him. The night they'd made love. When he'd been so certain that he could answer every doubt she had. Was this what she was talking about? That he thought he could take care of everything for her? Was her doubt really that he would ever let her take care of things herself? He shook that off because it was too dangerous to consider right now.

He started again. ''This doesn't change what's between us, Matty. Just because I decided the grant—''

The echo of the word in his own voice felt like a rock dropped into his gut.

''*You* decided. That's right. You decided it wasn't worth

the risk. Hell, you're probably right, too—you often are, which is one of your less endearing traits. But even when you're right and I'm wrong, I need to make my own decisions. And if there's a piper to pay, then I have to pay."

"Matty—"

"You can't spend your whole life rescuing me. I won't let you. You'd get tired of it eventually and I...well, I'm tired of it already. My self-respect can't take it. And even if I let you rescue me, I know it wouldn't work, not long-term. Not in a partnership. And that's what I want. That's what I need."

She was gone. Again.

Only this time it wasn't in a tornado of hurt and anger like six years ago. And it wasn't slipping away quietly before dawn as she had twice since they'd married.

It was calm and deliberate.

She even listened carefully when he tried to talk her out of it later that night. Listened carefully, then shook her head with tears glinting in her eyes, but her voice firm and repeated, "It won't work, Dave. It can't."

She'd packed some of her things, said she'd get the rest of them later, announced she'd arranged for Pamela Dobson to come look after him until he could get around. Then she stood at the door of his room and said goodbye.

He'd sat there, on the bed where they'd made love as if they were really starting a life together, and watched her go.

Chapter Fourteen

Matty sat across the desk from Taylor and waited for her to finish going over the papers she'd brought in.

"You said this is all covered under attorney-client privilege, and nobody could make me say anything against Dave, right? Not even if I'm not his wife anymore."

Taylor gave her an odd look. "I don't think it would come to that, Matty. I can't see any problem, since the grant commission signed this waiver and the money's been paid back. It's just that in the wrong hands, this could be made to look... Well, it *is*, uh, unusual."

"He did it for me. To rescue me." Matty blinked hard. "It's what Dave's always done. And I've let him. But not this time. Taylor, I want you to draw up those documents for me."

"Matty? Matty, are you in here?" It was Lisa Currick.

Matty wiped her eyes, then blew her nose. She'd been watching a tape. The song "They Can't Take That Away

From Me'' always did get to her, with Fred Astaire singing it to Ginger Rogers to let her know that with their romance apparently over he'll always cherish vivid memories of her in his heart.

So far she'd replayed it six times in a row, and she was nearing the bottom of a box of tissues.

Matty had heard Lisa knocking, and ignored it. Just as she'd ignored Cal's glares when he'd come in morning and evening the past two days. At least he hadn't said much. Except this morning, when she'd said she was sorry to be leaving him shorthanded, and she was sure she'd shake off this flu bug in another day or so.

He'd cast a skeptical glance at the residue of her eating habits. "Way you're acting, I don't want you around any Flying W stock, let alone heavy machinery."

The song ended again as Lisa reached the doorway. From the corner of her eye, Matty watched Lisa's razor-sharp look cover the empty soda cans, the drawn curtains, the jumble of movie cassettes. Without looking up, Matty rewound the tape to the song's beginning, knowing precisely how long to hold the button.

"Oh, great," Lisa muttered, apparently in response to the lyrics.

She crossed the room, swept an empty cracker box and a piece of paper towel off the couch and sat one cushion away, with the tissue box between them.

"Well," started Lisa, drawing out the word ominously, "how appropriate, a film festival. Joyce was telling me the other day that she put the tape of your reception—yours and Dave's—on a cassette. Sort of a belated wedding present."

"Tell her to throw it out."

"Don't you dare, Matty Currick." Lisa swung around to sit on the coffee table in front of Matty, squarely between her and the screen. "You scream, you holler, you keep crying your eyes out. But don't you give up. Not with all you got going for you."

Stunned, Matty stared at her.

"Even if he is my brother, if you think that man did you wrong, then you *do* something about it. You don't just fold up! If he's scum, you let the world know it. You owe it to yourself. You owe it to—"

"Dave is not scum!"

For half a second, Matty wondered where that shout had come from. Then she realized it had come from her. The other woman blinked, apparently as stunned by the outburst as Matty was.

Matty sat back, feeling drained of energy and emotion. "And he didn't do me wrong. It's complicated. Please, just go away. Please."

"Okay. I've seen what I came for—to see if you're in as bad a shape as Dave, and you're close."

Matty stifled the words to ask about Dave. She knew exactly what Lisa was doing, and it wouldn't work.

Another stanza of the song went by before Lisa stood, rooting in her large purse. "I have other people to talk to anyway, so I'll go. But before I do, I'm going to give you something to think about."

Before Matty could react, Lisa punched the eject button, silencing Fred's song, took that tape out, plugged in another one and started it playing. She was already gone before the screen flickered to life once more, now with another couple dancing in the center of the screen.

Certainly no Fred and Ginger, but with something disconcertingly compelling about the figures that didn't quite look like her and Dave.

It took a moment for her to realize that what made them look so different was the formal clothing, instead of their usual jeans, boots and shirts.

Their wedding clothes…her two-piece silk dress and his dark suit. Not hanging in a closet this time, but still so close there wasn't a breath of space between them, moving together, touching each other. Quick, small, fleeting touches.

And not only Dave touching her. The sleeve of her dress rubbed against his suit jacket, an unmistakably deliberate motion, even if the mind connected to the arm enclosed in that sleeve had no memory of it.

It wasn't the clothes that clung to each other, it was them.

Taylor Lindsey looked across the café's corner table and couldn't quite believe she was doing this. Couldn't believe she had laid in wait for Matty's ranch foreman at the Co-op. Couldn't believe she'd boldly asked Cal Ruskoff to have coffee with her. Couldn't believe she was about to meddle in someone else's life. Big time.

She'd seen Matty and Dave's misery for herself, but she'd had no idea things were so bad until Ruth Moski and Lisa came into her office this morning with worried frowns creasing their foreheads. These two smart, levelheaded women who both loved Matty and Dave had been very persuasive…and here she was.

Taylor cleared her throat a second time. "I'm worried about Dave Currick."

"He's still Matty's to worry about far as I know." Cal Ruskoff's square face gave nothing away.

"Of course he is. I meant as a professional colleague. I've heard some rumors…"

She paused, giving him plenty of opportunity to ask *What rumors?* He didn't.

Lisa and Ruth had been so adamant that she was the only one to do this part of the plan because their connections to Dave were too obvious. But she'd *told* them Cal Ruskoff had never looked at her with anything close to friendliness.

"Something about how Dave might have helped out Matty in getting that grant," she said carefully. "There's a rumor that an investigator might come up from Cheyenne to look into it. Dave could be in trouble."

"How much trouble?"

"I don't know. But I know people in Cheyenne, and I

heard there might be someone pulling strings. Someone in, say, an elected office. It almost seems like they're *looking* for a problem. And someone looking for a problem can twist things, so they appear—''

"How bad?''

"Dave probably wouldn't go to jail, but it might put a dent in his career.'' It wasn't a lie, precisely. She'd refused when Ruth and Lisa wanted to embellish—a felony! Ruth had to have been kidding. "Definitely take the gloss of his reputation, which is spotless right now. That would be such a shame.''

He quirked one eyebrow at her. "Seems to me you're the sort of woman who might be able to think of a way to get around something like that.''

Ah, here came the really tricky part. He clearly understood what she was driving at, but would he play along?

"Well, we—I—had thought that with Judge Halloran being a friend of the Currick family, and holding Dave in high regard, Dave would get a fair hearing if the judge handled it instead of this elected person pulling the strings. The difficulty would be letting Halloran know what's going on without it coming from, uh, official sources.''

She looked up through her lashes to be sure Cal had gotten that point. He had.

"Dave's a friend,'' she added. "I'd hate to see anything bad happen to his career. Especially now, when he's already so unhappy.''

He looked at his coffee cup, then back at her. "Matty's been a bear with a thorn in her paw all week.''

"She has, hasn't she? She came into the office and said—'' She cut off her own words. She was so relieved that she'd almost told him about Matty instructing her to forget the prenuptial agreement and draw up a separation agreement that gave her nothing from the marriage and pledged to repay Dave for every expenditure he'd made on her or the Flying W.

She liked the glint in Cal Ruskoff's eyes when he said, "Wonder if there's anything their friends can do."

His first day back to the office he came home after dark to realize Lisa had been in the house. It had to be Lisa.

Who else would leave photographs of him and Matty from childhood through their wedding reception, spread all over the neatly made bed in the master bedroom?

It was neatly made because he hadn't been sleeping in it. What sleep he'd been getting was on the couch, with the TV turned on, tuned to anything that wasn't an old movie or romantic in any way. Infomercials worked okay.

He also spent a lot of time on the porch outside the office, using his good foot on the railing to balance the chair on its back legs. When his thoughts started circling around too close, he'd let the chair come down, so his other foot hit the porch floor, shooting pain through his ankle.

Tonight, he'd walked into the bedroom to hang up his sports jacket and seen the photos. He couldn't stop himself from picking them up, one after another. Him and Matty at a youth rodeo, at a roundup, at the swimming hole, on birthdays, going to a dance, at graduations, looking at each other in a way that made any ordinary day a special occasion. He picked up another photo that didn't seem to fit with the rest of them. There was an odd expression on his face and Matty looked worried. It took a moment before he realized it was from the day before their last ride.

He dropped the photograph and walked out, not bothering to favor his bad ankle. The antidote of physical pain wasn't going to work now.

"Phone, Dave."

He wouldn't let himself glare, because everyone had been watching him these days as closely as people living by an active volcano watched the peak. But nobody could make a big deal out of a perfectly justified frown. "I told you, Ruth, no calls."

"It's your mother. From New Zealand."

The temptation to stick with the no-calls edict passed in a second. If he didn't talk to her, he wouldn't put it past his mother to have herself and his father on the next plane headed in the general direction of Wyoming.

"Dave? Are you all right, dear?"

"I'm fine. Everything's—"

"Lisa told me you and Matty have separated."

He cursed his younger sister under his breath, but kept his tone calm. "Separation's a legal term, Mother. We certainly haven't—"

"Oh, Dave, what did you do?"

It was what he hadn't done. But how could he explain it all to his mother when he was still struggling to understand it himself?

"It's not that simple, Mom. It's not like when we were kids, and Matty would get mad and then things would blow over in a day or two. She's not angry, she's…disappointed." He'd disappointed her, and that hurt.

He hadn't realized the silence had grown until his mother spoke again.

"I've been thinking about your saying that Indian Paint-brush reminds you of Matty. When I was first married and settling in on the Slash-C, I tried to grow Indian Paintbrush in the garden by the house. Grandmother Currick told me it wouldn't take there, and she was right. In some ways it's tough as anything—it can take late frosts, the dry and wind. But it needs to come up where conditions are right for it. A lot of times its roots grow right into the roots of other plants in its natural habitat, and it needs those roots to grow."

Rubbing his hand across his eyes, he sighed. "Mom, if you're trying to make a point, just say it, please."

"When you try to make Indian Paintbrush what you want it to be, it won't grow. It flourishes when it grows where *it* wants to grow—where and how it needs to grow. That's the same thing with people, and especially with relationships between people. But Indian Paintbrush *is* meant to grow in Wyoming, just like Matty. Just like you. And if you really believe the two of you belong together, that you need to grow into one another's roots in order to survive, then you better do something about it. But I'm not sure you do."

"You're not sure? What was all that stuff you fed me about opposites balance each other?"

"I meant I'm not sure you believe the two of you belong together."

"I've always believed that."

"No, you haven't, or you would never have been persuaded by anything your father and I and Grams Brennan ever said."

It's so unlike you to listen to other people. That's what Matty had said. Could the two women who knew him best both be wrong?

He ended the call with his mother, not even sure what he said. Because another thought had hit him—that photograph Lisa had left out and the odd expression on his face.

Fear.

He'd been afraid. Afraid of being responsible for Matty, especially responsible for her happiness if her dreams were just following his as the adults said. But another and deeper fear—that he'd disappoint her, that he wouldn't live up to the love that shone from her every time she looked at him.

How could he live up to that? How could he be sure he wouldn't let her down? How could he take care of her the way she deserved?

Take care of her...

Even if I let you rescue me, it wouldn't work, not long-term. Not in a partnership. And that's what I want. That's what I need.

He'd been trying to do it all on his own. It was why he'd been so scared six years ago—the idea of being the only one responsible for everything. And yet when she came back, he'd tried to keep things the way they had been before, tried his damnedest to make all the decisions, no matter how hard she fought him or how clearly she showed him she was capable of making her own decisions.

He'd recognized the signs. He'd noticed how she'd tempered her impulsiveness, how she'd thought of his parents more than he had, even how she'd gained skills and poise. Yet he'd stubbornly been trying to do it all on his own, even though that wasn't what she wanted or needed from him.

That was the thought that kept punishing him, even after he'd received a phone call that should have turned his thoughts to preserving his career.

Matty heard the phone ring as she stepped onto the back porch shortly before noon. The answering machine would get the call—she had muddy boots on, and she wasn't in the mood to talk to anyone.

"Matty? Are you there? It's Taylor" came the voice from the machine. "Please, if you're there. Please pick up."

Something in Taylor's tone had Matty lunging for the receiver with one boot off and one still on.

"Taylor? I'm here."

"Matty? Oh, Matty, I'm glad I finally got you!"

"What is it? You sound nervous."

"I'm worried. About Dave."

Matty's breathing stopped. "Is he hurt?"

"No. Nothing like that. But he's been called in to Judge Halloran's office for a one o'clock meeting...."

It took her a moment to process the rest of what Taylor was saying after that initial *No* released her breathing for a catch-up sprint.

"...and she told Lisa, who told me. The thing is, Matty, the judge asked for your grant application and your wedding license—yours and Dave's—to be put on his desk right after lunch."

"But...but the money was really Dave's."

"I know that. But it's a matter of professional integrity."

It was clear as crystal. Somehow the judge had found out they'd gotten married only to make her eligible for the grant. It was all her doing, and now Dave was going to pay the price.

"We've got to do something, Taylor."

"Oh, Matty..." Matty had never heard Taylor Larsen sound twittery before. "I wouldn't know what to do. I don't know what I *could* do..."

"Well, I know what I'm going to do."

She hung up the phone with a bang, yanked off her remaining boot and chucked it in the vicinity of the back hall before sprinting toward the shower.

"I want it noted on the official record that I officially object to this hearing being held in David Currick's law office, and that I—"

"There's no official record to officially object to," Judge Halloran told Bob Brathenwaite with fast-fading patience, "and I already told you this is an informal discussion to get this straightened out. With an anonymous call on an allegation like this, most right-thinking people would like to tell the caller to take a jump if he's not willing to come forward. But we don't have that luxury, so we've got to pursue it, but without taking up any more time or—"

"I'm the one you should be talking to, then."

Matty stood at the open door, one hand still on the knob, the empty reception area behind her creating a backdrop that to Dave's eyes was hazy at best. All he saw was her. She was pale. Her eyes looked puffy and reddened. She was gorgeous.

"Matty—" He half rose from his seat.

She looked only at the judge. "If you want to straighten this out, and do it quickly I'm the one you should be talking to. The only one."

"Your Honor, this—"

The judge held up a hand dotted with age spots. "You be quiet, and you *sit!*" The commands stopped Brathenwaite with his mouth open, and Dave halfway out of his chair. "Let's hear this young lady. But first, I need to know your name."

"This is Matty, Judge Halloran. Matty Brennan."

"I'm Matty Brennan Currick," she was saying at the same time.

Their enunciation of *Matty Brennan* overlapped perfectly, so her addition of *Currick* hung out there like a solitary flag in the wind.

But still she didn't look at him.

"Ah, of course. I remember now. From your wedding." The creases in the judge's face shifted like sand ripples in a windstorm. "Your wedding, ahem. Yes. There's been an allegation made, and I need to discuss it with Dave. If you will excuse us, please. Really, the secretary shouldn't have let you in."

"It's not Ruth's fault. She was away from her desk," Matty said quickly. "But the allegation isn't against Dave, it's against me. It's my name on that grant application. Any wrong—"

"Matty, don't—" He reached from his chair to take her hand.

She locked her fingers with his, squeezing, but kept talking, all her attention on the judge "—doing was mine. All me. And only me."

"I see. But it's Dave's professional standing that's been called into question. It's his reputation that could be at stake here, so I think it should be left to him instead of me deciding if you can speak for him. Dave?"

The other two men in the room couldn't know what this question meant. Yet the entire room seemed to go tense and quiet waiting for his answer. Or maybe the tension came from

Matty. She'd turned to look at him, their hands still linked, her eyes wide and direct. She knew what it really meant.

This hearing mattered to his profession, sure, but this question mattered to his life. To his heart.

She wanted a partnership. Where each partner rescued the other now and then, not just one partner rescuing the other. Could he let go enough to let her rescue him?

Again. A voice reminded him. Matty had certainly rescued him that dawn at The Narrows. But he hadn't had much choice then, and he'd fought her, trying to keep the control. He had a choice now.

A choice to trust her, to have faith in the woman she was. Only now did he understand what strength it took for a strong person to let someone else help.

"Yes." The word came easier than he could have imagined. It had been there all along, just waiting for him to wake up and use it. "Matty speaks for me."

The blue of her eyes as she met his look intensified, deepened to a color he'd never seen before. He thought maybe it was the color of their future.

She drew in a deep breath—a motion that instantly had Dave's body thinking of more carnal aspects of love—and faced Judge Halloran again.

"I was the one who planned the whole thing. Dave knew nothing about it."

The judge's eyes narrowed. "Ever?"

"Not until after we were married," Matty said firmly.

"That's not what the man who called in this tip said."

"Are you going to believe an anonymous voice or me?" She wisely didn't wait for an answer. "You can put me in jail, but Dave had nothing to do with this in any way, shape or form." Her grip on his hand tightened in warning. "He probably still doesn't know exactly what you're talking about, although he might suspect. But I fooled him along with everyone else. You can't punish him for that."

Dave caught the flicker of the judge's eyes toward the file

that clearly indicated Dave's repayment of the grant. He'd been halfway toward keeping Matty out of this entirely when she'd stormed through that door. Now the judge knew they'd both been involved. They both might get caught in the backlash.

And he didn't give a damn.

Matty had come to his rescue.

If he hadn't already loved her for most of their lives, he sure as hell would have fallen in love with her that moment she came flying through the door.

"Your Honor, please…" Matty said. "It's none of Dave's doing. My great-uncle got the ranch into such a mess that I thought for sure I was going to lose it. I couldn't stand that. Not after all the years of being away and dreaming of coming home, dreaming of coming back here and making the life I've never stopped wanting. I couldn't let that dream go. Not without fighting with every weapon I could think of."

"This is all very touching," Brathenwaite said with disdain. "But it's not germane. The issue is if they married for the purpose of defrauding the grant commission. It's clear they did."

"Based on what proof?" Matty demanded.

Brathenwaite ostentatiously looked around Matty to address Dave, "Currick, are you asking this court—"

"We're not in court," Halloran grumbled.

"—to believe that after a six-year estrangement that you simply picked up loving this woman where you'd left off? And *that's* why you married her?"

"Your Honor—" Matty started to protest.

Halloran cut her off with a wave of his hand. "I want to hear Dave's answer."

Dave looked at her as he spoke the words. "I'm not certain."

"What kind of answer is that?" Halloran complained.

"I'm not certain about a lot of things these days, Your Honor."

"Are you saying you don't know how you feel about the woman you gave an oath to love and cherish in my courtroom, young man?"

"No, Your Honor. I'm saying—in answer to Brathenwaite's question—that I can't tell you if I picked up loving her where I'd left off six years earlier or if I fell in love with her a second time." He turned in the chair so he faced her as directly as possible. "Fell in love all over again with the woman she is now."

"Dave." It was soft as a sigh, but he heard it, and felt it.

"Your Honor—" Brathenwaite's voice climbed an octave in outrage. "None of this is to the point—"

"Quiet." Judge Halloran steepled his fingers in front of his mouth and looked over the top of his glasses at them. "Let me see if I've got this straight. Are you saying when you two got married, and swore before God and the State of Wyoming to love, honor and cherish each other, that you were knowingly lying?"

"What?" Matty sounded confused.

Dave couldn't blame her. What was that old fox Halloran up to? This had nothing to do with what was in the file he had pinned under his elbows.

"Did you love David Edward Currick when you married him?" the judge rapped out in a voice that had quelled more than one courtroom hubbub.

"Yes."

"Do you believe he loved you at the time you married?"
She glanced at him and then away. "I...I don't know."

"The hell you don't, Matty. I loved you then, and I love you now."

"You keep quiet. I'm asking the questions. Do you love him now?"

"Yes—but that has nothing to do with—"

"Has everything to do with the oath you two took before me." Halloran made a show of straightening the papers and closing the file. Then he slid it to the side and put Dave's bucking bronc paperweight on it.

Matty looked from the judge to Dave and back.

"Is that it?"

"That's it."

"You're not going to punish Dave? Because it was all my—"

Judge Halloran held up a compelling stop-sign hand. "Once was enough for all that, young lady. Besides, I see no reason to bestir myself to dole out punishment when it seems Dave—and you—have punished yourselves plenty. See if you can't get the hang of loving each other a little better and forget all this other nonsense."

"I…" Dave watched the motion of her swallow, wishing his lips were on her throat. "Thank you, Your Honor."

He was unprepared when she abruptly released his hand and headed out the door at the same speed she'd entered.

"Matty!" he hollered as he started after her.

"Dave Currick, you hold on for a minute now."

"Judge, I've got to—"

"You can spare a minute to your career dammit, boy!"

The tone rather than the words halted him at the door.

"There's evidence in this file of damned foolishness. But if we knocked over every soul who'd been foolish there wouldn't be a one of us standing. Especially," Halloran continued ominously as Brathenwaite showed signs of reviving enough to sputter indignantly, "politicians. I don't see anything here to bother the ethics committee about—as long as you promise there'll be no more of this nonsense and swear you'll settle your situation with that young lady."

Dave grinned at him. "I swear, Your Honor."

"All right then, go— Go!"

Dave was thundering down the stairs from his office before the second command was even a word.

"Matty Brennan! Matty Brennan *Currick!*"

She stopped in the middle of temporarily empty Main

Street, turning to face him, her hands loose at her sides like a gunslinger.

"What do you want, Dave?"

This was bound to be a little dicey, but he'd never expected her to make it a showdown on Main Street.

"Are you going to stand and fight? Or are you a coward? That's right, I'm calling you a coward. Here in public, in front of everyone."

Everyone was stretching it. There were maybe a half-dozen spectators scattered within earshot. But that number was rising, and the way word traveled in Knighton, everyone would hear soon enough.

"I am *not* a coward. You pick the place to talk later, and I'll—"

"Now. Here. And you're right. You're not a coward. I am. At least I was." She gawked at him, mouth open, eyes staring, and he'd never seen a more beautiful sight. "What you said back there in the office—you can't take it back."

"I know. But it doesn't change the other things we talked about."

"Like unequal rescues? Seems to me you just added a major notch to your side on that account. Did such a good job that Judge Halloran's going to let me keep the rest of my hide."

"I'm glad, Dave. I'm so glad. But that doesn't—"

"Shut up, Matty," he said hoarsely.

For half a second, her eyes flared with anger at the order. Then they flared with something else as she seemed to hear the low note in his voice. Heaven help him, he was growing hard just looking at her. Right here on Main Street.

"I know you're grown up, Matty. I've seen what you've done with the ranch and I see how you are with people. But I was afraid to let you be too grown up, afraid to see how much you've changed. I kept thinking that if I could hold onto the girl Matty, the one who'd wanted to make a life here with me, then maybe you'd stay. But the woman

Matty…well, she'd spent all those years out in the wide world where she'd found things bigger and better and brighter.''

"You're wrong, Dave. The girl's the one who ran away. The one who let her hurt pride keep her away for six long years. It was the woman who had the courage to come back. It was the woman who pushed through that foolish pride and turned to you when she needed help.''

"Funny you should bring up need, Matty. Because that's something I've been thinking about a lot. When I told the florist I wanted Indian Paintbrush in your bouquet because it reminds me of you, she told me it's got certain properties. Like symbolizing how opposites can balance each other. That's some of how I need you, Matty. I need your impulsiveness to keep from being too stodgy. I need your stubbornness because I have it on good authority that I'm hard to budge once I get my mind set. I need you to keep me from trying to take control, even when I don't want to. I need you to make my dreams come true.

"Will you be my wife? Will you have me for your husband? In sickness and in health? Till death do us part? You rescue me and I rescue you.''

"What's goin' on?'' Hugh Moski asked loudly from the sidewalk.

"Shh!'' Ruth ordered him. "Dave's asking Matty to marry him.''

"Huh? Ain't it a little late for that? They had the wedding last month. You gettin' forgetful, Ruth? We had the reception in the Methodist Church basement. I was sure it was Dave Currick she got herself married to…''

"Of course it was Dave she married. Now be quiet, or we'll miss his proposin'.''

"Don't see how there's anything to miss by ways of a proposal when they already had the wedding!''

"Well, there's having a wedding and then there's really being married.''

"Well, now, that's the truth. Why didn't you just say that in the first place?"

Dave saw the smile in Matty's eyes before it touched her lips.

"They're right, you know. We had the wedding. Now I want the marriage. Matty, I love you. I want to spend my life with you. Whatever my life is, wherever it is, I want to be with you." He moved closer, not letting himself touch her yet. "You've already married me, now will you *be* married to me?"

"Yes, Dave, I'll be married to you."

Without any prompting from their audience this time, the bride and groom kissed. And it was a good thing it was in the middle of Main Street because it wasn't a kiss suited to a church building. Not at all.

"Funny how things turned out."

"What do you mean?" Matty stretched against him, and a slant of early afternoon light caught her hair.

Ignoring the questions and comments from the citizens of Knighton, they had driven straight to the ranch, cleared the bed of the photos by simply pulling off the bedspread and spent the past twenty-four hours there. Sometime during the night they'd made cheese sandwiches and ate them in bed while they'd looked over some of the pictures, recalling memories. Then they'd made some more memories.

"About Judge Halloran getting that anonymous phone call telling him something was going on about the grant to the Flying W. And all the paperwork showing up for him in a file. And even Ruth being away from her desk just as you came in. I don't think this was entirely by accident."

"You don't? But who—? Taylor."

"Taylor?"

"She's the one who called me and told me Judge Halloran was looking at the file. Plus, she told me when and where you were meeting. And she talked about disbarment and a lot of other things. To get me riled up, the rat! Besides, she had copies of the papers about you repaying the grant—I gave them to her to draw up an agreement about repaying you.''

"You don't have to—"

"I'm going to, Dave."

"Okay," he agreed, understanding that she needed to.

"Yes," she said breathlessly after kissing him. "I'm sure Taylor was involved."

"Who would have thought demure little Taylor Larsen would have it in her?"

Matty gave him a searching look. "Demure? Taylor? Have you ever really looked at Taylor? She's definitely a banked fire."

"Guess I've always been too occupied with the open flame of Matty Brennan."

"Good answer, Currick." He grinned, and that deserved another kiss.

"But Taylor couldn't have done it alone. Remember what Judge Halloran said about a man calling in the tip? Besides, his secretary told Lisa, who told Ruth who told me that the caller had the voice of—and I quote—one sexy man."

Matty's eyes widened. "Cal? You think Cal was involved? You think the two of them were in on it together? They *planned* it?"

"I can't see Lisa or Ruth being left out of a conspiracy," he said dryly. But she was moving against him, and he muttered against her neck, "It's over. Who cares."

"I care. What if something had gone wrong?"

"Even if it had gone to an ethics review board, it wasn't likely to get me more than a reprimand."

"Likely? Reprimand? Ooooh, wait till I get my hands on them."

"How about getting your hands on me first? Right after we discuss one more thing—this is the perfect time. Kids. I want six."

"Six!"

"I'm glad you agree. I knew we'd agree on something without negotiating."

"I did *not* agree. I simply repeated what you said. In case you didn't notice, I repeated it with astonishment. Six is a lot of kids."

"Yep."

"It's also a lot of being pregnant."

"And a lot of *getting* pregnant."

"Well, that's the upside. Tell you what, let's take it one kid at a time."

"One at a time, six times?"

"Dave…"

"Okay, okay."

"Deal?"

"Deal."

* * * * *

Watch for Taylor Anne Larsen's story in

MATCH MADE IN WYOMING

the next book in Patricia McLinn's
exciting miniseries

WYOMING WILDFLOWERS

On sale in July from
Silhouette Special Edition.
And now for a sneak preview of

MATCH MADE IN WYOMING,

Please turn the page.

Chapter One

"You and Taylor are standing under the mistletoe, so you have to kiss," Matty Brennan Currick proclaimed to Cal Ruskoff over the background noise of a party in full swing. Then she embellished. "Otherwise it's bad luck for the whole New Year."

As the owner of the neighboring Flying W Ranch, Matty was Cal's employer. Which was one reason why he was here at the Slash-C at her New Year's Eve party. She was also nearly the only friend he could claim, which was the other reason he was here.

"Never heard that," Cal grumbled.

"Me, either," Taylor Anne Larsen declared staunchly. She stood beside him, as if they presented a united front, at the same time angling her face away from him. He saw only her light red hair and the turn of her jaw heading toward a pointy chin.

"You haven't heard of it because neither of you grew up

around here. Dave!'' Matty snagged her husband's arm as he
headed toward the noisy hub of the party in the family room.

''Dave, isn't it true that if you stand under the mistletoe
with someone and don't kiss them, it's bad luck—*terrible*
bad luck for both people, all year long?''

Cal could see clear as day that Matty was focusing a compelling look on her husband. Dave Currick's lips quirked, but
he nodded solemnly.

''Terrible bad luck,'' he concurred. ''In fact, it's such
strong, awful, terrible, bad luck,'' said Dave with a remarkably straight face, ''that even if you're three feet away from
the mistletoe and don't kiss, you can get hit with it, so…''

He swept Matty to him with one hand at the small of her
back, and Matty cooperated fully. There was no time to look
away before their lips met in a brief but sound kiss. But it
wasn't the kiss that had Cal feeling as if prickles had gotten
under his skin—it was what followed. Still molded against
each other, the husband and wife exchanged a look that spoke
of remembering past moments and of promising there would
be more—and soon—that would be well worth remembering.

Cal didn't envy Matty and Dave having this. He just hated
feeling like a starving kid with his nose pressed against the
damned pastry shop window, watching what he wouldn't
ever have.

But maybe on New Year's Eve, a night somehow separate
from both the past and the future… For just a moment…

''Oh, hell,'' he growled, then pulled Taylor to him in much
the same embrace Dave held Matty.

Only, Taylor didn't lean into him, pliant and willing. She
remained straight, even arched slightly back against his arm,
as if to avoid contact with the front of his body. She didn't
entirely succeed, and they shifted to keep balanced.

Her head jerked back.

Shock.

That's what he saw in Taylor's wide green eyes. Shock.

He couldn't blame her. Taylor Anne Larsen was a nice

woman. Even if she was a lawyer. The kind of woman who wouldn't care for lies of either omission or commission. Polite, a little shy. He hadn't meant to shock her. It wasn't her fault he hadn't had a woman in too long to think about. It wasn't her fault that when he had thought about it lately her red-haired image had come to mind too often for comfort.

He pressed his mouth to hers.

Shock.

That was what he felt popping and sizzling and crackling through his bloodstream and nerve endings. Had to be.

Soft lips. Soft warmth. Soft skin when his mouth trailed off to one side. Soft hair that brushed against his cheek when he shifted the angle. And all around, a soft scent like…like something he couldn't quite name.

She gasped, and pulled her mouth free.

He didn't even realize he was reaching to kiss her again until she stepped back, abruptly leaving his arms empty.

"So now we're safe against bad luck for the coming year." Taylor smiled, but her voice wasn't steady. She stood barely beyond arm's reach. "Excuse me."

She took one step, then she looked over her shoulder, her gaze going from one face to another, and said, "I'm sure I'll see you again before midnight, Matty. And Dave. But I'll say Happy New Year now, Cal."

She walked away.

Something in Cal's chest felt tight and heavy. It took an extra couple of beats for him to realize she'd just declared that she didn't expect to see him again for the duration of this party. Didn't expect to, or didn't want to?

SILHOUETTE®
MAKES YOU
A STAR!

Feel like a star with Silhouette.

We will fly you and a guest to New York City for an
exciting weekend stay at a glamorous 5-star hotel.
Experience a refreshing day at one of New York's
trendiest spas and have your photo taken by a
professional. Plus, receive $1,000 U.S. spending money!

Flowers...long walks...dinner for two...
how does Silhouette Books
make romance come alive for you?

Send us a script, with 500 words or less, along with visuals (only drawings,
magazine cutouts or photographs or combination thereof). Show us how
Silhouette Makes Your Love Come Alive. Be creative and have fun. No
purchase necessary. All entries must be clearly marked with your name,
address and telephone number. All entries will become property of
Silhouette and are not returnable. **Contest closes September 28, 2001.**

Please send your entry to: **Silhouette Makes You a Star!**

In U.S.A.	In Canada
P.O. Box 9069	P.O. Box 637
Buffalo, NY, 14269-9069	Fort Erie, ON, L2A 5X3

Look for contest details on the next page, by visiting www.eHarlequin.com or
request a copy by sending a self-addressed envelope to the applicable address
above. Contest open to Canadian and U.S. residents who are 18 or over.
Void where prohibited.

Silhouette®
Where love comes alive™

Our lucky winner's photo will appear in a Silhouette ad. Join the fun!

SRMYAS1

HARLEQUIN "SILHOUETTE MAKES YOU A STAR!" CONTEST 1308
OFFICIAL RULES
NO PURCHASE NECESSARY TO ENTER

1. To enter, follow directions published in the offer to which you are responding. Contest begins June 1, 2001, and ends on September 28, 2001. Entries must be postmarked by September 28, 2001, and received by October 5, 2001. Enter by hand-printing (or typing) on an 8 ½" x 11" piece of paper your name, address (including zip code), contest number/name and attaching a script containing <u>500 words or less, along with drawings, photographs or magazine cutouts, or combinations thereof</u> (i.e., collage) <u>on no larger than 9" x 12"</u> piece of paper, describing how the <u>Silhouette books make romance come alive for you.</u> Mail via first-class mail to: Harlequin "Silhouette Makes You a Star!" Contest 1308, (in the U.S.) P.O. Box 9069, Buffalo, NY 14269-9069, (in Canada) P.O. Box 637, Fort Erie, Ontario, Canada L2A 5X3. Limit one entry per person, household or organization.

2. Contests will be judged by a panel of members of the Harlequin editorial, marketing and public relations staff. Fifty percent of criteria will be judged against script and fifty percent will be judged against drawing, photographs and/or magazine cutouts. Judging criteria will be based on the following:

   - Sincerity—25%
   - Originality and Creativity—50%
   - Emotionally Compelling—25%

   In the event of a tie, duplicate prizes will be awarded. Decisions of the judges are final.

3. All entries become the property of Torstar Corp. and may be used for future promotional purposes. Entries will not be returned. No responsibility is assumed for lost, late, illegible, incomplete, inaccurate, nondelivered or misdirected mail.

4. Contest open only to residents of the U.S. <u>(except Puerto Rico)</u> and Canada who are 18 years of age or older, and is void wherever prohibited by law; all applicable laws and regulations apply. Any litigation within the Province of Quebec respecting the conduct or organization of a publicity contest may be submitted to the Régie des alcools, des courses et des jeux for a ruling. Any litigation respecting the awarding of a prize may be submitted to the Régie des alcools, des courses et des jeux only for the purpose of helping the parties reach a settlement. Employees and immediate family members of Torstar Corp. and D. L. Blair, Inc., their affiliates, subsidiaries and all other agencies, entities and persons connected with the use, marketing or conduct of this contest are not eligible to enter. Taxes on prizes are the sole responsibility of the winner. Acceptance of any prize offered constitutes permission to use winner's name, photograph or other likeness for the purposes of advertising, trade and promotion on behalf of Torstar Corp., its affiliates and subsidiaries without further compensation to the winner, unless prohibited by law.

5. Winner will be determined no later than November 30, 2001, and will be notified by mail. Winner will be required to sign and return an Affidavit of Eligibility/Release of Liability/Publicity Release form within 15 days after winner notification. Noncompliance within that time period may result in disqualification and an alternative winner may be selected. All travelers must execute a Release of Liability prior to ticketing and must possess required travel documents (e.g., passport, photo ID) where applicable. Trip must be booked by December 31, 2001, and completed within one year of notification. No substitution of prize permitted by winner. Torstar Corp. and D. L. Blair, Inc., their parents, affiliates and subsidiaries are not responsible for errors in printing of contest, entries and/or game pieces. In the event of printing or other errors that may result in unintended prize values or duplication of prizes, all affected game pieces or entries shall be null and void. **Purchase or acceptance of a product offer does not improve your chances of winning.**

6. Prizes: (1) Grand Prize—A 2-night/3-day trip for two (2) to New York City, including round-trip coach air transportation nearest winner's home and hotel accommodations (double occupancy) at The Plaza Hotel, a glamorous afternoon makeover at <u>a trendy New York spa</u>, $1,000 in U.S. spending money and an opportunity to <u>have a professional photo taken and appear in a Silhouette advertisement</u> (approximate retail value: $7,000). (10) Ten Runner-Up Prizes of gift packages (retail value $50 ea.). Prizes consist of only those items listed as part of the prize. Limit one prize per person. Prize is valued in U.S. currency.

7. For the name of the winner (available after December 31, 2001) send a self-addressed, stamped envelope to: Harlequin "Silhouette Makes You a Star!" Contest 1197 Winners, P.O. Box 4200 Blair, NE 68009-4200 or you may access the www.eHarlequin.com Web site through February 28, 2002.

Contest sponsored by Torstar Corp., P.O Box 9042, Buffalo, NY 14269-9042.

SRMYAS2

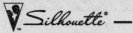

SPECIAL EDITION™

presents

PATRICIA McLINN

with her exciting new miniseries

These Wyoming women are as strong and feminine
as the men are bold and rugged....

Almost a Bride

on sale June 2001

Handsome rancher Dave Currick reunites with his old flame
Matty Brennan in an unconventional manner when he offers
her a marriage of convenience.

Match Made in Wyoming

on sale July 2001

Wyoming man Cal Ruskoff never thought love would pay
him a visit, until he's "set up" with beautiful Taylor Larsen
who draws him out of his shell.

**And look for a third "Wyoming Wildflowers" book
on sale December 2001**

Available at your favorite retail outlet.

Where love comes alive™